A Hue of Blu Marie-France Leger

Cover Design: Marie-France Leger

ISBN Paperback: 9798361151127

For more information, updates, and/or teasers, follow @mariefranceleger on Instagram.com or @maariefraance on TikTok.

Copyright © 2023 by Marie-France Leger
All rights reserved. No part of this publication may be reproduced, distributed, or transmitted in any form or by any means, including photocopying, recording, or other electronic or mechanical methods, without the prior written permission of the publisher, except in the case of brief quotations embodied in critical reviews and certain other non-commercial uses permitted by copyright law.

Author Playlist

Cry – Cigarettes After Sex

Romantic Homicide – d4vd

True Blue – Billie Eilish

Afraid – The Neighbourhood

Somebody Else – The 1975

Reflections – The Neighbourhood

Into It – Chase Atlantic

I Miss The Days – NF

Way Down We Go - KALEO

I Don't Love You – My Chemical Romance

Those Eyes – New West

Moral Of The Story – Ashe

You Broke Me First – Tate McRae

Mercy – MO

Remember That Night – Sara Kays

We Might As Well Be Strangers – Keane

Say Something – A Great Big World

A Hue of Blu

Disclaimer

If you're looking for a light, happy romance with a perfect ending, then this may not be the book for you. It deals with realistic situations and traumas.
If that is something that you're interested in, I'll be happy to see you along this journey of healing, heartbreak and growth.
Be kind to your heart, my darlings.

Mar.

To everyone stuck in a room void of light –
Be brave enough to open the blinds.
There is a world full of colour beyond the walls of your mind.

TW: Alcoholism, toxic relationships, mental health (specifically depression and BPD), body image, self-harm, mentions of OW/OM, and loss of a parent.

Part One
GRADUATION YEAR

*"I live; I die; the sea comes over me; it's the **blue** that lasts."*

Virginia Woolf

Chapter One
Blu

Year Four/Week One - Present

"Reservation's at eight, right Carter?"

I gripped my phone tightly, following the path of a fellow York student. Her hair was in a gelled, long braid, swaying back and forth like a boomerang.

And then it hit me in the face.

"*Jesus Christ,*" I muttered.

She didn't notice. I'm sure she had slapped a thousand and one people just today alone with that death whip.

"What about Christ, Blu?"

I rolled my eyes, entering the communications building of my college. Only this time, I kept a significant distance from everyone around me. *Like always.*

"Someone hit me in the face."

"No one hit you in the face," Carter stated. As if he knew me. As if he saw through my exaggerations.

Not many people did.

Not many people cared to.

"But yes, eight tonight. Cuisine Mercanti."

I nodded as if he could see, fully knowing he was sitting on his work laptop scrolling through a Tinder list of girls.

"See you later." I hung up the phone before he could say his goodbyes and scoped out the class numbers.

My pop culture seminar was in room two-twelve and this building already disgusted me. Cobwebs, exposed brick with gum stitched to the crevices of broken corners – *Eight months until graduation*, I repeated to myself. *Eight months until I run away.*

I had this professor last year, but the class was online so showing up was a bother. Mind you, I heard her voice, I knew what she looked like, but everyone else was a mystery.

A mystery I didn't care to solve.

"… And that is what Stuart Hall cited in the readings for next week, which I know all of you are dying to read."

Quiet laughter emanated through the cinder block encasing around twenty students in uncomfortable seats and miniscule desks.

"Hi there," my professor said. She had kind eyes – alert, but sweet. "Nice to see you. Take a seat."

My fingers wiggled into a wave as I flashed a rehearsed smile. "Plan on it."

A few people chuckled at that. I was good at eliciting reactions.

My bare legs hit the plastic chair before I could readjust the length of my black mini skirt. It was hot for early September, meaning fools just like the dirtbag in the corner were on the prowl to look up flowy dresses.

I matched this creep's eye-contact until he looked away, shuffling a deck of Pokémon cards underneath baggy sleeves. *Perv.*

That's when my eyes caught on something else, rather, s*omeone* else. His gaze held mine too, at least for a brief moment. A moment I picked up.

A moment I wouldn't forget.

Light brown hair, long enough to peek out underneath a baseball cap, but not messy. Blue eyes, laced with a hint of green. Chiseled face, angular like a model – no facial hair.

I was observant, a trait I possessed and loved to gloat about. Carter knew that about me; *nothing* slipped by Blu Henderson.

When someone interested me, there was no going back. For them, I mean.

I was untouchable, unattainable, charismatic and charming. I held my pride like a sword.

This man would be mine, whether he knew it or not.

For the rest of class, I watched him. He sat in the front row and I jotted down assumptions:

1. *Two earrings. One dangly cross, one pearl. Hipster, maybe. Edgy? Social media star?*
2. *White t-shirt. Navy blue pants. Nike blazers. Silver bracelet. Knows how to dress? A tad suspicious.*
3. *Art major. Tattoos. Michelangelo's "Creation of Adam" below his elbow – a rose next to it. Definitely art major.*

"What are your thoughts, miss blue hair in row three?"

4. *He's staring at me. His eyes are definitely blue. He has pretty privilege, he must. There is no way that –*

A girl tapped my shoulder, poked it rather. "Yes?"

"The professor asked you something," she whispered. Her voice was nasally.

Ah, so that's why he was looking at me. My eyes rolled around the room, meeting just about everyone's until they landed on his. I felt my professor staring, but that could wait. Just a second longer; I needed to know what it felt like to be in his sights.

"What was that, Professor?" I finally ripped away my gaze, a subtle smile playing on my lips.

Maybe she thought I was smiling at her. Maybe that was for the best.

"I asked for your thoughts on the Adorno reading," she started. "You were writing things down."

Yeah, I was. Not like it was any of her business. I quickly fanned my assumptions paper, then placed it down on its backside.

"Grocery list," I said, tapping my pen against the wooden desk.

Her face went cross. "I don't think right now is the time to –"

"– but if you're asking my thoughts on Adorno, I'd say his morals were skewed. His concepts on high and low culture are non-progressive." My eyes never left hers as I continued.

"By identifying jazz music as low culture, he's placing people into categories depending on their likes and dislikes, judging them, even." I turned to Nasal-Nelly beside me. "Do you like jazz music?"

God, I could've halted traffic with the red in her cheeks.

"I, um –" she swallowed. "It's nice. I – I do enjoy it sometimes."

"She enjoys it sometimes." I stated, flipping my attention back to the front. "And who am I to judge her partial enjoyment of jazz music? Adorno would. For that, I disagree with his beliefs. Thoughts concluded, Professor."

Someone in the back laughed loudly and I turned around to soak in the reign. A beast of a man wearing a fishing hat, plaid overcoat and dark denim was eyeing me with praise.

I saw it in everyone.

They saw it in me.

"Thank you for sharing..."

She wanted my name. "Blu, Professor. Blu Henderson."

Given any other circumstance, I would've shaken her hand. Seemed a bit inappropriate but I extended it anyway.

Like most people, she had the manners to receive the gesture, though it wasn't sincere. I just wanted to keep *his* attention a little longer. I knew I had it. I felt him looking.

Ten minutes later, class had finally come to a close with no substantial contribution from anyone other than me. I knew Prof. Granger had her own list of assumptions the second she saw me walk through that door. How could you not?

Dark blue hair, light brown eyes, rockstar attire, and a personality that demanded attention because I deserved it. Attention owed me.

It fucking owed me.

He stood up, collecting his black backpack and Air Pods. My God was he ever tall. You can never really tell when they're sitting down, but I would've placed him at 6'3. A full foot taller than me.

"Great to see you again, Jace," the professor said to him.

Jace.
Jace.
Jace.
His name stamped onto me like a tattoo.
"Likewise, Professor." That voice. *The* voice. Jace's voice.

His eyes were on mine for a fraction of a second before he ducked out of class. That look, it floated in my head. It bounced. It demanded.

He would be a part of me.
I would be a part of him.

I quickly flung my purse strap over my shoulder, darting for the door when Prof. Granger called out, "You're quite the character, Blu Henderson."

You're quite the character, Blu Henderson.
Of course I am, I wanted to say. *Glad you recognized*, I should have said.

Instead, I smiled. "See you next week, Professor."

When I finally exited the room, Jace was standing next to the water-fountain, filling up a glass tumbler.

He looked up at me.
I glanced at him.
And I walked away.

Chapter Two
Jace

Year Four/Week One - Present

"Can you get that?" Mom called from the living room.

I knew who it was before I answered the door. Baxter's Chevy was parked on the side of the road.

"Hey," I greeted, letting my brother inside.

He nodded, his tall frame filling most of the doorway. "What's up, Jace?"

"Nothing, just got back from school." I shut the door behind us, running my fingers through my hair. "Are we taking photos today?"

Baxter was a photographer, and the best one at that. Maybe I was a little biased because he was my older brother, but he was too talented to not get the recognition he deserved.

"Can't." He made his way around the hall, stepping beside the couch. "Hi Mom."

"Hey Bax," she smiled. She always had happy eyes around my brothers. "Nice of you to come by."

"Yeah, I was trying to call Will. Thought he showed up here after golf but he might still be on the course."

I leaned against the wall, crossing my arms. "Will didn't tell me he was at golf."

"Why would he tell you, kid?" Baxter laughed, leaning down to pet Sadie. "He's with the vets."

Our chocolate lab returned his cuddles, embracing the warmth my brother directed towards her. The warmth he rarely gave me.

"I'm twenty-one," I stated, as if I had something to prove. I always did. At least to my older brothers.

"Yeah, and the vets are thirty. Bit of a jump there, Jace."

Will worked as a financial analyst downtown. A few years ago, when he'd landed that position, my brothers and I coined his co-workers as "the vets" because they pranced around the office like veterans of war. I never thought Will would turn into one of them.

I never thought a lot of things would happen.

"Say," he started. "When are you getting a car?"

"When I can afford one."

He laughed. It was condescending. Everything my brothers did lately seemed to be.

"Can't afford shit if you don't work."

"Hey, language," Mom warned, lowering the television volume. "He's going to work when he graduates, aren't you Jace?"

This was always the topic of conversation. I hated that I felt inferior to Will, Baxter and Scott. Being the youngest of four brothers, there wasn't much room to grow even if I wanted to. In their eyes, I'd always be a kid.

In their eyes, I'd always be beneath them.

"Don't be sad about the soccer stuff, Jace. Sometimes things don't work out," Baxter said, as if I mentioned the sport in a silent exchange.

"I didn't say anything about soccer."

"No, but you're always thinking about it. Can't beat yourself up over stale bread. Get out there," he insisted, twirling his keys. "Find a new job. Find a purpose."

Find a purpose. As if that was the easiest thing in the world. To find a purpose when everyone around you already found theirs. When it was instilled on them since birth. When the one thing you loved, the career you thought you'd be working towards, crumbled beneath your feet.

"It's not that easy." I adjusted my shirt, glancing down at my arms. I'd been working out. I wanted Baxter to see that I wasn't a fucking loser.

He laughed, but it was sarcastic. "Nothing ever is. You make your own luck in this world, Jace." He pinched Mom's arm before heading towards the door.

"Hey!" she sniped, rubbing red skin. "You're twenty-six, Bax. Quit doing that."

He laughed, but it was genuine. "Old habits never die," then turned to me and punched my shoulder. "See you, kid."

Kid.

Kid.

Kid.

"My name's Jace," I mumbled, barely a whisper. Who would have heard it?

Who would have wanted to?

Chapter Three
Blu

Two Summers Ago

"Text me when you finish up," Fawn said as I knocked on Tyler's door.

"Yep. I'll recount the filthy details for you on the Uber ride home."

"You're sick," she laughed, ending the call.

Just in time, Tyler opened up and immediately pulled me inside. His hands were calloused from his construction job, the back of his tee stained from sweat.

"Mm," he kissed me, his tongue forcing into my mouth. "I needed this."

Of course he did. I was born to satiate. I tasted like fucking vanilla cream pudding.

His fingers circled my nipple, hardening at the touch. I made sure to wear something mesh and see-through. Tyler liked it.

"Couch," he commanded. I did as I was told and he had me bent over in seconds, the back of his hand slapping my right ass-cheek.

It hurt. It always hurt. But I smiled through the pain. Tyler liked it.

"Can you turn down the lights?" I requested. The darkness hid my imperfections. I was perfect, with minimal visibility.

But he didn't move. He pushed my legs apart with his foot, hiking down my skirt. I felt the pouch of my stomach droop down a little. I hadn't been eating much. Why did I have a pouch? *This won't do.*

He cupped my breast as he slipped his dick inside of me.

My stomach fat was present.

The lights were on.

He could feel it.

He could see *everything*.

I placed one arm over my belly, using my other hand to guide his down to my clit. He didn't do it. He wanted my tits.

"Fuck, Blu!" he moaned.

I couldn't feel him inside of me.

I felt the pizza from two days ago.

The salad from last night.

The water. So much water. Water for breakfast. Water for lunch.

He finished quickly, thank God. I managed to escape him seeing my hanging skin. *No crispy onion straws in the salad, useless carbs,* I made a mental note.

While he was disposing of the condom, I quickly yanked up my skirt and fluffed my hair. One of my buttons popped off but Mom wouldn't care. She'd be too drunk to notice.

Tyler had been my friend with benefits for a few months now. When I turned twenty-one, we'd met at a bar on Adelaide. He impressed me with his corporate position, I impressed him with my breasts. We fucked in the washroom and been hooking up ever since.

Most nights we were both incredibly wasted. But today he insisted on seeing me sober, maybe to fully feel how amazing it was to be inside of me. But it wasn't amazing for me.

The lights were on.

I grabbed the scattered contents of my purse and made my way to the door, sliding on my sneakers.

"I'll head out now," I called. Hovering in a man's place was the worst thing you could do. How embarrassing.

"I love that about you," Tyler once told me the third time we hooked up. "You never stay beyond your means."

What an insult.

Why had I come back?

He emerged from the bathroom as I was about to leave, his eyes scanning my body.

"You should try going to the gym, Blu. I have a membership if you want to come as a –"

I shut the door before I could cry.

I never saw Tyler again.

Chapter Four
Jace

Senior/High School – Four Years Ago

"Sarah asked me to prom last night," Morris bragged, lacing up his cleats. "Her prom-posal was too good."

I couldn't help but feel envious. I always did. Morris got every girl he ever wanted.

No one ever wanted the skinny, lanky kid with zits that covered seventy percent of his face. *How could anyone ever want that?*

"A little early for a prom-posal," I said, keeping the bitterness at bay. "How'd she ask?"

He sat in silence for a minute with the biggest smile on his face. I could tell he was thinking about it, about her. Only in my dreams could I envision feeling that way towards someone; only in my dreams would those feelings be reciprocated.

"She showed up to my house in this itty-bitty lingerie set, and she –"

"Wait what?" Connor piped up, throwing on his jersey. "How'd your parents not freak out?"

"They weren't home, dumbass," Morris said, throwing a sock at his face.

"How the hell was I supposed to know? Got pictures of her in it?"

"Watch your fucking mouth McCook," Danny interjected, curling a barbell with his right arm.

My eyes hovered longer on Danny's build. I looked down at my own. I let out a sigh.

"Sarah's Cumberland's woman, Danny. Why you so worked up?" Connor jested. "Got a crush?"

"Want me to throw this at you?" Danny waved the weight like it was a feather.

If only, I thought. *If only.*

"Why so glum, Boland?" Morris' voice called out to me. "You still got the year ahead of you."

I continued tying up my laces, looking down. I didn't say much to anyone. Silence was the best option. Silence didn't start arguments. Silence left no room for vocal judgement.

"I'm sure Tatiana will prom-pose to Jace," Connor started. "They'd look great together."

The room erupted in laughter. It was my worst nightmare.

Tatiana Orelwall was well over the average weight that any 5'1 girl should be at seventeen. She had a thing for porcelain dolls (she carried them everywhere) and her face was covered in cystic acne. We had that in common.

Danny was the only one not laughing, but he wasn't defending me either. No one really defended me. I barely defended myself.

Coach blew the whistle and everyone was on their feet. Everyone except me. I felt the sting of tears, but I didn't let them fall. No one should know me like that. I was already seen as weak enough.

A Gatorade bottle was tossed onto the floor in front of me. Max, I think his name was, sauntered over with a stoic expression. Max never smiled, never frowned either. He was just... Max.

"Pick it up, man. It's yours," he said.

"Pardon?"

He kicked the orange bottle to my feet. "For practice. I had an extra."

I didn't know what to say, I never did. So I snagged it and nodded a thanks. Thankfully, Max didn't mind. He kept walking past me onto the field.

That was the day that solidified the value of silence, at least for me.

Max didn't laugh at me.

Max blended in.

Max wasn't popular. Nor was he a loser.

Max was fit, but he wasn't jacked.

Max probably didn't care what other people thought of him.

I wanted to be like Max.

Chapter Five
Blu

Year Four/Week One - Present

I leaned back into the velvet cushion booth at Cuisine Mercanti.

"Have you decided on food?" the waitress asked. She was pretty. Carter was probably eating her up.

"I'll have the Sauvignon Blanc," I said, handing over the food menu. "Just drinks for now," my eyes roamed over her nametag, "Ellie."

I've come to learn that people enjoyed when you said their name. It was like an extra step at valuing a person's person. It made them feel seen. I did a great job of that.

"The six or eight oz?" she asked, her face a little brighter.

"The bottle," Carter answered for me, throwing a flirty wink.

She didn't reciprocate. Maybe it was because she had a boyfriend. Maybe it was because she was into me.

It was probably the latter.

She carried our menus and walked away before Carter could get upset.

"Don't be mad," I started, sipping on water. "She's probably taken."

He rolled his eyes. "No one likes me."

"I like you."

"You don't count."

"I'm the only one that matters," I chuckled, looking around the room. My eyes caught on two men in very expensive suits sitting at the bar. The hotter one was looking at me. The other was sporting clear inebriation.

"Carter, be subtle. See those two guys at the bar?" I queried. He nodded. "Which one is better looking?"

"The one on the left."

That was the drunk fuck. "Wrong answer."

He shrugged, rolling up his napkin. "It's just the truth."

I crossed my arms. "The one on the right is way better."

"You're only saying that because he's checking you out."

"Don't be stupid. You're better than stupidity," I replied, though I studied the two men a little longer.

The man fighting inebriation was more cut, his suit a little darker, a little cleaner. His midnight hair curled around his ears in a sexy, messy way. He was loud, his lips were plump. Yeah, he was good looking.

The one who stared at me, well, he wasn't horrible on the eyes either. Chopped hair, a bit of a beer belly. I unconsciously felt my stomach, adjusting the waistband of my skirt to smooth out any edges.

"Maybe you're right," I was ashamed to admit. "But he's not ugly."

"He's not." Carter glanced over at a group of girls sitting near the two men. "What about them? Do you think I'll have any luck?"

"Maybe. If you grow some chest hair and actually approach someone in person. Tinder's gotten you nowhere."

He flicked his flaccid straw condom at me. I dodged it.

"I'm not like you, Blu. I don't just approach random people."

I let out an exaggerated laugh, mainly to get the suit-mans' attention again. It worked.

"Carter, you're twenty-five. Don't be embarrassing."

"You're so sharp sometimes," he let out, a spark of anger in his eyes.

It would pass. No one could stay mad at me.

The waitress, Ellie, brought the wine to our table and set out two glasses. She showed me the bottle, standard practice, poured a little and it danced around my tongue.

"Great legs," I joked.

"She wasn't talking about the wine," Carter added. This time, the line landed and she blushed a little.

Ellie placed the bottle in the ice bucket and walked away, leaving me to congratulate Carter on his first success of the night.

"Very bold," I smiled.

"I learned from the best." We tapped glasses and he spoke again. "How was your last, first day of university ever?"

The thought sent a rush of adrenaline through me. Just eight more months. Eight more months and I would be free. I would take whatever inheritance my late father left me and shoot for the stars. By the stars, I meant Paris.

Since I was a little girl, I'd always wanted to go. There were stupid stereotypes that surrounded the place – "*Oh, Paris isn't that great. Paris is just a tourist location. Paris is this and that and this and that,*" but fuck the stereotypes.

Paris was a dream, that's what it was. The atmosphere, the Eiffel Tower, the environment... It was all new. It was mine to explore. I was determined to explore it.

Mom could no longer withhold the inheritance when I graduated university. It was written in his will when he left me. When alcoholism sucked away all the best parts of himself.

I sipped away the thoughts and redirected them to Jace. Jace.

Jace, Jace, Jace.

"I have a crush on someone in my class."

Carter looked up behind his glass. "You mean the class you just went to an hour ago?"

I nodded. *Was I speaking gibberish?*

"Can I ask how you managed to conjure up feelings so quickly, or do I even want to know?"

"I don't get feelings for people. It's just a crush." Feelings were for the breakable. I was strong.

"And what are you going to do about said crush?"

I sat up straighter. "I'm going to make him love me."

Carter threw me a sarcastic smile. "And then what?"

"I haven't thought that far."

But I did think about him. The entire subway ride to Mercanti I thought about him. He wasn't my usual type. He was an enigma. I could feel the challenge brewing – it excited me. In a world so mundane and grey, I was the sun that brought it to life. At least in my own damn universe.

"Shall we cheers to new beginnings?" I said, holding out my wine glass.

He agreed with me. They always agreed with me.

"Cheers to you, Blu Henderson. The girl who always gets what she wants."

How I wish that were true.

How I wish someone would notice.

I chugged down the rest of my glass and waved at suit man staring at me, then my chest.

A sense of adoration, desire and a pang of resentment ran through my core. I shoved away the latter and focused on the fact I was his object of desire. That's all that mattered.

In a world short of love, I had to be wanted.

I was wanted.

I felt wanted.

Never loved, no.

But I was wanted.

Chapter Six
Jace

Year Four/Week Two - Present

Blu sat next to me.

"Jace, right?" Her voice was demanding, seducing. Trouble.

I pressed my lips together and nodded. "Hey."

She was wearing a black hoodie that draped over yoga pants, white sneakers and her deep blue hair was tied in a messy bun. Her brown eyes flashed into mine as she settled into the chair, turning to me.

"Hi," she repeated. Her smile was nice. All her teeth were perfectly straight besides the front two; slight crowding issue. I had the same. I fixed it. I fixed everything.

"I said hey," I laughed, though I knew it came across rudely. I didn't correct myself. I sounded like my brothers. They never corrected themselves.

If she was offended, she didn't say anything. Nothing seemed to offend her.

I noticed her the first day of class. Her blue hair was like a breath of fresh air sitting between boring, bland walls. The way she answered Professor Granger had me on the edge of my seat – no one spoke the way she spoke.

"Sorry, I didn't hear you." She took out black headphones from her ears. I had the feeling she wasn't listening to anything.

I chose not to answer and began bobbing my leg. It was a nervous habit of mine, one I rarely realized I would do until it began to cramp.

The desks were pushed closer together, almost as if the universe knew Blu would sit next to me.

Blu Henderson, she'd said her name last class.

What kind of a name was Blu? A nickname, surely. One her friends must have given her, or her family. What was her family like? Why didn't I just ask? I was never good at asking questions. I was never good at saying much.

That was all Morris. That was all Danny. Connor. Reid. Price. Everyone.

Everyone but me.

I listened in class to Granger discussing semiotics. It was interesting enough, engaging enough, until *her* fingers touched my kneecap.

She looked at me. I looked at her. I thought I stopped bobbing my leg half an hour ago. I didn't.

Her hand stayed for a brief moment until she decided to retract it and face forward. I longed for her to touch me again. That longing was unusual.

When break came, she wasted no time to pose the question. "Do you do that often?"

"Do what?" I knew what she was referring to, but I wanted to hear her say it just the same.

"Your leg. You can't sit still."

I shrugged. "Just something I do."

"Hm." She leaned back, her brown eyes scanning mine. "You're very good looking."

If I had been drinking water, I would've choked. My cheeks began to heat up, but I burned the blush before it could surface. She probably caught it because she smiled.

"You look like a painting."

"A painting?" I asked. I wanted more of this. Whatever this was.

"A painting," she repeated, then turned to her laptop and began typing notes for the seminar.

We didn't speak for the rest of class. She got up abruptly to take a phone call and never came back, leaving me with the longing feeling of her fingers against my kneecap and the rush of her compliments.

By the time I got back home, it was late and I huddled into bed, drifting off to a list of paintings I could only hope she compared me to.

At least in my dreams, Blu's compliment was true.

Chapter Seven
Blu

Grade Eight – Ten Years Ago

"Your father's dead."

My mom didn't pull me out of school that day. She just uttered the words through a telephone call. It was my eighth grade teacher Mrs. Meleni that asked permission to take me home.

I didn't want to go home.

There wasn't much of a home to come back to.

When I walked through the door, Mrs. Meleni accompanied me. If there was a law against that, she broke it. But I felt safer with her by my side.

My mom was in the living room with a cigarette in one hand and a beer in the other. The radio was blasting punk rock and she sang her heart out as if her husband hadn't passed away.

As if my dad wasn't dead.

I was thirteen when I asked my mother how he died. She told me the alcohol took him. I know now that she meant he overdosed and the poison shutdown his brain.

Mrs. Meleni cried when she saw the state of my home. My mom was a functioning alcoholic, but an alcoholic nonetheless. She said if she could do basic household chores, show up to work and clean her car without losing it then why would she give up drinking?

I couldn't argue with her. I was voiceless.

Mrs. Meleni asked if I wanted to be taken to child services and I remember laughing at her. I said, "I'm a little too old for help."

What I really meant was, "Save me."

When I went to my father's funeral, my mom sobbed like a two year old who lost her favourite toy. I don't know that she ever loved my father. I don't know that she ever really knew him.

Did I?

Did he even love her? Me?

Why would he leave me if he loved me?

The house stopped stinking like booze. Dad was a spiller, Mom poured her drinks in lidded cups. The floors weren't sticky anymore. I guess that counted for something.

Dad left a hefty inheritance for Mom and me, only he specifically stated in the will that I'd receive my share when I graduated. Back in the day, he had founded his own contracting company. He was smart, my dad, in his own way. He was sick too.

But I was thirteen. What was a thirteen-year-old going to do with thousands of dollars? I had no use for the money. Not then, anyway.

After the funeral, Mom disappeared for a few days. I think she went to Aunt Lisa's; she came back wearing a red overcoat and some knee high stockings. Aunt Lisa's was a strip club, I'd googled.

That night, I slept in my dad's bed. I wanted to feel what he felt, every night, waking up and hating his life so much that he poisoned himself from the inside out.

Was I so bad? Was I a hard kid to take care of? Was I too needy? Too clingy? Too weak?

His room was dark and dismal, various shades of dark blue stamping every corner of these walls. Navy drapes, indigo sheets, chipped spruce paint.

Was blue a happy colour? I could no longer tell. He was sick, but he was out of his misery. A bittersweet dichotomy of some sorts.

I drifted off to sleep thinking about who I was. Who I wanted to be. What I wanted to achieve. Was I going to end up like my parents? One dead, another teetering between breathing and breathless?

I chose neither.

I chose Blu.

A part of me died that day.

Her name was Beatrice Louise Henderson.

Chapter Eight
Jace

Senior/High School – Four Years Ago

Six months after I changed my life, I asked Riley Montgomery to prom.

People underestimated the change your body could make in six months.

Six months and my Accutane treatment finally clear up my acne.

Six months I worked out every part of my core until I was numb.

Six months of wearing a clear retainer.

Six months of motivational podcasts.

Six months of erasing the scrawny, lanky shit I used to be.

Six months and I got my dream girl.

I remember when I first noticed Riley noticing me. I'd just gotten off practice when her and her friend Marla approached from the bleachers.

"Great job out there, Jace."

I didn't even think she knew my name. But she did, and she was talking to me.

"Thanks. We got another game tomorrow night if you want to come?"

She liked that I invited her, and I savoured the new confidence I found in myself. Old Jace would have never talked to Riley Montgomery. Riley Montgomery would have never talked to old Jace.

The next night, she came wearing my jersey number on her cheek. We won 3-0 and I rode the high a little longer than I'd ever rode it before. Before she could say anything, I took her face in my hands and kissed her senseless. It was the second time I spoke to her, and my hands were gripping her waist. She let me explore more of her later, but I wanted to wait until prom.

I saw something with this girl. She saw something with me.

No one saw that before.

A few days after I asked Riley to prom, the guys were getting changed in the dressing room.

"Boland copped Riley, d'you hear Danny?" Connor piped, slapping my chest.

"Good on you," Danny said.

He had a crush on Riley for a while, but I got her. She liked me. Not him. I felt a sense of power from that.

"You fuck her yet?" Morris asked, as if he had every right in the world to know my business.

I shook my head.

"She doesn't want to touch you, eh Boland," Connor joked. His stupid antics went over my head. Shit wasn't funny.

"Didn't Samantha Cordon give you syphilis last year, Cumberland?"

The boys growled with laughter while Connor ducked out of the room, unable to meet my eyes. Again, I felt like I'd won. The guys loved me. For once, they weren't laughing at me.

They were laughing with me.

Five minutes later, the dressing room had cleared out entirely. Or so I thought.

"Feels nice, doesn't it?" It was Max who remained.

"What?" I slung my bag over my shoulder. "What feels nice?"

"Feeling like you belong."

A surge of heat soared through my body. A pang of annoyance coupled the emotion. "You're fucking weirding me out, Max."

"You're better than this, Jace."

"You don't know me."

"You don't know yourself," he countered, shaking his head. "You think fitting in with a bunch of assholes is going to fulfill you? What are you looking for?"

"A way out of this conversation," I snapped, turning my back on him until I exited the room.

Who the hell did he think he was? Acting like he knew me? Questioning everything I worked towards, everything I worked for? I barely said five words to this guy. He would've said less than three.

"Baby," Riley said as soon as I reached her locker. "You look a little down."

I cupped her cheek and kissed her lips, taking in all that she was giving me. All that belonged to me.

Leaning in close, my breath tickled her ear. "Come back to mine."

I fucked her that night.

I couldn't wait until prom.

Connor said she didn't want to touch me, well, I proved him wrong.

I proved everyone wrong.

That's all that mattered.

Chapter Nine
Blu

Year Four/Week Two - Present

My ethics and media class was a drag.

Most of my courses were online so I didn't need to brave this shithole of a campus, but this one was by far the worst.

Prof. Flowers was anything but a dainty stem and leaf. She wore these weird overcoats that had swirly designs on them, her boots were clunky and muddy as if she lived in the wastelands and her hair was constantly uncombed.

Oh, yeah, her personality wasn't that great either.

She banked on participation marks for grades, and sadly I was walking a thin line between passing and failing my degree so attending was the only option.

I couldn't fail. I had a plan. I had to leave.

This building stunk of mildew and there was only a slim window in the corner of the class, tucked away behind a podium housing old books.

But today was different.

It was different because there was a new face.

"Funny seeing you here," I told Jace, plopping my bag next to his. "Switch in?"

He nodded. It became his signature sign. I think it meant he liked me.

"Yeah, the class I was in was ridiculous," he said, stretching out his long legs. My eyes trailed the length of his trousers before meeting his gaze again.

"Which class?" I asked, mainly out of formality. There were plenty of things I wanted to know about Jace, none of them involving school.

"I honestly don't remember the name. The professor called out everyone and quizzed us the first day."

"You're right, that's lunacy."

"Tell me about it."

"What did she quiz you on? I mean," I relaxed into my chair, "What is there to even quiz you on?"

He scoffed, running slender fingers through his hair. I noticed he changed his earrings. Both were diamonds.

"I think she was trying to make a statement."

Interesting. I leaned in. "Isn't that everyone's intention?"

He caught my eye and a glimmer of *something* passed through his gaze. "Is that what you're trying to do?"

"Is it working?"

The muscles in his jaw flexed and finally, for the first time since I'd met him, he smiled. It was a small gesture, one I could tell was reserved for the people he was impressed by (or impressed upon). But he smiled at me. That was a good enough answer as any.

"Alrighty class, I see some new faces!" Prof. Flowers started, throwing a look at Jace. He was the only boy in our class besides Hugo, a transfer student from somewhere overseas.

Faces. Plural. There was only one. And he was sitting next to me.

"Would you like to introduce yourself?" she piped.

"I'm not very good at introductions," he began, "But why not."

This grabbed everyone's attention. His voice was deep and low. Given the fact that he was the only man in this bleak environment, half the girls were wide-eyed and interested. I knew first-hand. I was one of them.

A brunette in the corner twirled a lock of hair around her finger. Another pushed out her boobs from a too-tight top. She was far in the back, though. He wouldn't see her.

I did.

"My name's Jace, I'm a fourth year communications student and uh," he paused, looking down at a crack in his desk, "I love soccer."

Most people waved, a few mumbled hellos, Prof. Flowers smiled. I studied. I studied all of him.

He was silent, but not shy. Maybe he liked to present himself as such, but there was something to him that screamed attention. Now attention could go one of two ways – either you sought it out, or it found you. I couldn't tell if he was both, neither, or somewhere in between.

"Cool, cool," the professor clapped, then quickly switched on a Ted Talk for the next half hour.

During this time, I decided to scout out any potential competition in the room. Call me crazy, but I needed to be the one he wanted. If someone was prettier than me, he would like her. Wouldn't he? Every guy chose looks over personality. At least, everyone I had ever been with.

They were all the same.

That's when I noticed a little belle sitting in the corner, quiet with doe-eyes. She was stunning, sporting that girl-next-door look. I didn't look like that. I tried too hard.

She would peer over at him occasionally, then glance back to the screen. God, did this guy not see the effect he had on people? Imagine looking like a model-off-duty without even trying. Imagine having to build up a strong personality in order for people to see you.

I chanced a look at Jace and could see his eyes flutter between the screen and girl-next-door.

Fuck.

I looked again. He was looking at her.

Are you fucking serious? Absolutely not.

I ripped a page out of my planner and pulled out a sharpie, scribbling a note on the back:

Have coffee with me.

Four words.

Four words he wouldn't refuse. He couldn't refuse it. *He can't refuse me.*

I folded it into a perfect square and slid it to him, smirking once before returning my attention forward.

Now I didn't need to look to see that he was no longer captured by girl-next-door. He was focused on me. I felt his burning stare as he pulled out a pencil and wrote something, then passed it back.

The palms of my hands were sweaty. Why was I sweating? Was I nervous? No. I never got nervous. Nerves were for the weak.

Silly me, I thought. What did I have to worry about?

Name a time and place.

I was Blu Henderson after all.

Chapter Ten
Blu

Year Four/Week Two – Present

Of course I suggested that we hang out after class. I needed to know him. Time was running out.

He ordered a latte from the café barista at Plane. It was a trendy spot on campus, though I'm not sure how. Maybe I was just a hater of all things. Maybe I *liked* being a hater. But not of him, he interested me.

Truthfully, I despised the taste of coffee. It was either too bitter, too burnt or too sweet. It also reminded me of the many times Dad said he was going sober. Another excuse, wasn't it? To soften the blow before he took his last breath.

Ah, that was a long time ago. Best not dwell on the parts of your story you couldn't rewrite.

But this moment, here with Jace, I had the power to control it. I didn't care about this fucking place, or any place, so long as there was one where we could talk. Where I could get to know him.

It was weird, this growing fixation with a man I'd known for two weeks. I didn't have his number. I knew nothing about him. Everything that intrigued me was conjured up by the assumptions I made in my head.

I was always a clever girl, a creative one too. Maybe that was my flaw. Maybe I fell in love with the potential of people, not who they really were.

Maybe this wasn't the case. I hoped like hell it wouldn't be, otherwise my best efforts would be useless, and I would've wasted my time.

Again.

"Tell me about yourself, Jace."

We sat by the bookshelf in the back corner. *"The lighting is better here,"* I'd told him. He didn't give a damn about the lighting, I could tell.

But I did.

He needed to see my features.

He needed to take me in.

His fingers wrapped around the ugly paper cup every shop insisted on using nowadays. Their "mission" rang clear in my head: *Save the turtles! Stop global warming! No littering!*

Best to redirect concern towards the rich who flew in private jets for a fucking tootsie roll.

"What do you want to know?" he asked.

God, his voice was nice. So, so nice.

But mine... Mine was dominant, demanding. I was in charge. He should learn that.

Using the tips of my fingers, I gently pushed aside the refresher I'd ordered and rested my chin atop my free palm. "Everything."

"That's a loaded question." He placed his lips on the rim and sipped. I watched it play out in slow-mo. I watched everything. "Be more specific."

You don't get to demand anything from me, I wanted to say. "What's your favourite movie?" I settled on instead.

"American Psycho."

Huh. I happened to love that movie. "Let me quiz you."

He leaned back into the wooden seat, folding his arms. "Shoot."

Before I began my trivia, I scanned the skin beneath his elbow crease. Michelangelo's "Creation of

Adam" was tattooed beside a shaded rose, I noticed it the first day of class. I wanted to ask about that, about the silver ring on his pointer and pinky. I didn't ask that. I was too busy talking about fucking psychos.

"How many kills did Patrick Bateman have?"

He tilted his head to the side, letting out a sharp laugh. "I didn't psychoanalyze the movie. I just enjoyed it."

Must be nice, I thought. To enjoy things without looking too deeply as to why you enjoyed them, why they existed – why they made you happy.

"What's your favourite movie?" His turn.

Without missing a beat, I responded, "Sleepy Hollow."

"Gothic." He leaned forward, Michelangelo's Creation folding into invisibility. "Have a thing for monsters?"

Ha. "Not quite."

There was a brief pause before we spoke again. Just for a moment I felt awkward, tense. I felt… Incapable.

Had I read this wrong? He was supposed to be nervous. Why wasn't he nervous?

"So you asked me to coffee to discuss films, or what?"

I looked up, astonished that he had the balls to even question me.

"I asked you for coffee because I think you're attractive." I didn't give him time to react before I said, "Do I make you nervous?"

I already knew the answer.

I made everyone nervous.

"No."

I laughed out fucking loud.

Did I hear him correctly?

"What?" My head was shaking so fast I could've snapped my neck. "What do you mean, *no*?"

Now it was his turn to laugh. And his laugh...

Was so –

Fucking –

Nice.

"Maybe I make you nervous." He crossed his arms again, leaning back on his chair. "After all, you're blushing."

No I wasn't. "No I'm not." I covered my cheeks. They were hot.

Shit.

"Can I ask you something?" he said, staring at me with eyes like crisp fern.

I swallowed. "Mm-hmm."

"Is this normal for you?"

"Is what normal for me?"

He pressed his lips together, his jaw flexing once again. I felt exposed, raw, stripped of the self I tried so hard to maintain.

"You try to intimidate people." He inhaled and exhaled within two breaths. "You don't need to do that with me."

"Intimidate," I released, as if he were speaking a foreign language.

"Don't get me wrong, Blu. You are quite intimidating. Most pretty girls are."

"Most pretty girls are," I repeated.

"You're hearing me correctly."

He thinks I'm pretty.

He thinks I'm pretty.

He thinks I'm pretty.

I must be pretty.

"Not very good at taking compliments, are you?" he assumed.

But it wasn't a compliment, was it? It was a fact. Jace thought I was pretty. He was stating, not suggesting. No improvements needed to be made. Did they?

"I want you to be honest with me."

He nodded in response. It started to become my favourite thing about him. The only gesture I really knew.

"What would you change about me?"

The way he stared made me uncomfortable. Looking at me like I was some sort of alien, someone unrecognizable. I was still here. Was that too vulnerable? Was that too much to ask?

"That's an odd question."

"Don't answer it," I snapped, curtly. "I mean it."

"You asked the question."

"Did you have an answer?"

"I don't know you well enough," he admitted. "I don't know you at all."

A decision fluttered in front of my eyes. How did I get to know someone? It'd been a long time since I let someone in. There was good reason for that. The choice was there – let him in or leave him be.

I chose the former.

This time would be different.

"Do you want to?"

That smile returned, a slight dimple piercing the right side of his cheek. It was something new. I hadn't noticed it before.

That was an answer within itself.

Chapter Eleven
Jace

Year Four/Week Three – Present

After coffee last week, I gave Blu my number. Rather, she placed her phone in my hands with the contact list ready for my name.

Class started in an hour and my commute to campus was half of that. Luckily, Will was passing through York to attend a meeting so he gave me a lift.

"How's school?" he asked me, sipping an americano. He drank five of those a day.

That question alone made my heart palpitate. He cared enough. That was plenty.

"Good."

"Speak up about it, Jace. How are classes?"

No, he cared a little more than enough. I smiled. "Classes are fine. I met a girl."

This piqued his interest. "What's her name? What's she like? 'Bout time baby bro."

And just like that, the thrill paused itself.
Baby bro.
Kid.
Kid. Kid. Kid.
Would they ever see me as an equal?

I wasn't that far off in age. Baxter was twenty-six, Will was twenty-seven and Scott was twenty-nine.

Not. Far. Off.

"Yeah she's cool. Bit bold, though. Her name's Blu."

He adjusted his position and drove with his knee, folding the cufflink around his wrist. "Blu? Like the colour?"

"Like the colour." She popped into my head and I smiled. "She's got blue hair, too."

"Huh. Interesting. She one of those art freaks?"

"What makes them freaks?"

He scoffed. "Aren't they all? I mean, you have to be some level of weird to paint the shit that they paint."

I felt myself getting offended. "Baxter was an art major. He's a photographer."

"Baxter's a Boland. There's a difference."

If there was one thing I hated about Will, it was his entitlement. If someone didn't work in finance or business or whatever the hell he studied, they were automatically beneath him. He judged me the most out of all my brothers, even if it was silent commentary.

"What's the difference?" I genuinely wanted to know.

"He doesn't have coloured hair like your Blu."

My Blu.

Why did he say it like that? Why did I like it?

I felt a tad protective. "It suits her."

He laughed condescendingly, taking a right turn into the campus parking lot. "I bet it does," he unlocked the car door, "Maybe you'll meet Red next, or Orange. Try all the colours of the rainbow by the end of fourth year, yeah?"

I slammed it shut and walked away, hearing the stupid exhaust pipe he installed fade into the distance.

Why the hell did it have to be this way? Was I always going to be picked on forever? By own family at that?

I felt turned off. I felt it creeping in. Every step that I took towards the classroom was a step I wanted to take back. Maybe I should've occupied my thoughts with someone named Kendra or Emily. Maybe I should text Riley –

No. *Don't ever fucking text Riley again.*

Class started in fifteen minutes, meaning I was early. I was always early. There always seemed to be one or two consistent faces present, but I didn't know their names. I didn't care enough. They were nobodies.

I was a nobody once.

Never again.

Fifteen minutes alone with my thoughts was a long time. Blu always walked in late, so I had minutes to reflect. She'd asked me if I wanted to get to know her. She'd asked me a lot of things that day.

It was odd. Most of the things we talked about were superficial; Blu struck me as anything but. I felt her holding back. I felt something. I didn't ask. She was the one who wanted to go to coffee with me.

Maybe Blu liked me.

Nah.

Yes. *Yes.* Was that so hard to believe?

Did I like her? No. I didn't know her. Could I like her? I mean, she wasn't my usual type.

Riley had blonde hair.

Blu had blue hair. Dark blue, almost black.

Riley had green eyes.

Blu had brown eyes.

Riley had a petite build.

Blu was curvy.

I couldn't like her. She wasn't my type. Will would never approve.

She walked in five minutes after I halted any growing feelings. Her smile was crooked. She waved at me.

"Hey Jace." Her phone was clutched in her hand and that's when I thought about it.

She never texted me.

Why hadn't she texted me?

You don't fucking like her, why do you care?

"Hi," I responded, shifting my body away. It was forced. I forced myself to.

Slowly, she lowered her handbag and eyed me with trepidation. It radiated off of her. I didn't want her to notice that it was bleeding off me as well.

"Everything okay?" she asked. Her voice was smaller, almost docile.

I nodded in response. That's all I ever did. If I would've opened my mouth, what would I have said?

"I'm questioning my feelings for you." *I don't have them.*

"I sort of like you." *But I don't know you.*

"My brother won't approve of you." *But do I care about what he thinks?*

Yes. I cared about what everyone thought.

She settled beside me and didn't speak, opening her laptop. I did the same, scrolling through journal articles on one tab and Twitter on another.

I glanced over at her laptop and saw that she was looking at plane tickets. The background was Paris, I think, but she exited out right before I could confirm the destination.

"I'm sorry I didn't text you," she said, her eyes sincerely apologetic.

And that's when I knew I was a dick. A liar.

That's when I recognized how fucked up I was, because I responded with, "I didn't notice."

For fuck's sakes, Jace.

I noticed everything.

Blu didn't talk to me for the rest of class.

Chapter Twelve
Blu

Freshman/High School – Ten Years Ago

Six months after Dad left, I dyed my hair blue.

It was a harder process than I could have ever anticipated. My hair was naturally dark brown, so bleaching it broke it, essentially.

I tried box dye after box dye, toner after toner until finally it turned into a brassy orange colour that grabbed onto the turquoise Manic Panic Mom picked up for me.

She didn't know what she was buying, just that it would give me something to do. Something she didn't need to do for me. Something that would occupy my own happiness all on my lonesome.

My hair turned into this horrible green shade. It looked like sea moss, or moldy Jell-O. Could Jell-O get moldy? I believed it. I believed everything back then.

My elementary school friends distanced themselves from me. No one wanted to associate with the girl who lost her father, let alone one taken by alcoholism. They already made assumptions about me. Said that I was probably drinking at the age of thirteen. I think Mrs. Meleni spilled the beans to someone about the state of my home, and that person spoke to another person who gossiped and bam.

I was a freak.

And now, I was a freak with blue hair.

Those assumptions changed the trajectory of my life. No one would make bad assumptions about me again. I didn't belong to my father's legacy, nor my mother.

I was Blu Henderson. Not Beatrice.

When people asked me why I dyed my hair blue, I told them it's because I recently discovered a movie called Coraline. It quickly became my favourite since the main character had this bright, cobalt hair. I liked her. I saw myself in her.

Lost.

Neglected.

Sad.

No one needed to know that I dyed my hair because I felt close to my dad; in some way, those walls, those curtains, those sheets – it was all I had left of him. It was all he left me with.

I got bullied, surely. Every kid does. I embraced it, though. I bullied those scoundrels back. After all, we were the same age. The rats weren't above me, they were beside me. They just buried their ugliness better.

Then one day, I met Fawn Vanderstead.

She moved from some town three hours away because her parents landed a good job at The Factory.

She was rich and pretty.

She got bullied too.

Like I said... *Rats.*

I wanted to be her friend. Maybe it's because I wanted to be like her, or have the things she had or dressed the way she did. Never had I ever approached someone the way I approached Fawn, but when I did, I knew we'd be friends.

Sometimes two people, completely opposite and far apart were tied by an invisible chord. No one could see it but the people inside the knot. That knot was too hard to break, so we didn't break it. We let it tighten around us, we let it shape us, until we morphed into someone new. Someone better.

Someone Blu.

"Do you like my hair?" I'd asked Fawn who at the time, was standing by her locker painting her nails a pretty pink shade. Well, pretty enough. I never liked pink.

She looked up at me with big brown eyes. They kind of reminded me of my own. Her hair was black and slicked back into a nice ponytail. Long, unlike my chopped, turquoise mess.

"I hate it, actually," she deadpanned. I was about to turn away when she grabbed my wrist and spun me around. "But we can fix it. My aunt is a hairdresser. Come over after school."

So I did. And the day after that, and the day after that.

Fawn became my lunch buddy, my dinner partner, my everything.

It sounded dramatic, but when you had nothing, the people you gave yourself to filled the void that was left stripped and barren.

Fawn repaired me. Her aunt repaired my hair. I mended the broken pieces of myself.

But broken pieces always remained, especially when they sat right underneath your skin. It looked like flesh, felt like flesh. Shards became soft. Glass became smooth.

Pain became happiness. Happiness became pain.

Pain became comfort, and that comfort was bliss.

Chapter Thirteen
Blu

Year Four/Week Four – Present

"I'm not talking to him again," I stated, sipping on a glass of prosecco rosé. "*Ever again.*"

"You have class with him," Carter said.

"Two times a week, Blu," Fawn added.

We sat in a leather booth at the back of Teladela, a fusion cuisine Fawn insisted we tried with no room to argue.

I rolled my eyes. "So what?"

"Run me through what he did again." Carter gripped his beer, watching me with criticism. Or maybe it was empathy. I could never tell the difference.

Truthfully, I didn't even want to replay the events of last week. It was an embarrassment. I was an embarrassment.

How dare he speak to me like that? What did I ever do to him? I was complimentary, direct and assertive. My intentions were crystal clear.

I set up the perfect story. I did everything right. And yet, he was cold and distant. "*I didn't notice,*" he'd said when I apologized for not texting him.

He didn't think about me at all.

"I got on his nerves, and now he wants nothing to do with me." I wished I hadn't said it out loud. Saying things out loud made them very real.

Fawn narrowed her eyes, matching Carter's. "Why would he hate you? You're like, the nicest person ever."

"I wouldn't go that far," Carter smirked. I knew it was out of love. At least, I thought so.

We all chuckled but it didn't ease my concern. Was I not enough? Did he really even like me to begin with? Oh my God, this was all in my head, wasn't it?

"I don't want to put myself in a position to be embarrassed, guys. I was probably too forward." I caught myself rambling, but I couldn't stop. I wanted someone to hear my innermost thoughts. I didn't want to be alone with them any longer.

"Should I be more silent? Quiet? Should I take a different approach?"

"Whoa, whoa, whoa, Blu," Carter leaned in, placing a hand over mine. It was shaking. I was shaking.

"Why are you spiralling right now?"

That felt like a slap. "I'm not."

"You kind of are, babe," Fawn took my other hand in hers. "Why do you always expect the worst?"

Before I could respond, Carter chimed in. "You're projecting, Blu. You're seeing what you want to see."

"Why the fuck would I want to be rejected, Carter?"

"I don't think you want that. I think…" he looked over at Fawn, "I think I agree with her. You had a string of shitty experiences so you don't expect this to be different."

"It won't be."

"See!" Fawn pinched my wrist. "See."

My cheeks heated. Maybe I did project. Maybe I did see what I wanted to see. But how could my poor, little brain do that to me? I wanted nothing more than to be loved.

• • •

I deserved it. The world owed me.

"What do I do?" I asked. It sounded desperate. I was begging for advice, a way out. "Do I give up?"

"Why are you so invested in this guy, Blu? You've known him for a month," Carter questioned.

A damn good question at that.

I made a mental pros and cons list the day that I met him and again after coffee. Honestly, there were more cons than pros. The desire to win someone over trumped everything. It always did.

Pros: He's hot, he's tall, he's mysterious.

Cons: He's twenty-one. I'm twenty-three. Definitely some maturity issues. He doesn't say anything, he doesn't give anything, he's kind of... boring? No, that's not the right word. Basic? Figure this out later. I don't know how he feels about me. I don't know that I ever will. Every girl looks at him when he walks by. I think he pretends to be oblivious. I see that in him. I can't date someone like that. I don't even want to.

I recited this list out loud as my friends stared at me with open jaws.

"You don't even know a single thing about him," Carter stated, shaking his head. "This isn't even about him, Blu."

"What are you talking about?"

"Hi, excuse me!" Fawn called over our waiter. He perked up. Fawn was gorgeous; talking to her was a privilege, I'd come to realize.

"Can I get another glass of prosecco please? Oh, and maybe two vodka shots."

A Hue of Blu Marie-France Leger

He nodded and tapped his temple, as if he was communicating that he remembered her order. Or, rather, he would remember her.

My face soured. "I don't even like vodka."

"It's not for you, babe." She looked over at Carter. "If we're going to listen to this insane story of you liking a boy out of potential, then we need some liquid T.L.C."

"Out of potential?" But I knew what she meant. I wanted to hear her explain it. Talking had gotten me nowhere, clearly. No one understood me.

She tapped her bright blue acrylics on the white table cloth and cleared her throat. "Since knowing you Blu, I've come to realize three major components of your personality."

"Here we go," I groaned, even though I'd asked for this.

"One, you're wild and arrogant and ruthless."

"I –"

"I have the mic. Don't interrupt me." She wiggled a finger at Carter who looked amused. Dazed, almost. Infatuated? He never looked at me that way.

"Two. Where you are bold and impulsive, you're also the kindest, most generous girl I've ever met. You wear your heart on your sleeve. You value love over everything, even in the absence of it."

Even in the absence of it.

"Three…" She had a hard time meeting my eyes; I knew what was coming.

"You've lost a lot. You downplay your pain. You act like it doesn't exist, that it isn't a part of you, when it became you."

The drinks arrived on a silver platter, interrupting the zone Fawn had built around this table.

A Hue of Blu   Marie-France Leger

I couldn't look away from her; she couldn't look away from me.

Fawn had been my friend for ten years now. She'd seen the relationships, the hookups, the toxicity of what I'd accepted because I didn't know any different. My home life was non-existent [still is] and everyone resented me. My mind made it worse.

After high school graduation, I convinced Mom to take out ten thousand from the trust Dad left me. He'd told Mom to only release it after I graduated post-secondary, but she cared more about me staying out of her way.

She broke a promise that day. To her husband, to herself, to me.

I asked her to break that promise.

I guess we were two sides of the same coin – tarnished, rusted and bruised.

I guess I was more my mother than I thought I was.

Fawn and I both took a gap year. We travelled for six months across Australia, fucked some boys, kissed some girls, drank disgusting beer that surfers paid for and attempted to scuba-dive. *Attempted*, being the keyword.

When we got back, we both picked up jobs at convenience stores. Conveniently [see what I did there], they were just five minutes away from each other so we would grab Subway every afternoon on our lunch breaks. We never had the same one, but we pretended we did.

"We need to go back to school," she'd said to me one day, chomping on a cold-cut-combo.

"I agree." I was eating the same. I always copied her. She was better than me.

"York?" she suggested. "It's close enough. It's no U of T but it'll suffice."

It wasn't a top university, no, but she was right. Anything to help me move forward in life. I was stuck. The same horrible habits never perished. They grew and festered and boiled. Something needed to change.

At the time, I didn't realize it was myself.

"Earth to Blu," Carter snapped his fingers in front of my face, drawing me back to reality.

"I didn't mean to offend you," Fawn murmured. "If I did, it wasn't intentional. I just –"

"You didn't offend me." Liar. Everything offended me.

Rejection.
Judgement.
Words.
Actions.
My past.
My present.
Myself.

"So how do I move forward?" I almost forgot that it was Jace we were talking about.

"Let go of any expectations." Carter pushed the fresh glass of prosecco my way. "Instead of trying to win him over, get to know him. Then in two weeks, give us reasons as to why you actually like him beyond something surface level."

I grabbed the stem of my drink and downed it in one gulp. Getting to know someone came with an invisible list of requirements. At coffee, I didn't actually want to get to know him, let's be honest.

Jace was a contact high.

I wanted to enjoy that feeling for as long as possible. I always did. With everyone.

I didn't give a flying fuck about his favourite movie, nor the meanings of his tattoos. I wanted him to see that I cared, even if it wasn't genuine.

Getting to know someone came with vulnerability, and not just on his part, but on mine. Was I ready to do that? Did I even want to?

Carter gripped my fingers. "I guarantee that you don't like him, Blu. You like what he represents."

"And what does he represent?"

A tired sigh escaped his mouth. "A challenge."

Chapter Fourteen
Jace

Year Four/Week Four – Present

Blu was early today.

She glanced up at me the second I walked into class, but she didn't look like her usual self.

Over the last four weeks, I'd noticed how well she dressed. It was a weird thing to notice about someone, especially when she held little importance in my head for the first fourteen days. But after coffee, I almost began to piece the puzzle together – the puzzle that was Blu Henderson.

Her hair was always down in dark waves. She wore a lot of lace tights, black mostly. I wished that she didn't wear purple eyeshadow; it made her eyes look tired.

Today though, she looked more tired than ever before.

I decided to sit next to her.

"Morning, Blu."

Her head was on the desk when she turned to me, barely lifting a movement. All she did was acknowledge my presence before settling back into position.

Goddamn, was this how I acted? Was this how she saw me?

"Long night?" I asked, taking out my MacBook.

Her face was buried in her arms, but she nodded and returned her attention to me. Brown eyes poked out from beneath her sleeves, a small smile on her lips.

It felt like a victory.

"I was out," she explained, then yawned. "Had one too many glasses of prosecco."

A heat burned my cheeks. I realized I knew so little about her friends, her social circle. Was she with another guy? Was she seeing someone? *Why did the thought bother me?*

I decided to ask. "On a date?"

Now her eyes fully met mine, glossy and bloodshot. If I didn't know any better, I'd say she was still a tad drunk.

"Not a date." A simple response, she'd said, with no further explanation.

If not a date, then a hookup. If not a hookup, then a meet-and-greet. If not me, then who? Who was she out with?

I turned away before I could ask any more questions. She wasn't my problem. She was barely anything. We were acquaintances at best, strangers who knew of each other in school circumstances.

Strangers who didn't feel like strangers.

"Okay class, today I want to start off by pairing you off." Professor Flowers turned on the projector, loosening a silver tie around her neck. "Choose a partner and answer one of the four questions on screen."

A few girls looked at me. Every time that happened, a flash of serotonin skyrocketed through my body.

I was attractive. I was good-looking. I became everything I wanted to become. I worked hard for this

– my face, my body, my everything. Gone are the days of the scrawny twig, Jace Boland.

Before I could open my mouth, Blu slapped a palm on my desk, leaning up from her slump.

She said one word.

One word that sent all the waves of serotonin into overdrive.

One word that no one had ever said to me in my entire life. A word I craved to hear. A word that did not exist to my ears.

"Mine."

Chapter Fifteen
Blu

Year Four/Week Four – Present
"Mine."

His fingers were so close to my hand, so close. If I extended my pinky just a little further, it would've touched his thumb.

"Okay," he nodded.

I won.

The girl-next-door's face dropped. Maybe she expected to be his partner – don't know what kind of delusional world she was fucking living in.

"What question do you want to do?" Jace asked, opening a Google doc. "I was thinking number two. It's the easiest if you did the readings."

Oops.

He tilted his head, narrowing his eyes. "Did you do the readings, Blu?"

Caught red-handed, I guess. *I accept my defeat.* "One too many glasses of –"

"Prosecco. Got it," he snapped, glancing one last time at the projector before typing away.

"I can help, you know," I leaned in closer, re-reading the question. "I've done Crenshaw's readings before."

"But it's not about before, is it?"

"Why are you being rude?" It slipped out of my mouth, but I didn't regret it. He was being an asshole and he needed to know.

He laughed, well, more like a scoff. It was condescending as hell.

"You ask to be my partner, but you don't prep for school. Did you expect me to do all the work?"

Fuck. This. Guy.

I sat in silence while he typed away, crossing my arms and analyzing my surroundings. Not looking at him was the easiest thing I could do. Maybe he had a point, but there were nicer ways to say it. I liked direct people, fuck, I was direct myself.

Direct, not sharp.

There was a difference.

Ten gruelling minutes of nothing passed before Prof. Flowers clapped her sandy, bony fingers and began asking the pairs for answers.

I was in and out until it reached girl-next-door. She had a soothing voice, like an angel or a priest. Whatever fucking way you look at it, she seemed innocent.

Men loved innocent girls.

It was a weird thing they enjoyed. Like, this goal of taking someone's virginity was the ultimate trophy, and if you had been touched you were some fucking harlot.

It ground my gears, watching her. She had perfect hands, a symmetrical face, she was small and fragile like a glass mirror.

In some ways, maybe she and I were the same.

Breakable.

"Okay, Blu and Jace," Prof. Flowers targeted. "What question did you select?"

"Question two," Jace responded. For himself, not for me.

"And what answer did you come up with on Crenshaw's reading?"

Jace began to talk but I wanted to sew his perfect fucking mouth with a needle and thread.

And that's what I did.

"Crenshaw discussed racial discrimination," I began, silencing whatever tooth-lipped comment the man beside me had to say. "White male privilege and power is still being pressed upon women, depicting them as incapable and unworthy due to the colour of their skin. Because of this, women have a hard time coming into their identity in fear of being judged."

Contrary to what Jace believed, I had done the readings. Two years ago, Prof. Wentworth. I didn't forget a thing.

I never do.

"Great analysis, Blu." Prof. Flowers quickly moved on without acknowledging Jace.

For the rest of class, I didn't either.

Chapter Sixteen
Jace

Year One/York University – Three Years Ago

"I can't believe we're here, babe."

Riley sat on my dorm single, flipping through our high-school graduation yearbook.

"Oh my gosh," she squealed, bobbing up and down.

I glanced at her tits, then her face. "What?"

"My lipstick still hasn't faded on the paper. See?" She showed me the puckered outline of her lips pressed below her signature.

I decided to give her a kiss of my own, which turned to her blowing me, which turned to me fingering her before my roommate Bryce came in.

If he suspected we were fooling around, he didn't show it. I met him briefly at the orientation but he was a quiet guy; kept to himself, sort of reminded me of Max.

Sort of reminded me of myself before I made the switch from loser to heartthrob.

"You're so big," Riley had whispered in my ear before she left the room.

I know, I thought. I know.

"Hey man," I addressed Bryce who was settled at his desk, textbook already flipped to a wordy page.

He nodded at me. That's it.

I walked up to him, glancing over his shoulder. I felt him tense up. "What class is this for?"

"Our intro class." He highlighted a few lines, scribbled some letters in the margin, and hiked his glasses higher. "We have a quiz next week."

"Yep," I said, pushing away from the desk. "That's next week's problem."

"That's not how you want to start university," he advised.

I remember it was a jab to the gut.

I remember because I'd said that to Morris first year of high school when he downed seven shots at a Summer's Eve party.

I remember because Will had said it to me when I'd followed in Morris' footsteps.

For some reason, that one line struck a cord with me and I threw myself into books and soccer. They became a priority of mine.

Soccer.

Academics.

Riley.

Nothing else mattered. I had tunnel vision for the things I wanted. The things I wanted knew I wanted them.

One night, Riley came over when I was studying for an exam. She'd dressed up in sexy lingerie and showed up in a trench coat, kind of like the girls you see in movies.

Little did she know, Bryce was there helping me study. She didn't drop the coat, thank God, but she was pissed for reasons I could not explain.

"You're always studying now," she complained. "I never get to see you."

"I always see you." It wasn't a lie. She came over at least four times a week.

"I mean, *see me*, see me," she glanced at Bryce. "The nerd is always here."

I slid my textbook from my lap and pulled her into the hallway. "That was rude, Riley. He's really been helping me."

"With what?"

"With my classes, baby. I practice every day. I have a tournament coming up and a scout from The Academy is coming. I need to maintain my GPA to keep my scholarship."

She rolled her eyes, huffing with annoyance. "I just miss you, you know."

We kissed in the storage room closet for half an hour until our lips were both raw and red.

"I love you," I'd said. At the time I really meant it.

"I love you too, Jace," she repeated back to me.

Two weeks later, she surprised me with EDC festival tickets.

Two and a half weeks later, she took the tickets back. Said she needed to sell them for extra cash.

Three weeks later, I found out from her Snapchat story that she never sold the tickets and was sitting on some other guy's shoulders at the festival.

A string of "I'm sorry" texts followed the aftermath of her breaking my heart without actually telling me she was going to do it.

No warning.

Just selfish acts from a selfish girl.

A girl who could lie about loving me.

Four weeks later, The Academy scout watched me play the worst game of my life.

And one month later, my dreams of pursing a career in soccer were crushed indefinitely.
All because I fell in love.

Chapter Seventeen
Blu

Year Four/Week Five – Present

"Mom!" I called out, "I'm home!"

It was purely theatrical of me to yell that. I did it every single time I walked through the front door, fully knowing she was either passed out in her bedroom or too drunk to notice.

"Mother, I collected the mail," I said, waving a grocery store catalogue and a credit card bill in the air. Again, all for the theatrics.

"What do I need to pay this time?" She stumbled out of the bathroom, her black hair a ratty mess. "I'm off today."

She said it like I asked. I stopped asking a long time ago.

"Your MasterCard." I noticed a bowl of soup next to the sink. Mom liked to place dishes there to make me aware of the fact it needed washing, just that she didn't want to do it.

At least she ate today.

The back of her hand swiped her eyes as she took a swig of brown liquid from a Dasani bottle. "I paid it already."

"Then maybe you should think about switching to e-bills instead of regular mail." Like clockwork, I took the remaining lumps of soup and flushed it down the drain. "It's better for the environment anyways."

"Aren't you noble," she muttered, plopping down on the couch.

I just shrugged even though I knew she wasn't looking. She never really looked at me, sort of just through me, and she was the only one I never demanded attention from.

I knew she'd never give it.

"I'm going out with Fawn later."

Netflix was blasting, a reality T.V. show I'd never seen before. I'm surprised she even heard my voice.

"Enjoy."

She never asked what I was doing, but I told her anyway. It made me feel like I actually had a parent to talk to.

"We may do cocaine off a phone case." I placed the bowl in the dishwasher and ran it. "Or psychedelics."

She didn't respond to that.

"Heroin could be fun," I added, sitting on the loveseat across from her.

She didn't meet my eyes when she said, "Just don't drink."

And then she laughed. She laughed as if someone was tickling her ribs with a feather.

Five minutes later, she fell asleep and I watched her. I studied her angles, her sunken bone structure, the forehead creases that were stamped into her skin even in rest.

She'd been beautiful once, my mother. I wouldn't say she's terribly ugly now. It could be the poison rotting her from the inside, but her features were distorted beyond belief.

I had to wonder if I went down that same road, if I married an alcoholic, would I become one?

Would I have children with one? Would those children succumb to the urges I couldn't fight?

Did my mom want this life for me? For herself?

I glanced around the room. Mom was sleeping on the corduroy couch Dad left for us. Well, everything Dad left for us because he left us.

Just seven more months, I repeated like a fucking mantra. *Seven more months and I'll be gone.*

A few hours later, I was painting my nails when Fawn walked into my room, shutting the door behind her.

"Nora's asleep on the couch," she said, placing her purse on the dresser.

"Yeah, I know." I extended my hand out to admire the red manicure. "I left her there."

"At least she's not on the floor."

At least.

"Still haven't texted Jace?"

His name was like sludge on my tongue. "Jace has better things to do. Like police my life."

She rolled her eyes, taking a dab of acetone on an angled brush and grabbing hold of my pointer. "You're being dramatic."

I let her clean my cuticles while she spoke.

"He called you out on the fact that you didn't do your work. Why are you so mad?"

"Because I don't like him talking to me like he knows me."

"Blu, maybe he had a bad day."

I ripped my hand away. "Why are you defending him?"

"I'm not, but you always make people out to be the villain if they're not eternally nice to you." She squeezed a pump of hand lotion into hers. "Not everyone's out to get you."

I let her work the solution onto my fingers, contemplating my thoughts. Without getting to know Jace, I would never understand his moods if he had been in one, let's say. I'd never know if he was sad or happy or willing to talk or craving space and silence. I'd just assume. I always assumed.

"Should I invite Jace out tonight?" I asked, expecting a no, hoping for a yes.

She nodded repeatedly and handed me my phone. "Is that even a question?"

"God, I can't believe I'm doing this." I opened my contacts and selected his name. "I've never texted him before."

"He's just another guy, Blu. Don't think too much about it."

>7:03pm – Blu: Guess who?

>7:09pm – Jace Boland: Spiderman??

I rolled my eyes and showed Fawn the text. I hated that she was smiling. I hated that I was holding one back.

>7:12pm – Blu: Seriously?

>7:13pm – Jace Boland: You told me to guess...

>7: 15pm – Blu: You're insufferable.

>7:18pm – Jace Boland: Haha. What's up Blu?

I don't know why that gave me butterflies. The fact that he knew who it was right away made me think he was almost waiting for it. Our conflict from last week seemed resolved; no hard feelings. I liked that.

"He bounced back fast," Fawn peered over my shoulder. "He definitely doesn't hate you."

My confidence came flooding back. "Who could ever hate me?"

> 7: 22pm – Blu: Come out with us tonight.
>
> 7:28pm – Jace Boland: Us?
>
> 7:29pm – Blu: My friend Fawn and I, come. Pls.
>
> 7:30pm – Jace Boland: Little short notice.

Disappointment found its way to my heart. I showed Fawn the text.

"Wait, he's typing!" she exclaimed.

> 7:32pm – Jace Boland: Send me the addy. I'll be there.

Chapter Eighteen
Jace

Year Four/Week Five — Present

"You're not staying for dinner?" Mom asked, taking the roast out of the oven.

I thumbed the back of my earlobe, making sure the cross earring was secure. "Got plans."

When Blu texted me, I felt a weird surge of excitement. After the way she handled my attitude in class, I almost wanted to test it out further. Call me a bad guy, but poking the bear thrilled me.

Fucking Blu. Never once did I doubt her intellect; that was apparent the first day of seminar when she was called on by Professor Granger. That irritation I felt was real, *at first*.

I hated being used. Had circumstances been different, *and she wasn't Blu Henderson*, that anger would've shut me away entirely. But she didn't do the readings. And yet, she still outshone me.

For the first time, I wasn't mad about it.

A part of me had been waiting for Blu's text, parts of me that I didn't fully understand yet. But I knew if I didn't go, I'd never understand the feeling I had around her.

"What plans? Are you meeting your brothers at Deaks?"

Deaks? "They're going to the bar?"

"Yeah," she looked confused, taking off her oven mitts and setting them on the counter. "To watch the World Cup."

A pit formed in my stomach. "They didn't invite me."

"Oh, well I wouldn't take it personally, Jace. They're just –"

"They're just what?" I snapped, looking my mom dead in the eyes. "Older? More mature?"

Before she could say anything, I grabbed the extra set of car keys and felt a slight tinge of satisfaction. *See, I can drive. I can fucking drive. I'm old enough to do that.*

"Where are you going?" My mom asked from the dining room.

Dad walked in at the same time as I opened the front door, brief case in hand, thermos in the other.

"Hey kid," he said.

Kid. Kid.

Kid.

Kid. Kid. Kid.

"For fuck's sakes!" I swore, slamming the door behind me.

I could hear commotion from the inside of the house, but truthfully, no fucks were left to give. As I reversed the Honda, my phone vibrated with a text from Blu.

8:15pm – Blu Henderson: When are you coming?

My hands gripped the wheel, taking a left towards Deaks as I cleared the message and exhaled the growing vexation.

Sorry Blu, this is going to have to wait.

***

Scott, Will and Baxter were sitting at the bar. A pitcher of beer was placed in between them, half empty. They were laughing.

They were laughing without me.

"Jace?" Scott was the first to notice. That was a shock.

He pulled me in for a side hug, patting the barstool next to him. "What are you doing here?"

Gladly, I took a seat. "Just wanted to spend some time with my brothers."

"Welcome, welcome," Will spoke, as condescending as ever.

Baxter shouted at the T.V., slamming down his pint with a heavy hand. He didn't say anything to me.

No acknowledgements, just normalcy.

Normal to treat me like a ghost. Normal to forget I existed.

"How's school? Haven't seen you since the summer." Scott took his eyes off the screen for a split second to address me.

Little did he know that meant the whole world and more.

"When do you graduate?" Another question, he'd asked. My heart was full.

"Could I have some beer?" I nudged my head towards the pitcher.

"Oh fuck, for sure man. Jean!" Scott called the bartender, a lanky fuck who had no muscle. "Can I get another glass for my brother here?"

For my brother.

My brother.

Damn right I was.

"ID please," the bartender demanded.

In any other circumstance, I would've been pissed. Pissed like I was earlier to be reminded of my age, my youth, the contrast between me and my siblings.

But Scott acknowledged that I was his brother.

I pulled out my ID and flashed a smile, happily showing him that I was of age.

That I belonged.

The whole night we drank and chatted. The whole night I felt fulfilled. I thought about Blu, mainly because my phone continued to vibrate in the back pocket of my jeans.

I didn't touch it once.

If I could feel this way forever, that I fit in with the people who mattered most…

I'd never check my phone again.

Chapter Nineteen
Blu

Year Four/Week Five – Present

"He's a no-show, Fawn."

There wasn't an emotion in the world to encompass how I was feeling. Anger didn't cut it, rage didn't surpass it. I was – I was…

I was *hurt*.

"I'm sorry, babe. He's an asshole." She waved a hand at the bartender, ordering a round of shots. I didn't know which kind. I didn't care.

When the liquor came, I downed both in one gulp. I still didn't know what the taste was.

"At least you know now, right? You don't have any expectations…" Fawn was trying to comfort me, but we were at Play, one of the best nightclubs in the city.

I didn't need comfort.

I needed a distraction.

"Dance with me, Fawn!" I yelled over the loud music, pulling her with me towards the multicoloured floor.

The first man I noticed – who noticed *me* was tall with dark hair. He had rounded armpit stains soaking through his grey t-shirt, but two drinks in hand. *One of them must've been for me.*

"These aren't roofied, right?" I joked, taking hold of what I could only assume to be a vodka-cran.

I couldn't hear what he said. I didn't need to. After gulping down the drink, he came up behind me and fell in sync with my movements.

Fawn held my hands as she swayed her petite body to the beats; the man behind me cupped my breasts as I grinded.

The night faded in and out. My mind was taken over by the right things.

Drinks.

Pleasure.

Desire.

No Jace.

No fucking Jace.

"Can I get you another drink?" the man behind me asked, his hot breath caressing my ear.

"Please."

When he left, I grabbed Fawn by the wrist and pulled her to the bathroom. *God, I was yanking her everywhere tonight.*

"No need to be rough," she said, rubbing the skin I'd just been gripping.

"Is that guy cute?" I demanded, my eyes adjusting to the dim lighting of the bathroom corner.

"Who?"

"The one I was dancing with."

"Um," she was hesitating. Why was she hesitating?

"He's not, *not* cute."

"So he's ugly."

"I didn't say that, Blu."

"You might as well have!" I snapped. "Holy fucking shit… Holy fucking shit, shit, shit, shit. I can't believe this. I hooked up with a loser!"

"You didn't kiss him, did you?"

Did I? Wait… Did I?

"I don't think you kissed him…" Fawn said, looking around the room like a lost little deer.

"We're in the bathroom," I sniped. I couldn't understand why she was being so stupid.

"I know? I didn't ask where we were? Why are you fighting with me?"

I didn't know. "I don't know, I'm sorry." I paced around the white-tiled flooring. "I'm sorry, Fawn. My emotions are all out of whack."

"Is it because of Jace?"

Yes. I refused to say it out loud.

"You can talk about it, you know." She leaned against the sink when some girl walked in. *Tumbled* in, rather.

"*Sooooo pretttyyyy...*" she slurred, pointing at Fawn first and then me. Like usual. Like always.

My gaze followed her into the bathroom stall until she shut the door and began hurling.

I turned the faucet on and splashed cold water onto my face, ignoring all the foundation, mascara and lipstick that began to pill and melt away.

"What are you doing?" Fawn's eyes were wide as she came up behind me. "Stop that."

"It's a dark club. No one can tell I'm ugly underneath all this."

"Blu, what the fuck, enough of this shit!" She scrambled for the tap, shutting it off and forcing me to face her. "He's one guy!"

"One guy who doesn't like me!"

"One guy out of a million who would if you gave them a chance! Christ Blu," she rubbed her forehead, the inebriation fading into the black.

"I'm calling Carter to pick us up. We're leaving." Fawn marched towards the door, slinging her purse over her shoulder, placing her phone against her ear.

I could hear her ranting to Carter behind the wall, but tuning it out seemed like the best option. All there was left to focus on was the gurgling sounds of the drunk girl who called Fawn pretty.

Not me. Fawn.

Why didn't he come? Why didn't he like me? Was I that horrible? Was I that unlovable that someone could never see the good parts of myself?

Were there any good parts left?

I sunk to the muddy, disgusting ground and felt one with the floor. We were similar, the cold tiles and me.

Stepped all over.

Dirty.

Only there to provide a smoother transition for people to get to their destination.

"Come on, Blu. Carter's ten minutes away." Fawn was standing in front of me, holding out her hands.

All I could do was look up at her. Her perfect, sculpted body, her slender fingers, a face cut like diamonds.

"Why do you like me?" A tear escaped the corner of my eye. For once, I didn't wipe it away.

"We're not doing this here."

"If you want me to get up, you will answer me."

"I'll lift you, babe." She crouched but I moved further away. The girl from the bathroom emerged and said nothing, washing her hands.

She was embarrassed.

That made two of us.

"You can't lift me. I'm fat."

"You're not fat," the drunk girl said, looking at me through a mirror. That's why it made sense. Mirrors were distorted.

Fawn was pleading, I saw it now. *I* put her in distress. *I* was the problem. On a night that we were supposed to have fun, *I* ruined it. Because of one guy. One guy who didn't like me.

One guy out of a million who *should*.

Chapter Twenty
Jace

Year One/York University – Three Years Ago

"Got dumped, eh?"

"Why'd you call, Will? To patronize me?" I paced around the dorm, counting down the minutes until Morris brought over some weed.

The second he told me he was visiting from Western, I jumped for joy like a little bitch. There was no distraction in the world that could take the incessant, persistent, god fucking awful pain away.

Nothing worked.

No one worked.

"Hey man, I'm trying to be here for my baby bro –"

I hung up the fucking phone. Right on time too; Morris had just walked in.

"Jace fucking Boland," he gripped my shoulder and pulled me in for a hug, "It's been too long."

"Good to see you, Cumberland." I hesitated to ask about the weed. Truthfully, I cared more about it than him in this moment.

He moved further into my dorm, kicking off his shoes. "Where's blondie?"

I'm going to lose it.

"D'you bring the weed?" I asked. His comment warranted it.

"Got the goods." He fished a small, transparent bag out of his back pocket and tossed it over. "About three joints in there, I think."

There were only two.

Fucking two.

"Where's the third?"

He wore a dumb expression, his blonde hair getting into his eyes. This was the guy everyone liked in high school, this fucking bonehead.

This is the guy I worshiped.

He should've worshipped me.

After Morris tore his ACL, he gave up on soccer completely. Unlike me, it was his choice to do so. I was forced out of it.

I wasn't good enough.

"Oh shit, ha-ha." His laugh sent me to Hell. "It's behind my ear."

This fucking moron.

"Can we smoke in here?"

I already started, lighting the tip of the pre-roll and inhaling the distraction into my lungs.

For the first half hour, Morris offered up life details I didn't care to know; how his criminology degree was going, the brunettes he'd fucked, his rich family buying a new boat.

After a while, I turned on some music and slumped into the desk chair, realizing that Morris was on my fucking bed and he was the guest.

"Off the bed, Cumberland."

His hands flew up in protest but he followed my request, laughing to himself about something I didn't care to ask about.

I didn't ask about a single thing that had to do with Morris Cumberland for two hours.

"So," he let out a puff, "You and Riley still together?"

I was calm, high, on cloud nine. Then he goes and asks this.

"Why? You wanna fuck her?"

His face dropped. "Uh, no, the fuck ha-ha."

I didn't look at him when I said, "It's fine. She's fucking someone else."

Honestly, no clue what Riley was up to. Three weeks had passed since she screwed me over. Two weeks had passed since The Academy scout chose McTavish and Laundry over me.

"Sorry to hear. When'd this happen?" Morris was trying to be sentimental. He didn't give a damn. He'd probably slide into her DMs tomorrow.

"Few weeks back, don't remember." Twenty-one days, sixteen hours ago.

He shrugged, coughing into his flannel. "Don't worry, Boland. Plenty of fish in the sea."

And I wanted *one*.

One who didn't want me.

Chapter Twenty-One
Blu

Year Four/Week Six– Present

Thank God for reading week.

If I had to see Jace at school, I would've ripped his head off.

There had been an apology text. "Sorry about that Blu," he'd said twenty-four hours later. Might've been twenty-five. "I had a family thing."

A long paragraph was typed out on my behalf, but I thought better than to send it.

Men didn't respond to desperation. They responded to silence.

After sending a dozen roses to Fawn's doorstep, I followed up with a box of chocolate and fuzzy peaches. *I was the best boyfriend ever.*

When she opened the door, her golden shimmer robe sparkled like the sun.

"How many times do I have to tell you, I don't eat chocolate," she smirked, holding the door open with her foot to let me pass.

"But I do."

Fawn lived in a condo downtown, courtesy of her parents might I add, but she was a good enough person that I didn't judge her for it.

She had a pair of slippers waiting for me by the door; blue fuzzy smile slides with fur trimming.

I placed the treats on her kitchen island and backed towards the living room, kicking my feet up on the ottoman.

"I don't need presents. I just want you to know you deserve better than what you're putting yourself through."

I stared as she surveyed the candy, poking the packaging like it was a live animal.

"It's for consumption," I stated, turning on Netflix.

"I know what it's for." She finally caved and tore open the fuzzy peaches, taking a handful before meeting me on the couch. "Why must you tempt me like this?"

"Someone's got to do it."

We watched a couple episodes of Peaky Blinders before my ovaries started to hurt for the main actor, and my eyes subconsciously fluttered between the T.V. screen and my phone.

He wasn't going to text me. I didn't answer his text. Why was I still looking?

"Do you want to talk about what happened last week?" Fawn asked, reading my mind. She was good like that. She cared.

I think.

"Haven't we talked about it enough?" I felt like I'd exhausted my breath. "It was a shitty apology from a shitty guy."

"Sure, but you're still hurt."

"Nope."

"It's okay to be hurt, Blu."

"No, it's not." I leaned forward. "I barely know this guy, he ghosts me and I throw a hissy fit like some sad girl who got broken up with by her fiancé of twelve years."

"Well, when you put it like that..." she teased, but I found no amusement.

I shook my head. "It's not acceptable."

Her laugh broke the tension in the air. "Oh my God, Blu, for once can you just admit that you had feelings for someone? Why don't you just tell him? Get it off your chest?"

I reached out to touch her forehead, then her cheek. "Are you feeling okay? Do you need me to take your temperature?"

"Stop it, I'm serious." She swatted my hand away, leaning back into the cushion. "Communicate with him. You have two classes with him this whole year. What are you going to do? Avoid him?"

"Yes."

"No, Blu, no. Text him and ask what family thing he had. Text him and ask for a reason. He committed to plans and he ghosted you, so you have every right to demand why."

"Is that not an invasion of privacy?"

"Maybe. Find out. If he doesn't text you back, then avoid him." She tapped my phone and tossed it over. "Get some closure, at least."

Maybe she was right. Maybe I just wanted to text him for my own selfish reasons. But as soon as I clicked open our conversation, the shame came flooding back.

"What do I say to make me not sound totally desperate?"

"I just told you. Ask, *nicely,* if he's okay and if the whole family thing was resolved."

Huh, that's actually not a bad way to go about it.

9:16pm – Blu: Everything all good now? With the fam?

I showed Fawn the text and she nodded in approval. "Want to watch one more episode? We can order takeout."

My nerves were all over the place as I hit send, staring at the delivered button longer than necessary. That button held a lot of power.

One word. Delivered. It got to him. He would see it. I was vulnerable.

Twenty minutes passed before my phone screen lit up and my heart stopped.

9:36pm – Jace Boland: Better, yeah. Thanks for asking.

I was so pissed, my ears were ringing. "What the fuck am I supposed to say to this?"

"Um, I mean…"

"Wait, he said something again." I checked the conversation, butterflies banging against my ribcage.

9:37pm – Jace Boland: Blu about the other night, really sorry again. Can I make it up to you?

"He asked if he could make it up to me," I practically scream-shouted. Fuck, I was being so cringey, so fucking cringey.

"Well?"

"Should I let him?"

Fawn got up to retrieve the delivery, pulling her robe tighter together. "Up to you. How much do you care?"

That one question struck like lightning.
How much did I care?

As my eyes re-read his last message twenty, thirty, forty times before I responded, I realized how much this mattered to me.

How much did I care? I asked myself again, before texting back:

9:45pm – Blu: What did you have in mind?

Chapter Twenty-Two
Jace

Year Two/York University – Two Years Ago

I met Mel in second year after I got banned from a campus bar for vaping in the establishment.

She was sitting on the wrought-iron stairwell when I stumbled out of the door.

"Pull your pants up," she'd said to me.

My attention turned to the mysterious woman looming in the night. The fire from her cigarette was the only thing illuminating her features.

"Excuse me?" I addressed her.

"Your pants are halfway down your ass. Pull them up."

I looked down, ready for a fight, ready to tell her she was wrong. Little did I know, she was right.

"How'd that even happen?"

"I'm not sharing my secrets with you," I countered. There was a tinge of flirtation in my tone, completely unintentional.

She stepped out of the darkness, handing me a cigarette. I didn't take it. I stared at her instead.

"Like what you see?" she asked, taking another drag.

Her hair was chopped just underneath her ears, dyed a merlot red with orange streaks. Dark bags swept the creases below her eyes, a splatter of freckles painting her face.

A silver chain dangled underneath a ripped cardigan, pink lace stockings to match the tank top beneath her shirt.

I'd never been more intrigued.

I'd never been more terrified.

"I have a girlfriend," I admitted, thinking of Riley. Thinking about how poisonous it was to say that.

Seven months was a decent amount of time to sit on what she'd done. She suffered without me far too long. When she came crawling back, crying on my shoulder that she made a mistake, I was there for her.

I was doing her a favour. She needed me.

The stupid fuck who she fooled around with called her the night she rested in my arms again. Where she was meant to be. He went on some tangent about how he couldn't live without her, how he never should've let her go.

I laughed. Did he not know she was on speaker? Was he not aware that she was nestled comfortably in the crook of my neck?

Everything I wanted was mine again. Riley, in some way, filled the void I'd been searching for. Maybe I wasn't good enough to go pro in soccer, but I had my girl back. I coached scrimmages, played with my friends on the weekends. It was still my passion, even if it was no longer my dream.

I'd create a new one. *I always do.*

"Did I ask if you had a girlfriend?" She walked closer, her Doc Martins grazing my Nike's. "I'm Mel."

I scoffed, taking a step back. "Did I ask for your name?"

It was rude. It sounded rude. But I didn't want her to think she had the upper hand. And just when I thought she'd walk away, she smiled.

"You and me," she nudged my shoulder, "You and me are going to be friends."

***

Year Four/Week Six– Present

I clicked speakerphone as I typed my message to Blu:

> 9:36pm – Jace: Better, yeah. Thanks for asking.

"I can't believe she texted me back," I released, hitting send. "I wouldn't have texted me back."

Mel was on the other line, outlining a commission piece for one of her clients. "I wouldn't have either."

"Hey, need I remind you that you approached me, Melinda." I loved using her full name to get her heated.

"And I regret it every day."

I chuckled, returning my attention to the bland text I just sent. "It was dry, wasn't it?"

"Extremely."

"Well, what should I say?"

"What do you want to say?" A second voice joined the call, addressing me with a high-pitched squeal. "Hi Jace!"

Mel's girlfriend. "Hey Ellie, how goes it?"

"Good, good, love." I heard a smooching sound and felt a rush of pride course through my veins. Mel deserved the happiness. She was one of the good ones.

"Sorry, Jace. Continue. What'd you say?"

"I didn't say anything yet. I want to make it up to her, though."

"Seriously?" Something clattered on the ground, followed by Mel's hushed cursing. "*Fuck.*"

My fingers hovered over the keyboard. "Screw it, I'll just say exactly that."

9:37pm – Jace: Blu about the other night, really sorry again. Can I make it up to you?

"How do you seriously intend on making up for the fact that you ghosted this poor girl?"

Poor girl? She didn't know even her. Maybe Blu was rich. Maybe she owned a boat, like Morris. Maybe she had a cottage in South Hampton, like Riley. All assumptions. All things I had to learn.

"I can invite her over."

This, Mel laughed at. "To what? Fuck?"

I rolled my eyes. "No. Damn Mel, I thought you knew me better than that. I'm a nice guy."

She sighed. "Be honest with me, Jace. What are your intentions with her?"

Being put on the spot was something I was never fond of. It was a weakness of mine, to think on my feet, to show emotion the second it came to me. What were my intentions? Did I even have any?

"Too early to say." That was a safe response.

"In her mind, she's probably went through a thousand routes."

"That's her mind, Mel, we aren't the same. We think differently."

"Maybe, but you're like a hue of each other."

I relaxed my neck against the pillow, taking Mel off speaker to concentrate on her words. She was always so insightful. She was the one girl outside of my family who actually gave a shit enough to prove her loyalty.

"Somehow, this girl got under your skin enough for you to tell me about her. Like, remember what happened the other day in class?"

When she put me in my place. Yeah, how could I forget. "What about it?"

"From what I gather, you two seem so similar but don't want to admit it. That maybe, you both orbit around each other – a hue of something."

She paused for a second, then screamed so loudly the phone almost knocked from my ear. "Wait! That's such a good idea! Thank you Jace."

A laugh bubbled from my throat. "Mel, did you take shrooms today?"

Silence.

Then laughter.

"How'd you know?"

We shared the glee, talking about her recent paintings and upcoming art show.

That's when the idea hit me.

"Can I bring a plus-one?"

As if we shared the same brain, she responded, "I thought you'd never ask."

9:45pm – Blu Henderson: What did you have in mind?

10:02pm – Jace: 1067 Goblet Street. Saturday @ 7pm. Wear something nice.

Chapter Twenty-Three
Blu

Three Winters Ago

"You're... You're telling me this now."

Kyle and I had been dating for a year, and he just dropped the bomb on me that four months ago, he'd had a threesome with some first year girl and his best friend.

His best friend who we just went out with the other night.

His best friend who constantly told us how good we were for each other.

His best friend who had a fucking girlfriend too!

"The guilt was eating me alive, Blu. I didn't want to hurt you, I –"

"You didn't want to hurt me, Kyle?" Tears burned my eyes but I reserved the right to cry. He didn't deserve to see them fall.

"No, baby – I mean, *Blu*, I didn't."

"You thought that by telling me four months later, you'd be sparing my heart?"

"Well," he scratched the back of his neck, looking around my room like some fucking treasure was hidden behind the beige walls. "I just... You were doing so much for me and I couldn't keep it from you anymore. You deserve so much better. I don't deserve you."

Then the stupidest thing happened.
He started to cry.
"I don't deserve you," he repeated.

Slowly, he made his way towards the edge of the bed, crouching down between my legs.

"What are you doing?"

"I don't deserve you." He wrapped his arms around my middle and set his head against my breasts.

Then the stupidest thing happened again.

Only I was the stupid one.

I began comforting him.

Him.

The person who broke my heart.

The person who cheated on me.

I was playing with his hair. Scratching his back. Feeling his skin against my bare legs.

Wanting him.

Craving this closeness. The comfort we'd shared for three-hundred-sixty-five days.

"It's okay, Kyle." *It wasn't. But neither was I.*

"I don't want to get back together," he whispered against my stomach, his lips hiking up the edge of my shirt. "I just want you to know how much you deserve."

His fingers slipped up my pyjama bottoms. "I wish I could've been that for you."

"Why…" He slipped a finger inside of me, pulsing up and down. "Why… um, can't you… be?"

Gently, he pushed me down onto the bed, his body covering mine with protection. A brief moment of security.

I knew it would end soon enough.

"Because you're too good for me, baby." His jeans were off before I realized, his dick inside me once again.

"You're so…" In and out. In and out. "You feel so good."

He finished three minutes later.

I laid on my bed half naked, staring at the ceiling, cursing myself for letting this happen again.

I was to blame.

I let people take advantage of me.

I was in the wrong.

"I'm –" He zipped up his pants, hand on the doorknob, no remorse in his eyes. "Fuck, Blu, I'm sorry. We shouldn't have done that."

"No," I whispered. "We shouldn't have."

He was gone within thirty seconds.

I don't know how long I stayed in that position for. The sun began to set until the darkness outside my window covered the lower half of my body.

"*Good enough to fuck,*" I stated.

"*Not good enough to love,*" I accepted.

Chapter Twenty-Four
Blu

Year Four/Week Six– Present

After plugging in the address Jace sent me into maps, I found out that my destination was an art gallery called Prix.

We hadn't texted since he asked to meet me; I just responded to his message by giving it a thumbs up.

And now, I found myself on a random Saturday in mid-October, pulling my beige trench coat a little tighter before stepping into the space.

Art galleries were like charcuterie boards; rare that you found the time to spare, to prepare and roll salami into roses and cut cheese into perfect cubes – but when you had the time, it was worth it.

This art gallery was not an exception. This art gallery was a charcuterie board.

The room itself was small, dimly lit and a tad claustrophobic with all the people crowding paintings, but there was a charm that sucked the breath from my lungs.

A wooden table was placed in the center of the room with none other than…

A goddamn fucking charcuterie board.

"Ha-ha," I laughed, letting go of my jacket seams. "What are the odds."

"Hello," I was greeted by a very tall, very slender woman with red nails and scarlet lipstick. "Is there a piece you've commissioned?"

Wait, what? Was this a private event?

I cleared my throat, happy that the dim lighting was disguising the blush in my cheeks. "I'm meeting someone."

"Oh, wonderful!" She smiled so brightly I could've caught on fire. "I'll get out of your hair then."

You weren't in my hair. What a dumb saying.

My eyes trailed the length of the walls as I contemplated texting Jace. *So stupid*, I thought. I was literally here, exactly where he wanted me to be, and still refused to message first.

After two minutes of hovering awkwardly by a stone statue, I moved towards one of the only paintings that caught my eye.

There were a couple of people standing in front of it, so I stayed back, analyzing the canvas and its simplicity. My head tilted to the side as I followed a single black line that swirled around a red dot, another grey line interconnecting with another black line, and a zigzag of electric blue – blue like my hair, that penetrated the vacant spaces between the swirls.

None of the lines touched the red dot, only a gradient shade of scarlet and white fading within each other that protected its perimeter. That's when I got curious. Narrowing my eyes to the display description, the painting read: "Controlling Chaos."

"Do you like it?" a voice behind me asked, soft yet assertive. They wanted a yes.

I gave them exactly that without even turning around. This was not a time for smart remarks. This was no game. This painting was wonderful, and it deserved the recognition.

"It's unique, unlike the others in here." *I wouldn't be me without a little edge.*

As I turned around to face the converser, I was met by those bluish green eyes, light brown hair swept back perfectly and his signature cross earring paired with a simple pearl. He was wearing all black, a button down paired with slim slacks and oxfords. A silver bracelet dangled on his wrist, winking at me.

"Jace," I released, unable to hold his name in my mouth any longer.

Beside him was the person in conversation, no doubt. Her voice matched her face – kind, but intimidating, colourful yet mysterious. Her red hair was pinned back, two orange strands cascading down her face.

She was much taller than I was, but much shorter than Jace. Everyone was. He was built to tower over people.

"I'll take the compliment," she said, extending a hand. "Mel Klorfor. I'm the artist."

Her nails were sharp, sparkling like silver diamonds. They were much better than my black acrylics, more expensive looking. I made a mental note to re-do my nails at an actual salon this time, not my stupid press-ons from Amazon.

"Jace Boland." He, too, extended a formal hand as if we'd never met before.

For a second, I thought I was going through a simulation, wondering if the past few weeks were a product of my imagination, until he smiled at me.

I took his hand, savouring the way it felt against mine, then released his fingers.

"Blu Henderson," I addressed Mel. "Tell me more about this painting."

We both walked up to it, her flats sweeping the concrete, mine clinking like bells.

"What do you think it means?" she asked, turning her questioning eyes to me.

The longer I stared at the canvas, the harder it was to make sense of it. *Controlling Chaos*, I wondered, pondered, dove deep into my psyche to pull out an answer.

There were none. I hated being wrong. My guess was blank.

"Does he know?" I took a look at Jace who was standing directly behind me, almost too close. If I took one step back, my heel would be pressed against the point of his toe.

I tried my luck.

I was right. He was a few centimetres away from wrapping his hands around my waist.

That was all I cared about. Not a damn painting.

"I actually don't." His voice was low, reverberating through me like a volcanic eruption. "Care to explain, Mel?"

The tip of his finger trailed the length of my forearm before he pulled away, taking a step back.

He did that on purpose.

I took a step forward, creating more space between us. If that's how he wanted it to be, then fine.

He scoffed. At first I thought it was condescending, but when my eyes met his, they were playful and light. My lips turned up at this.

"A friend of mine is a businessman, and he asked me to paint something powerful like him," Mel began, "His words not mine." We all laughed at this and I felt a sense of unity, a rush of belonging.

"He explained to me how every aspect of his life felt controlled by outside sources. He works to live so that he can please someone above him. He eats well so that he can maintain a good physique. Then, he repeats this cycle, every day. Those are the black lines you see."

She pointed to the rings circling the red dot, then moved her finger to the grey lines. "This is the grey area, the parts of his life that bring him mundane happiness, and these zigzags," she trailed her fingers up and down the blue lines, "the chaos. The inevitable. The heartache."

For a few minutes, she continued to speak about the intersecting lines, how they were relevant to a man I'd never met and I listened to every single word. The way she spoke about something she was evidently so passionate about made me reflect on my own life, what drove me, what made me tick.

I used to love photography. Before the alcoholism took over my father, he'd bought me a disposable camera for my seventh birthday. At first, I threw it on the ground and broke it. I wanted Barbies, like everyone else.

He bought me a new one. Said that I should be different, I should stick out from the rest because life was boring and the world was going to end. Make it as vibrant as the girl he saw me to be.

I don't think he really saw me as anything, but at least he pretended.

I didn't know I'd only have three more years left with him. If I'd known, maybe I would've broken the second camera and the third or forth.

Or maybe I wouldn't have given up photography at all.

Everywhere we went, I took that ugly yellow rectangle with me and snapped photos of grass, the sky, a bird in a tree and a kid on a swing. Everything was art in its own way; if you just opened your eyes to see. Lately, my tendency was to keep them shut.

Now the only art I knew were the paintings in museums, the graffiti on brick walls, the tattoos on my skin. I kept them hidden. Only the people I slept with knew I had them, maybe not even then. Were they really paying attention to something more than my bare flesh and nakedness?

In a way, I wanted to keep them concealed. The scars beneath the black ink were no longer a part of me – I assigned them a new meaning. These tattoos became the only art that reminded me that art existed, that it was beyond canvases and paintbrushes. That maybe, buried within it all, there was a little girl with a disposable camera who missed her father.

Her father who didn't miss her. Who *couldn't* miss her.

"What's the red dot mean?" I asked, swallowing the memories.

Mel smiled. "It's him. This white around him that puts space between what he can control, and what he can't. He's safe here, in this hue of red."

He's safe here, in this hue of red.

Mel and Jace were pulled into conversation by a couple next to us. They didn't address me. I was unfamiliar to this territory. They seemed to belong, Jace with his fancy attire and Mel with her sparkly silver nails.

My trench coat covered a black turtleneck dress, but I felt more comfortable being covered, hiding the parts of me no one could see.

A Hue of Blu

I took a step away from the conversation I was not a part of, and stepped towards "Controlling Chaos."

Every line, every swirl, every sharp edge didn't touch the red dot. This hue of red was an impenetrable forcefield, protecting him from the outside world. The outside pain.

In that moment, all I could do was pray and wonder...

Will I ever find a hue of Blu?

Chapter Twenty-Five
Jace

Year Four/Week Six— Present

After I'd made my rounds, saying hello to all of Mel's friends and prospective buyers, I took Blu to the pizza parlour around the block.

"You're hungry," I stated, rather than questioned. "You've got to be."

Truthfully, it was me who was hungry. Mel was such a bubbly person, so outgoing and carefree. Her friends were a reflection of her image – equally as vivacious and full of life.

Mine didn't belong in a scene like that.

Mine were just as hollow and empty as I was.

"You're assuming I'm hungry," Blu said, wrapping her jacket around her like a scarf.

"What's underneath that?"

"Underneath what?"

I pinched her elbow, rubbing the thin fabric between my fingers. "You haven't taken it off all night."

If the pizza parlour lights weren't glowing neon red, I could've sworn her cheeks were as cherry as they were. Maybe I shouldn't have asked.

"It is cold, I get it." It wasn't really, but I was wearing a long sleeve and pants. The lie was passable.

I held open the door, allowing her to walk in ahead of me. The scent of her perfume trailed after her, stopping me in my tracks.

"What perfume is that?"

She turned to look at me, her brown eyes wide. "Uh, I don't think you'd know it."

"Try me."

"It's *Her* by Burberry." She stared at me. I stared at her. "Why?" she asked.

Classic. Fucking classic.

Riley wore the same perfume.

I waved at the pizza guy by the cash, pulling open my wallet.

"What can I get you, sir?"

Blu stepped behind me, scanning the rows of pizza displays but didn't say anything.

"What do you want?"

She shook her head. "Nothing."

I narrowed my eyes. "You good with pepperoni?"

"I'm not hungry."

I turned back to the pizza guy. "Two pepperoni slices, please."

He punched it into the cash and gave me the total. Honestly, I didn't even see it, just tapped my card and found Blu sitting at the stools.

She seemed... off. Sad? Shy, almost? Not like I had much experience being around Blu, but this was definitely noticeable.

"Everything okay?"

"Why'd you ask about my perfume?" she questioned, whipping around to face me. "Is it bad? Is it too much?"

Whoa, whoa, whoa. "Blu, no," I let out a strained laugh. "No, not at all. Just a familiar scent."

At this, her face softened, her eyes lightened and she relaxed into the stool. "Oh, okay. It's like, one of my worst fears."

"To smell bad?"

"Well, yeah. Isn't that what attracts people? Scent?"

"And who might you want to attract, Blu?"

Her cheeks reddened. I didn't need a damn neon light blocking my way to see that.

I smirked, leaving her there, wanting me, and fetched the pizza.

While I was waiting, two girls walked in, definitely drunk, hand-in-hand. They were pretty, wearing tight dresses and lace-up heels.

They smiled at me, I smiled at them, my eyes lingering longer on the taller one.

"Order up," the pizza guy announced, handing over two white paper plates.

"Thanks man." As I turned around, I almost made a head-on collision with the tall blonde who positioned herself right behind me.

"Sorry," she purred, throwing her hands up. "You're so hot, I needed to say something."

If I wasn't here with Blu, maybe I would've returned the compliment. Maybe I would've shared my pizza slice with her. But I had company, and I wasn't that big of an asshole.

"I appreciate it. Stay safe," was all I said before returning to the stools and handing Blu her slice.

"*You're so hot*," she mocked, twirling the plate with her pointer.

I laughed. "You heard that?"

"She was loud enough."

"Hm." I took a bite of my pizza, grimacing at the grease that swiped my teeth before wiping my mouth with a napkin. "Good flavour."

"Before now, I didn't think you even ate pizza."

My eyebrows scrunched as I took another bite. "Seriously? Why?"

She shrugged, staring at her slice like it was a fucking anaconda. "You've got a good body. Usually fit people shy away from this shit."

Huh. I guess it was a compliment. She didn't know how hard I worked for this, though. "I eat a lot. Just can't put on weight."

"Must be nice."

That line.

That one line.

Holy fuck, how could I have been so blind?

"Blu," I chewed slowly, pushing her pizza towards her. "What have you eaten today?"

She sat erect, pulling her coat tightly again. I'd noticed one of her nails was missing. She tried to bury it in her palm.

"I ate," she replied.

"Yeah? What?"

"I had a salad earlier."

"What kind?"

"What does it matter?" Her tone was clipped. She wanted me to drop it.

Fat chance. I knew an eating disorder when I saw one.

"Have one bite and I'll stop pestering you."

In that moment, I realized how glued her eyes were to the slice of pizza. Did I make this worse? Was I making this worse?

I didn't know what to do. I'd been in this situation before. Being the skinny, lanky twig in high school, seeing all my friends buff and padded with stories they wouldn't be embarrassed to tell in front of a crowd of people. It made them manly. It made me spineless.

My hand fell to her bobbing knee. She was anxious.

Her eyes flitted from the pizza to my touch; her leg stopped shaking.

She swallowed. "One bite?"

I squeezed a little tighter, gently rubbing my thumb against her skin. "One bite, darling."

She lifted the crust to her mouth, taking a generous bite of meat and cheese, then turned her face from mine.

Embarrassment. I've felt it one too many times.

My fingers cupped her chin, turning her to face me. There was a sting in her eyes, an emotion she was holding back.

"I'm sorry, Jace." She dropped her head low, her jaw tight in the cup of my hand. "You must think I'm some kind of freak."

A freak.

Was that what I thought I was? When I assumed people thought that of me? I was consumed by this feeling for so long. I saw it now.

She was my match. An equal. A broken piece of myself, a mirrored shard of glass.

I didn't remove myself from her touch. Not once. "Quite the opposite, actually," my gaze softened, "You and I have a lot more in common than I thought."

Chapter Twenty-Six
Blu

Three Summers Ago

"What are you looking at?"

Kyle and I were descending the escalator at Yorkdale mall when two brunettes stepped on the opposite side to head up.

I knew exactly what he was looking at – *who* he was looking at. He did it often enough.

It bothered me often enough.

Never once did I address it, though. Addressing it made it real and I would've preferred to live in blind ignorance, but a part of me felt the need to snap.

"Just the Topman display." His reply was so casual; if I'd been oblivious I might've even believed him.

Little did he know how observant I was, how life forced me to pay attention to all the little things. When people believed you couldn't see them, the parts of themselves they attempted to hide resurfaced.

My gaze lingered on the two brunettes, both in athleisure wear – tight leggings, cropped zip up hoodies and ballcaps. Of course their bodies were slim and toned, just like everything Kyle wanted.

Everything I wasn't.

As soon as we reached the bottom of the escalator, I sped ahead until I reached the first bathroom. Kyle called after me but I was safe in the stall, safe to store my thoughts in my head and lock them away until need be.

I never wanted those thoughts to breathe, but they always came. They persisted. They wanted to be there.

Eat less.

Drink more.

Raw veggies. Water. Grapes.

No grease. No junk food. No food.

No food.

No food.

As soon as I heard one of the hand dryers go off, my fingers were down my throat, forcing out the bacon and egg hash I made this morning.

It was an awful, shitty feeling.

Not throwing up, that was the relief. But that desire to be small, to impress, to feel wanted and beautiful. A full time job, I'd say. It consumed me.

If I'd only been a twenty-six waist instead of a twenty-nine; if I'd only drank vodka-sodas instead of blue lagoons. So much sugar, so many useless, empty fucking calories.

When I finished in the bathroom, my body felt light, like a feather in a burning forest. All the anger and resentment I felt towards Kyle dissipated slowly when I saw his eyes.

"Baby, you look sick. Are you okay?"

He kissed my face, as if he didn't think about macking two girls ten minutes ago.

"I look sick?" I questioned, smiling brightly. "I thought I looked great."

He tapped my ass. "You always look great."

I didn't hear that last remark, or any remark other than the fact he suggested I was ill.

If you only knew what I did for you, Kyle.
If you only knew what it took.

Chapter Twenty-Seven
Blu

Year Four/Week Seven— Present

I needed to go home after the pizza parlour. I couldn't see Jace.

Needing to do something was very different from wanting. I wanted to see him, that's all I wanted. But the right decision was distance, I wasn't blind.

When I refused to eat, an oddly comforting recognition formed in his eyes. He'd said that we had more in common than he thought. Did that mean he, too, struggled with poor eating habits? Or he has? Was he just trying to be nice? He didn't owe me that.

No one did.

After that comment was made, I searched for something in him; a sign that I didn't see before, a hint that showed me just how broken he was.

There was a sea of blue in his eyes, clear blue like calm waters. He was calm, all the time. The levelness in his voice never exceeded fifty percent – he wanted to be perceived that way.

That's when the realization hit me that everything about him was a façade. I don't know what did it, what clicked in my brain, but I felt more alone in that moment than I had in so long.

I had an urge to open up to someone who was fabricating a reaction, someone who probably had no idea what it felt like to be living in a universe of competition.

As I walked to Prof. Granger's class, I made note of all the outfits I wished I could wear if I had a breast reduction, the jeans I could finally fit into, the men who would pursue me.

I wanted to be an object of desire. I craved it. I needed to know that I was worthy of love.

But no one else needed to know that.

"Hi, hi, excuse me!" someone to my left called.

I pulled out my earphone and turned my attention to a chipper blonde with a yellow raincoat. "Yeah?"

"I just wanted to say I love your jacket." Her smile was kind, her sentiments kinder.

I grabbed her hand and held it tight. "I love your face."

She blushed and walked away, leaving me with a serotonin boost that would last two seconds because it wasn't a man who complimented me.

I caught a glimpse of my outfit in one of the glass windows as I passed the courtyard, allowing myself one second of appreciation for my individuality.

There was nothing wrong with being basic, dressing in the same clothing that every other girl in the city of cities wore. Me personally, well, I couldn't get behind that.

My jacket was a black wool coat, ankle length with grey hemming. I'd gotten it off a mannequin at Zara; the lady told me they didn't usually do that but she'd make an exception for me.

Women were always nice to me.

Maybe they felt sorry for me.

Maybe they questioned why I didn't feel sorry for myself.

A Hue of Blu

Marie-France Leger

The rest of my outfit was all black – black turtleneck, black jeans and black sock boots. A red scarf was the pop of colour that brought out *Blu Henderson*, the confident girl with a sad soul.

My phone pinged as I opened the doors to my faculty building.

3:55pm – Jace Boland: Turn around.

His hand cupped my elbow as he positioned himself in front of me, holding me steady. God, I couldn't meet his fucking eyes. They looked through me, they analyzed me. They saw something I refused to see.

"You didn't respond to my text," was all he said in the one minute of quiet silence between concrete walls.

He had texted me after the pizzeria, asking if I was okay and if I needed anything, to Facetime him. I thought it was odd that he even wanted to video chat, he didn't strike me as the type. Then again if you looked like that, no angle was a bad angle, even on camera.

I scratched the skin underneath my fingernails, staring at the floor. "Lots of schoolwork and stuff, didn't really –"

His fingers lifted my chin to face him, to meet that bluish-green gaze I'd been trying to avoid. "Eyes are up here, Blu."

I was completely immobile, paralyzed being this close, being this vulnerable to someone who wasn't mine. There was no way he cared enough; there had to be an ulterior motive here.

"Talk to me."

My lips were dry when I said, "Class is going to start soon."

"It already started, darling." He slid his phone out of his back pocket and showed me the time: 4:04pm.

"Then let's go." I began to walk and he let me, but didn't follow. "Are you not coming?"

A slow shake of the head. "I'm craving some coffee. Might skip today."

We now stood at two ends of the hall, staring at each other like a stand-off. Who was going to break first? Who was going to follow who? Who would fold?

"Enjoy," I forced out.

"I will."

But we both didn't move.

For a few seconds, it felt like eternity until a group of people burst through the second floor staircase and exited the hall.

"Who do you go to class for, Blu?" he asked, his tone suggesting he already knew the answer.

I stood up straight, not wanting him to hear it. "Myself."

A small smirk stamped his face. "Don't lie to me now."

And with this, he pushed the glass door and held it open, waiting for me, knowing I'd follow.

And like the coward, pathetic, attention-craving sadist I was –

I folded first.

Chapter Twenty-Eight
Jace

Year Two/York University – Two Years Ago

I don't know when I started being good with girls.

A piece of me was still living inside that shy, scared, fickle boy who knew nothing about anything and watched Netflix with his mom on weekends.

Honestly, after I got with Riley things changed. She was the confidence boost I needed to feel like I'd won, like I deserved a trophy after I got off Accutane and sorted out my appearance.

When we got back together, it felt like another reward. I'd saluted a fat 'fuck you' to the guy who took her from me and relished in the moments I had with her.

But as time went on, I realized I was waiting for something that would never come. I had the girl, but not really. She was there, but never present. She listened, but never cared. It was something to pass the time, *I* was something to pass the time.

I'd gone out with Bryce one night after Riley said she was feeling under the weather and couldn't go to Brixton with me. Bryce, being as introverted as he was, said no at first until I pushed his polo-wearing ass out of the dorm and into a corner booth.

"Two Belgian Moons, please," I told the waitress, a pretty blonde with a tiny waist.

Her eyes trailed down to my arms, stopping at my tattoos, circling through to my white tee, my silver bracelet, my rings – fucking all of me. All of me.

"What's the occasion?" Bryce asked, stretching out his arms.

We'd been going to the gym together since first year and he'd become more of a friend to me than Morris, Connor, Danny, hell even my own brothers.

"You hate Riley," I stated, leaning back against the hardwood. "Tell me why."

He laughed. "I don't hate her, man."

"You're never around when she's there."

"That doesn't mean I hate her. She's just not..." Bryce always chose his words carefully. I admired that about him. "She's not my type of person, that's all."

"Okay, but why?" I pried. I needed to know. I needed to hear that she wasn't good for me anymore. I couldn't make that decision myself.

He let out a sigh. "Because you're my type of person, Jace. And I care about what happens to you."

"So this is about me?"

"Yeah, obviously."

The drinks arrived on a black tray. The waitress slid both over to me, completely ignoring Bryce's presence.

"How the hell d'you do it, man?" he gawked, taking one of the beers from my end. "They just flock to you and stare. It's nuts."

Never in my life did I picture someone saying that to me. Seeing someone envious of my ability to pull girls without even trying, by just existing, by breathing. It was everything I thought I wanted.

When I was nothing, a shell of someone, a small spec of dust in comparison to all my friends, no one paid a morsel of attention to me. I envisioned this for so long, and now that it was happening, the feeling was surreal.

And yet, I felt an overwhelming urge to grab Bryce and shake him, to tell him he's as good as they come. That he was smart and helped me through so much shit. He didn't need the looks to get a wife, he should just be happy with who he was.

But if I wasn't going to practice what I was preaching, then there was no sense in saying it aloud.

I sipped my beer. "She's not going to change, is she?"

It was the realization I came to when Riley came back for the second time. When she was lying on my chest, her best friend slumped on the beanbag chair next to us, her fling on the phone begging for her. She loved an audience, she loved being wanted, being watched. I was just a part of her show, a cinematic masterpiece she tried to craft within herself.

I was an actor. A marionette on a string. She controlled me. I never wanted to be controlled again.

"You let her back in." Bryce took a swig of Belgian, cracking his neck. "She's probably thinking that no matter what she does next, you'd take her back."

I shook my head. "I don't want that."

"Then don't have that, dude. Just break up with her."

"Like, now?"

His eyes trailed one of the bartenders collecting empty cups. My eyes followed. For a second, I wanted to steal her attention, then thought better of it. There were plenty of fish in the sea. People like Bryce deserved them all.

"Jace, she basically dumped you over fucking Snapchat. A call is generous, a text is kindness."

As much as it pained me to do so, I crafted the message two and a half beers later, read thoroughly by Bryce, and hit send.

> 10:02pm – Jace: Listen Riley, I can't do this anymore. I feel like ever since EDC, I've been fighting for your attention and it's not fair to me. I love you, but I'm not waiting around anymore. I hope you feel better.

I blocked her number right after that and accepted the round of tequila Bryce bought me in celebration. It was a weird thing to celebrate, breaking up with someone, closing a chapter that needed to be closed.

There was almost a bittersweet taste to an unhappy ending. Everyone knew it was coming, but was still unprepared. I thought I'd feel great, but I felt worse.

That was the moment that I found out how to be good with girls. When I pushed aside the inebriation with three cups of water and a plate of fries, marching up to the blonde waitress and asking for her number.

Of course she gave it to me, with ease too. Of course she was back in my room every single day for the next week.

Of course it didn't last, because nothing ever did for me.

But over time, I learned to be everything that everyone wanted. I learned to match the energy of others, to morph into whatever they liked and remained that way until I didn't need to anymore.

That was the moment I realized how to win people over.

That was also the moment I realized how little of myself I had left, when I was trying to please everyone else.

Chapter Twenty-Nine
Blu

Year Four/Week Seven— Present

We ended up back at Plane.

It always amazed me looking around, seeing new faces everywhere I went. The campus was big, thousands of students bustling about with their own lives, own agendas and personal stories.

And yet here I was, back at a coffee shop when I hated coffee, trying to figure out Jace.

"You sure you don't want anything?" he asked, pulling out his wallet.

"Positive."

"You know one day –"

"*Hi, I can help whoever is next!*"

We made our way to the cash, stopping beside the pastry display. "Can I have a latte, please? For Jace." Then his attention was back on me. "One day, I'm going to get you to like coffee."

My eyes lingered on the snickerdoodle cookie. I ripped them away before Jace could see. "Hell might freeze over before then."

He laughed, that signature laugh that sent butterflies to my stomach. His whole face lit up like a Christmas tree.

"Do you think you're going to Hell?"

My eyes opened wide. "What?"

"Just an honest question," he shrugged. "Do you?"

"I mean, uh," I scratched my scalp, cracking up at the fact this was the conversation we were having. "Probably."

"For what?"

"For what?" I repeated.

"Latte for Jace!" the barista called.

As we walked over to the sugar cart, Jace asked again, "Yeah, for what?"

He placed his drink down on the counter while I leaned against the table, watching his slender fingers remove the lid.

"I'm more curious about you," I began, regaining my footing. "They say the quiet ones are the most surprising, have the most to hide. Will you surprise me, Jace?"

My confidence came in waves, you see. In a crowded environment like Plane, I could blend in with the atmosphere. No one could see through me when there was so much else to look at. Alone with Jace, that was a different story. No one but him could see me, and that was a terrifying thought.

His eyes never left mine as he stepped forward, placing a firm hand on the surface beside my hip and emptied a sugar packet into his cup.

My breath hitched as he leaned in closer, his words tickling the curve of my ear. "Something tells me I already have."

And with the weighted presence of his body dangerously close to mine, he disposed of the packet and led me to a two-seater booth underneath floating shelves.

"So back to the Hell question," he stated, settling into the ladderback chair.

"Are you religious?" I asked, half-laughing, half-flustered from just a few moments ago. My legs were pressed together underneath the table.

"Nope, just curious." He took a sip from his cup. "If it makes you feel any better, I'll probably be in Hell with you."

"What would drag you down there?"

"Envy, most likely. I'm a pretty jealous person. Want what I can't have, have what I don't want."

I folded my arms across my chest, leaning back. "Everyone has a bed. You're saying you don't want a bed?"

He chuckled, his dimple poking through. "Not material things, darling. I'm talking about people."

"What do you mean?"

He inched forward, wrapping his fingers around the width of his drink. "It's never the people I want in my life that come around. I feel like I'm waiting for someone to understand me, and no one ever does."

Before I could answer, react, fucking blink he tapped the table with his knuckles and said, "I've got to use the bathroom."

And so I sat, staring at the empty seat across from me, watching strangers through a glass window drift like ghosts through campus.

That small piece of information that Jace let me in on, a shred of vulnerability he finally showed me felt like a landslide of progress. *"I feel like I'm waiting for someone to understand me, and no one ever does."*

What made him say this? Made him open up? Was it the fact that I showed him a piece of myself? A piece that I never wanted anyone to see? Or did I even have to show him for him to know that I was struggling? What was left underneath Jace Boland that I could unlock?

As soon as he sat back down, I reached out and grabbed his hand. It was a forward gesture, a tactic I used many times before to make a man nervous. It never fazed me. But this, my touch featherlight over his, felt like the scariest thing in the world.

My index grazed over the ring on his pinky. "I understand you."

His eyes were fixated on my hand, his fingers frozen. For a second, I thought he was going to yank it back and leave me embarrassed and shattered. But suddenly, he squeezed my hand gently, and removed a brown paper bag from his jacket pocket.

He slid it over to me, keeping his grasp interlocked with mine.

I unwrapped it, peeling off the white tissue until I saw the snickerdoodle cookie from the pastry display.

I thought... I thought he didn't notice. I thought he didn't see me looking. *I'm the one who notices everything. I'm the one who pays attention.*

No one had ever paid attention to me before. Not like this. Not ever.

"Jace —"

"I understand you," he whispered. "I understand you."

Chapter Thirty
Jace

Year Four/Week Eight– Present

Halloween was tonight and I texted Blu asking if she wanted to come out with me and my friends.

I knew she probably had other plans, but I went ahead and shot my shot anyway.

A few guys from first year were having a house party in the village, and Bryce and I were going as Spiderman and Venom. Clubs were overrated and overpriced, even though girls loved that shit. Couldn't be me. If Blu had plans to blow her life savings on twenty-dollar watered down mixers, I could save her from that.

> 5:18pm – Jace: Halloween party tonight. Want to come?
>
> 5:32pm – Blu Henderson: Where?
>
> 5:38pm – Jace: Campus village.

I texted her Bryce's dorm room number because that's where we were pre-drinking. Never in my life did I think Bryce would meet Blu; never in my life did I think I'd be the one providing that opportunity.

Over the last week I'd contemplated whether or not she was someone I wanted in my life, someone of value and importance. It was a stupid thing to analyze, but I rarely let people in. Nothing good ever came from it, nothing good ever will.

But the more I thought about her, the more I realized she was actively living in my head. There were no distinctive feelings to describe the emotions I felt, just that they were there. That was the push I needed to text her.

"She coming?" Bryce asked, slugging back a cider.

I checked my phone to see that I had two missed texts from her.

> 5:40pm – Blu Henderson: I'll pass for tonight, have fun though!
>
> 5:41pm – Blu Henderson: Thanks for inviting me ☺

It was a bit of a sucker punch to the face, honestly, reading those messages. I thought after the last couple weeks, we made some progress getting to know each other beyond something superficial. But then again, girls always made Halloween plans in advance so I shouldn't have been surprised. *Don't take it personally, Jace. It's nothing personal.*

"Guess not." I grabbed a Bud from the cooler and leaned against Bryce's desk.

"Disappointed?"

I met his eyes, those curious brown orbs. "What answer are you expecting?"

He shrugged, his Venom mask tight like spandex over his forehead. "The truth."

I couldn't help but laugh. "You look like a fucking idiot right now. I can't take you seriously."

"Look in the mirror, man. You're in a skin-tight Spiderman suit."

"And I look amazing." The beer was cool on my tongue as I swallowed down the fizz, staring at my phone. "She's probably going to a club."

"Why don't you ask her?"

"Because I don't care."

I didn't need to look up to see that Bryce had rolled his eyes. "But you do."

We stared at each other for a few moments before the unyielding curiosity took over. "Fuck it, I'll just ask."

> 5:55pm – Jace: No worries, you got big Halloween plans?

The temptation to silence her notifications was weighing on me. Halloween was always a ball and I'd never had to worry about a girl before, not that I was worrying about Blu. Riley and I had been together last Halloween so she was on my arm. *Whose arm would Blu be on tonight?*

> 6:01pm – Blu Henderson: The biggest. Think wild inebriation, strippers and a dildo cake with vampire fangs 😜

A dildo cake with vampire fangs? Where was this girl going? Did I even want to know?

"I'm done with the questioning," I told Bryce after hearting her message and switching off my phone. "Don't think I'm going to like the answers."

He lifted his can in the air to cheers me. "You'll have fun tonight, man. When have you not?"

And just like that, a laundry list of occasions popped into my head.

When I was bullied for being too skinny, too ugly – an acne ridden loser.

When Riley broke me.

When my brothers devalued our relationship.

When my dad would yell. And I mean, really yell.

When I wasn't good enough to play pro.

When I wasn't good enough.

When I wasn't good enough.
When I wasn't good enough.

I pulled the Spiderman mask down over my head and shoved the rest of the drinks in a backpack, holding the door open for Bryce.

Halloween was my favourite form of self-expression. You could be anyone you wanted, put on a costume and people wouldn't judge you, wouldn't try and look any deeper than what you showed them.

Maybe it was a good thing I wasn't seeing Blu tonight – she'd shred away this suit and pull out the pieces underneath.

Tonight, I was Spiderman. Tonight I saved the world.

Tomorrow, I'd be Jace Boland. The man who wished the world would save him.

Chapter Thirty-One
Blu

Year Four/Week Eight— Present

"Should I tell him I was joking?" I asked Fawn, forking a piece of chicken in my Pad-Thai.

"No," she swallowed some noodles. "He's probably at that party right now. Never text a guy when they're at a party unless they text you first."

He wasn't mine and yet I claimed him in my head. The thought of him being out with a bevy of girls sent nails down my esophagus. But again, he wasn't mine.

"I should've just went. He literally invited me."

At this, Fawn set aside her take-out box. "First of all, if you went, I would've been very pissed. And your chocolates and flowers would not have cut it."

I laughed.

"Blu, it's good that you denied him for once. He's probably thinking you'd just come at his beck and call no matter what."

He was definitely thinking that. But still, I couldn't shake the butterflies that came with his invitation.

Jace wanted me there.

He wanted to be around me.

"If I wasn't here, I'd be there. You know that."

"I know," she stared at me hard for a few seconds. Every time she did this, I knew she was contemplating something. It freaked me out.

"What?"

Her hand was in mine, squeezing gently. "You're worth so much more than you give yourself credit for."

Fire burned the back of my eyes but I refused to cry. Ever since the beginning of our friendship, I felt like Fawn saw right through me. All the little cracks, the rocky exterior, the crumbled foundation of my life – she knew.

She loved all the pieces of myself that I hid from the world.

She loved me when I didn't think it was possible.

She never made me question if I was worthy of it, because to her, loving me came as easy as breathing.

"I love you, Fawn." I wasn't much of a sap, but after three glasses of wine and a food coma, sweetness oozed out of me.

She tapped my knee and pressed her lips into a smile. "Love yourself more."

And just like that, she hit play and resumed The Conjuring, leaving me in the corner seat of her couch with a wonder in my brain.

Love yourself more.

Was that made to be an insult? I did love myself, didn't I? I showered, I made my bed, I cut my nails and did my hair. My skin was always washed, my clothes neat and pressed. If I didn't love myself, those chores wouldn't get done.

And yet, all my material possessions felt like scraps of paper.

Love yourself more.

As if I didn't think about all the things I could change about myself – to improve my appearance, my health, my facial texture. That was love. I was trying to fix broken pieces. I loved myself.

Love yourself more.

I walked away from Kyle, didn't I? Maybe he stayed a lot longer than he should have, but eventually I left [when I had no choice]. I left.

I left.
I loved myself.
I loved my –
I loved…
I hated myself.

***

My phone rang at 2:14am.

Luckily, I wasn't next to Fawn because my ringer had been on full blast.

My eyes adjusted to the dark surroundings of her living room, the purple fuzzy blanket draped over me on the couch.

Every time I stayed over, she knew to set aside a space for me alone. Sleeping next to people was never something I enjoyed, even if that someone was my best friend.

I reached over to grab my phone from the coffee table, checking the caller ID: Jace Boland.

Immediately, I sat up, answering. "Jace?"

He was panting when he said, "I just got clocked in the face. Where are you?"

My eyes flew open. "Someone punched you? Are you okay?"

"*Shut the fuck up I'm talking!*" At first I thought he was addressing me, but quickly realized there was someone else with him. "Blu, where are you? Can I come see you?"

Before I could answer, he repeated my name again. "Blu? You still there?"

He was drunk. He was so drunk.

"Yeah, yeah. I'm…" Fuck, Fawn's not going to like this. "I'm at my friend's place. I can send you the address."

"Send me the address, I'm on my way."

I hung up and texted it over immediately, devising the best course of action to tell Fawn what I'd just done.

2:27pm – Jace Boland: Be there in 10.

Well, I couldn't prolong it anymore. I tiptoed into Fawn's room and found her cuddling with a body pillow, her eyes sewed shut. She was one hundred percent out cold.

Even when I exited the room and the door shut a little louder than expected, I could hear soft snoring penetrating through the wall.

I decided to shoot her a text anyway and let her know that Jace got hurt and needed a fix up. Fawn understood things better than anyone. She'd do the same if she were in my position.

But a part of me still felt so shit for inviting him over to someone's home, a home that wasn't mine.

I didn't have time to dwell on it though because Jace had just texted saying he was pulling up.

2:35pm – Blu: Just text me when you're at the door. Floor 8 room 803. Don't knock!

My palms were sweaty. Why were my palms sweaty? This felt intimate, wrong. It was like two kids playing together after hours, hiding in the shadows so their parents couldn't see. I'd done stupid things like this before, but never in my best friend's home.

And yet, a part of me was racing with excitement at the thought of seeing Jace. Why had he called me? Why had he even invited me tonight? Did he like me? *Could he?*

My phone vibrated in my hand and without even checking, I slowly opened the front door to meet him.

"Holy fuck," I said, barely a whisper.

His light brown hair was disheveled over his forehead, a huge gash cut his forearm, still bleeding, and his right eye was already bruising.

"Blu I –"

"Shh," I placed a finger over my lips, pulling him inside. "Fawn's sleeping."

"Who?"

"Never mind." Luckily, the bathroom was a few steps away from the entrance and the furthest away from Fawn's bedroom.

Jace gripped the doorhandle for support as he followed me into the small space, plopping down on the edge of the bathtub.

I shut the door and locked it, leaning against the counter to analyze his injuries in the light.

"What the hell happened?"

He laughed.

He fucking laughed.

And what's worse?

It was the most attractive thing I'd ever seen.

There was something about a guy who was scraped up post-fight that made a girl squirm. Call me crazy, but if you asked anyone, they'd agree. I knew it wasn't the time to be thinking such outlandish thoughts, but fuck. He was too damn beautiful.

"My friend was talking to some guys' ex and he didn't like that very much," Jace began, shaking his head with amusement like his lip wasn't sliced open. "Tried to jump my buddy and I stepped in. Next thing I know, my ass ends up in a thorn bush."

He held up his arm to show me the bleeding gash down his skin, staining the red and blue lining of his Spiderman costume.

"I didn't know you had tattoos," he slurred.

My arms were wrapped around my middle, covering the small space of skin between my pyjama waistband and tank top.

I felt more naked now than ever.

"Let me wrap up your arm," I offered, bending down underneath the sink. Anything to ignore the conversation of what they meant, when I got them, *why* I got them.

I found Fawn's medical kit and rummaged through the contents. Jace's stare was burning through me, I could feel it in my bones. His eyes were scanning my body, scoping out flaws, scouting out insecurities. *God, why the fuck did I have to wear boxer shorts on the night I saw him? He could see everything. He could judge everything.*

"Heal me," he said, tilting his head to the side. A slight grin formed at the corner of his lips as I walked towards him, taking hold of his arm.

"Is your friend okay?" I asked, bandaging his wrist first.

"Why are you asking about him? I'm the one who got fucked up."

I laughed because it was the stupidest thing he could've said. "How much did you drink tonight?"

"Enough that this didn't hurt."

"Maybe you really are Spiderman."

"Maybe you can be my Mary Jane."

I stopped for a second, realizing how close we'd gotten. Those long legs were extended on either side of me, placing my body in the middle of them. Heat radiated off his core, or maybe it was me. Maybe I was too aware of the proximity that I felt sparks.

"Heal me," he repeated under his breath, his fingers finding the back of my calf.

Fuck. Fuck. Fuck.

This wasn't in my head. This was happening.

I pretended not to notice, bandaging up his forearm. Blood soaked into the gauze, turning the white netting into pink.

"I think Spiderman is more than capable of healing himself," I teased.

His bluish-green eyes flicked down my face as he said, "Sometimes it's nice to be taken care of."

A frog lodged itself in my throat. "Yeah, I'm uh…" His skin was warm. It wasn't just me. "I'm doing the best I can."

His hand slid further up the back of my leg, trailing behind my knee, resting on my thigh. "Come closer and do a little more."

My breathing hitched as he gently pulled me down, my knees kissing the cold tile floor. I was eye-level with him now, his stare bleeding into mine with inscrutability.

"You're drunk, Jace," I breathed out, fighting the urge to lean forward. I did the opposite. I'd been on this side of the coin one too many times.

"Where were you tonight?" He searched for something in my eyes, like always, then drooped his gaze downwards. "Where's the vampire fang dildo cake?"

I chuckled.

He smiled.

Now his hand found the small of my back, but he didn't move me forward or push me away. It just rested there. It was meant to be there.

"I didn't do anything for Halloween."

"No?"

"No," I pressed my lips together. "I was kidding."

"Don't make a habit of lying to me now, darling."

God, every time he said that, I melted. This was bad. This was really fucking bad. He knew what he was doing, he knew it got under my skin. And yet, I let it. Every single time, I let it.

Jace stabs me.

I twist the knife.

Who's to blame?

"Why did you call me?"

This time, he leaned back, removing his hand from my skin. I craved it. I felt empty without it. I wanted his touch again.

He didn't look at me when he said, "I don't know."

You're joking. "That's it?"

"Yeah, I just…" Now he stood up and I felt like my heart was halved in two. "Just drunk and wanted to see you, I guess."

I guess.

I fucking *guess.*

My face was hot. "Because I give you attention?"

"What?"

This was my past repeating itself, wasn't it? I saw all the signs and I chose to ignore it. I was convenient.

I was fucking convenient.

"You feel bad for me."

"Blu, Blu – No, what? Where is this coming from?"

I couldn't help it. The tears fell. I moved away. "Why the fuck did you come here tonight? Answer honestly."

He couldn't say anything. He didn't have a response. He came because he wasn't thinking clearly and he knew I'd pick up. He knew I'd bend whatever rule I was following for him. Fawn was right. At his beck and call.

At his fucking beck and call.

Two loud knocks made me jump. Fawn was awake. *Shit.*

I quickly unlocked the door and found her tired eyes staring back at me, then quickly averted to Jace. "Why are you in my bathroom? What's going on?"

"He was just leaving," I spat, dragging Fawn out of the doorway so Jace could get out.

His long stride made it to the front entrance before he turned to Fawn and apologized, then threw me a glance.

"What?" I snapped. It was sharp, I knew it was. But anger seethed through me. Rejection. Pain. I didn't know where it was coming from. All I knew was that it lingered.

He let out a clipped scoff, shaking his head. He turned the doorknob and before leaving, said, "Stop assuming that you know how I feel. You're hurting yourself at this point."

Then he was gone.

I cried on the floor for fifteen minutes, letting out ridiculous sobs to Fawn. The worst part was, I couldn't even explain why I was crying. I didn't know.

All I was sure of was that the person to blame, the one who twisted the knife and kept it lodged in my heart… that wasn't Jace.

That was me.

Chapter Thirty-Two
Blu

Year Four/Week Ten – Present

The first time I sliced my skin was three months after Dad died.

I'm surprised I didn't do it sooner.

It resembled euphoric bliss every time I took a blade to my flesh and felt something other than mental drought.

The second time was when my first boyfriend, Zac, threw the gold watch I'd gifted him at my eye. I had hugged another boy. It was my mistake.

The third time was after Kyle had gotten too drunk and forgot the meaning of consent.

And the last and final time was a year ago, when I realized I'd gained twenty-two pounds and couldn't fit into my Rag & Bone jeans.

I realized after I stopped self-harming that directing my pain to the parts of my body that did nothing wrong was fucked. Why would I damage my beautiful skin when my heart was already bristled and stone? One ugly thing was enough.

When I turned eighteen, I got a rose tattoo on my wrist to cover up the pain my father left behind. Then, butterflies on my forearms to stamp the spots I wrecked in his wake.

The words "Rise Again" were written on my inner bicep, right where Zac had gripped my arm so hard it bruised. He'd punctured a piece of my soul that day. I'd never let myself forget it.

After Kyle had violated me, I got a heart tattoo to remind myself that I still had one.

Then the weight came and I made a small incision on my lower stomach, just above my hip. Maybe the fat would have dripped out of me like honey, that was my first thought.

It didn't.

I got a bumblebee tattoo instead.

The rest of my patchwork were meaningless tattoos. I'd only gotten them so that I could stop hyper-fixating on the reasons why I inked my skin in the first place.

Jace knew I had them now. My only hope was that he was too wasted to remember what he saw. Maybe he just assumed they were for the aesthetic, I mean, I could always lie and say that was the case.

But ever since Halloween, I avoided interactions with him at all costs. I skipped the classes I had with him last week to catch up on school work, only attending my Tuesday seminar which was environmental media. Paying attention for the first time in two months was a blessing because the content wasn't actually half bad.

Prof. Barnaby was a wholesome old man who pronounced every syllable and wore colourful suspenders. Today was no different.

I sat down next to the printers at the back of the class, scrolling through a Pinterest board of photography ideas when the chair pulled out next to me.

"This seat taken?" the voice asked.

Before I even decided to look up, I rolled my eyes. "That's such a line."

"It was an honest question."

Huh. My interest was piqued because the mystery stranger still hadn't sat down.

I was met with a set of leaf-green eyes, a tallish man with brown hair, a plaid overcoat and a varsity tee underneath. His curls were covered underneath a black ballcap and a key chain hung around his neck.

"Sit," I smiled, wondering why I'd never seen him before. *Oh wait, it's because my mind has been consumed by Jace Boland for the past sixty days.*

"I'm Vince, by the way." He opened up his laptop, an Asus covered in random stickers, and turned to me. "Blu, right?"

"Everyone seems to know me before I know them," I stuck out my hand to shake his. "Blu Henderson, yeah."

His palm was soft against mine. "With a name like Blu, it's kind of hard to forget."

"And the hair," I twirled a cobalt lock around my finger. "Don't forget the hair."

He placed a hand over his heart as if he were wounded. It made me chuckle.

"I could never," he said. His smile was cute, no dimples though. Not like Jace.

"I'm glad I finally got the chance to talk to you. You always sit alone."

"Well, I was sitting alone before you came along so nothing's really different."

He leaned back, taking off his cap and flipping it backwards. "Touché. Was it wrong of me to sit here?"

"It's a free country, love. Sit where you want."

"Love," he smiled. I knew he'd like that.

Prof. Barnaby finally decided he was ready to teach and switched on the PowerPoint slideshow. "Right class, who's presenting today?"

A girl raised her hand and shuffled to the front, setting up her project. I stared at her trying to assign a name that fit because I had zero clue what it was.

"She looks like an Abigail," I whispered to my new friend. "Doesn't she?"

He squinted as if he were looking through a magnifying glass. "I can see it. Her name's Liz, though."

"She doesn't look like a Liz."

"Do I look like a Vince?" he queried, forcing me to stare at his features.

I shook my head. "No, you look like a Caden or a Cory. Something C."

"Cunt?" he jested.

I hated that word. But when he said it, it sounded more like a pre-teen who just discovered Urban Dictionary so I let it slide.

"Do I look like a Blu?"

His eyes travelled from my forehead to my cheeks, my chin and then hair. "I think it suits you perfectly."

The rest of class, Vince and I played Google games and competed in Solitaire matches behind our laptop screens. He won the first few rounds but I made a comeback eventually. I always did.

A part of me wondered what his motives were. I was sure I'd find out soon enough whether he wanted to sleep with me or if I was just something to look at. But for now, I relished in the idea that someone of the opposite sex could actually enjoy my company.

When class ended and he walked me out, the first sentence that left his lips was, "Want to grab a bite to eat tomorrow?"

"I have class at four but I can meet you after that?"

His grin was bright. "Sounds good. Can I get your number, Blu?"

I plugged it in without hesitation. Maybe Vince could be a good distraction. He was decently tall, rather plain style but it wasn't horrible. He was kind of cute, in a nerdy, soft-boy way.

Yeah, I could learn to like him.

He could learn to like me.

Everyone did.

Everyone but Jace.

Chapter Thirty-Three
Blu

Year Four/Week Ten – Present

"Tell me about him, what's he like?" Carter asked, buying us two white chocolate mochas from the coffee cart.

"There's nothing to it, I just met the guy yesterday."

"Vince, right? That's his name?"

"Yes," I said, rolling my eyes. "Finally someone you remember."

"I'm sorry, Jace is just not a memorable name. Kind of like Sam, or John, you know?"

The warm liquid burned my tongue almost immediately. "Apologize to all the Sam and John's of the world."

"I'll get around to it." He kept my pace as we walked through The Square. "Tongue okay?"

I made a face. "Why? Want to kiss me?"

His expression was equally disturbed. "Save that for Jace."

As angry as I was with him, the thought of our Halloween night came back to mind. Him holding me close in the bathroom, his piercing stare penetrating all the walls I'd fought so hard to keep up. There was something about him, from the very beginning, that kept me sane and insane all at once. I fucking hated it.

Fawn approached just as we turned the corner to enter The Market, dragging a tall man behind her wearing a beige puffer.

"Guys, so sorry I'm late. Bryce was shaving." She pulled me in for a hug, acknowledging Carter before introducing us to her new man. I think?

"Hey, I'm Bryce Beckworth." He extended a hand, formal like me. He was raised right, I thought. Only I wasn't, and I had to learn the art of pleasantries along the way.

"Blu," I smiled, switching my drink to the opposite hand. "Henderson."

If I wasn't staring at him directly in the face, I wouldn't have realized that he was frozen like a fucking icicle.

"Something wrong?" Fawn asked, realizing too.

"Um –" His features were bright red, and definitely not from the cold. "Wow, this is actually really awkward."

"Awkward?" Carter asked.

"Awkward?" Fawn repeated.

"I'm so confused," I muttered.

From the way he was staring at me, there was definitely some familiarity on his end. Fuck, had I hooked up with him at a party… Or a club? I mean, he was decently attractive; it was definitely probable. If that were the case, awkward indeed.

"Blu, you said?"

"I did," my gaze travelled to Fawn who was tense beside him. "Look, if we ever –"

"No, no – Fuck, uh, my roommate – *old* roommate and best friend is Jace." He scratched the back of his neck, looking around as if someone could save him.

Why was he looking around for help?

I was the one who felt like my knees were about to give out. My lungs were collapsing. This was not happening.

"Jace," I let out, my tongue dry. "Jace Boland is your best friend?"

"Nice to officially meet you, Blu," he blurted, choking out a laugh. "This is crazy. Small fucking world."

"How…" I pinched the bridge of my nose, looking at Carter, then to Fawn, then cussed. Like, three times. "How the fuck did you two meet again?"

"I told you, Hinge." Fawn was mortified on my behalf. I could sense it. But in the few times that she mentioned Bryce, she said they'd had some good dates. Mind you, they'd only been talking for a week and a half, but he was a gentleman. *Her* words.

"I'm sorry, I'm making this weird. It's not weird, I don't care, I'm just surprised," I lied.

I initiated a walk to the first vendor cart I saw – some crystals and magnets. There was no way I could just stand there and stare at an extension of Jace Boland, someone close to him that was probably texting him at this very minute.

But wait… That meant that Jace mentioned me. I mattered enough for him to tell his best friend. Why did I matter if I didn't? I did.

I mattered to Jace Boland.

And it still wasn't enough.

My eyes caught a mulled wine station with holiday cocktails listed on the menu. The drinks were ten dollars too expensive, but I didn't care. Something strong was calling my name, something that could ease my discomfort and make me whole again.

"Anyone want an espresso martini? Anyone?" I looked to Carter, then to Fawn and quickly scanned over Bryce. He was a bit shorter than Jace with black hair. His eyes were bright blue, sort of like Jace, but not.

Jace. Jace. Jace. God, when the fuck would he get out of my head? When would I stop being reminded that he exists?

"I'll have five espresso martinis, please." I slapped my card on the counter, hoping, praying that these drinks would be made within ten seconds.

It was impossible, but so was seeing my best friend dating Jace's best friend.

What. The. Fuck.

"*What the fuck*," I whispered. No one heard me. Everyone was paying attention to their own shit. For once, it was a blessing. For once, I wanted to be invisible.

"Five?" Carter said, the extra drink finally registering. "Who's drinking the fifth?"

One look was all it took to get him to understand. One silent exchange that allowed my best guy friend to see how dangerous this situation was about to become.

If Fawn and Bryce worked out, that would mean one thing –

Jace Boland would be around.

There would be no escaping this, escaping *him*.

Jace Boland was here to stay.

And five espresso martinis would never be enough to drown out the war brewing between my head and heart.

Chapter Thirty-Four
Jace

Year Four/Week Ten – Present

Blu walked to the class door with some guy.

> Blu said goodbye to this guy.
> Blu smiled at this guy.
> *Who the fuck was this guy?*
> She stepped inside and scanned the room, trying to hide the fact that she was looking for me. *I'm not an idiot, Blu*, I wanted to say. *I'm right here.*
>
> She wore a grey scarf and a black coat, her tan knee-high boots contrasting the evident disdain she was sporting today. In my head, I commanded her to sit beside me. Words needed to be said.
>
> After Bryce told me that the girl he'd been talking to was in fact Blu's best friend Fawn, everything clicked. It made sense, just never registered before. She'd mentioned the name Fawn, but I hadn't been listening. My attention had always been on Blu.
>
> "What did you guys talk about?" I'd asked. "Did you mention me?"
>
> He said they made pleasant conversation, cordial would be the right word. After he brought up the fact we were friends, he sensed that Blu didn't want to discuss anything that had to do with us – or whatever the fuck *"us"* entailed.
>
> So he dropped it. Classic Bryce. I would've pressed. I would've wanted to know what Blu was thinking. But then again, he didn't feel the way I did. No one felt the way I did.

I watched Blu drop into a front row seat, placing her belongings on the chair next to her. Nah, that wouldn't do.

"Blu," I called. Fuck my pride. "Come here."

It was loud enough that a few people turned their heads, but friendly enough that they wouldn't pay any mind to the situation.

Her big brown eyes turned to me, hesitating, but respecting my wishes. She gathered her bag and coat, plopping down next to me.

"Hi," she said, flatly. "What is it?"

I cleared my throat, sitting erect. "We haven't talked. I want to talk."

"About what?"

"Not here."

"Then why am I sitting with you?"

My eyes narrowed. "I don't know, Blu. Why are you sitting next to me?"

"You asked," she countered. "I can get up right now."

I opened an arm, nudging my head to the worst possible desk she could've chosen upon entry. "Feel free, darling."

As soon as she stood, I realized she wasn't playing. My hand flew out in front of her, wrapping around her wrist gently.

She stared at me, lowering her posture back into the chair.

"I like you better beside me," I stated, surprising myself.

And not a truer statement was spoken.

"You confuse me," she said, shaking her head.

Valid. "I confuse myself."

"I never know how you're feeling."

Chapter Thirty-Five
Blu

Year Four/Week Ten – Present

"So, what did you want to talk about?" I asked, keeping up with Jace's long stride down the hall.

"I just wanted to apologize for Halloween," he started, glancing over as we walked through the building. "I shouldn't have called, honestly. I was too drunk to be thinking clearly."

So none of that mattered, then. The way he held me, the way he looked at me, the things he said.

I kept silent, even though my heart was shattering, yet again.

He stopped in his tracks, halting me with him. I never understood how he did that, how he knew when something bothered me. It was like a sixth sense.

"I remember everything, Blu. I know what I said to you before I left."

His words banged against my skull. "*You're hurting yourself at this point,*" I quoted. "Yeah."

He shook his head, feeling the bottom fringe of my scarf. It was a small gesture, but intimate all at once. As if he wanted to touch a part of me, but not my skin; just something connected to me, something on my body.

"Do you like me, Blu?"

The cold wind slapped me in the face as he asked the question. It might as well have been his hand.

"No." *Liar.*

"Don't say that."

"I don't know you well enough."

He swallowed. "Because every time you try to, you get afraid. Like, you think I'm some bad person, that I'm going to fuck with you and hurt you or something. We can't keep doing this dance."

My heart hammered in my chest. I felt my phone vibrate in my pocket but I didn't dare check. "I don't think you're a bad person. I never said that."

"Then why won't you open up to me? Are we always going to spend time together without actually saying anything? You don't eat, I'm supposed to pretend I don't notice. You hide your skin, I'm never supposed to ask why you're wearing a jacket inside?"

Tears burned my eyes, I think one might have slipped out because his face softened. He flexed his jaw, taking a step forward. His thumb contacted my cheek before I could make a movement, brushing away the sadness that found its way to the surface.

"When you're ready to talk, I'm here," he offered, but his eyes were focused on something behind me. "I think someone's waiting for you."

Immediately I zipped around, seeing Vince waving at me from behind the college pillar. *Fuck.* I forgot we had plans. He even reminded me on our walk to class, but I spaced. Every time I was around Jace, I fucking spaced.

Now, more than ever, was the worst time to go. But now, more than ever, I needed to be away from him.

"He was the guy you were with earlier," Jace stated, like a fact from Wikipedia.

"Yeah, that's um, Vince from my environmental media class."

He nodded, saying his name like it was cement on his tongue. "Vince." His jaw was square and tight as he pressed his lips together and turned around.

"Where are you going?" I asked, knowing damn well his route to the subway was the direction I was walking in.

A ghost of a smile played on his lips as he stopped, facing me, then Vince. "Does he know who I am?"

I shook my head, furrowing my brows. Why the hell would he know Jace? For what purpose?

"Well," he wiggled his fingers into a wave, aimed directly at Vince, then met my eyes with intensity. "I'm sure he'll find out soon enough."

And with that last comment, Jace was gone.

Chapter Thirty-Six
Jace

Year Four/Week Eleven – Present

After missing Thursday's class, I called Blu the following Monday.

I don't know what came over me Wednesday night, seeing her with some guy, some fuck who dressed the same as Morris and Danny.

He had a good build. He was tall, nice hair. Seemed like a decent dude.

I was better, wasn't I? Blu wanted me. I knew her. He didn't.

A part of me wanted to keep the knowledge I had of her as my own personal trophy. Knowing her was all I had over this guy.

"Jace?" She always answered the call with my name. I found it endearing.

"Hey, how's it going?"

She was silent for a few moments, probably wondering why the hell I was calling her at 8:09pm on a random weeknight.

"Good, what's up?"

We always did this. Pretended like nothing happened, no conversations took place days prior. It's like each morning was a fresh start and we wouldn't be affected by prior circumstances.

"Just wanted to see how your date went."

"It wasn't a date."

"No?" I readjusted my position on the mattress. "He's a good looking guy, Blu."

Why the fuck did I always do that? Like, I wanted her to say no, of course I did. I wanted to be the only one she thought was attractive. So unrealistic, so fucking delusional.

"Okay…"

Stupid, stupid, stupid.

As I opened my mouth to make an even bigger fool of myself, a "call waiting" alert vibrated my phone: **Scott Boland.**

"Blu, I got to go. I'll see you in class."

I hung up before she could say goodbye, not that there was much of one to exchange, and answered my oldest brother's call.

"Hello?"

"Want to have dinner Wednesday night?" he suggested amidst the distant sounds of a T.V. playing.

My whole face lit up. Scratch that, my whole fucking world. Mom must've told him I wanted to spend some time with him.

Last week, I'd sat down with her and had a heart to heart. Dad wasn't even a piece of the puzzle anymore. All he did was come home, whine and complain about some aspect of his life and repeat. All his problems somehow involved yelling at Mom and me, as if we were the punching bag he possessed.

My brothers, they were all I had of a father figure. It sucked, it really fucking sucked that I couldn't spend as much time with them as I wanted to. But they didn't want to spend time with me. That was the worst part.

I was too young.

I wouldn't understand their careers.

I wasn't good company.

I was inconvenient.

Fuck was it ever painful sometimes. I never wanted to beg for someone's affection, let alone my brother's time. I just couldn't take it anymore. The house was too quiet, my mind was too noisy. Mom was the closest thing to me, and for a while, that was sufficient.

But when we sat down over dinner, something switched in my brain. I realized how lonely things had been, not just for me, but for her. Maybe if I spent more time with my brothers, Mom and Dad could repair a love they lost. Maybe they could have alone time, go on dates – I wouldn't be a burden, a part of the problem. After all, I wasn't planned. Maybe they really did see me as some kind of nuisance.

That's what I led with talking to Mom. She cried. I held back tears. I never cried in front of anyone.

"You're not a nuisance, Jace," she tried, stroking my cheek. "I'm sorry you've been feeling so down."

I shrugged. "It's not really you, Mom. I don't know. I just feel like Bax and Will and Scott, they don't really care. And, you know, we're brothers. It's tough being alone all the time. Seeing my friends with their brothers and not having that."

"Will and Bax are always so busy, baby. You know that. But I can talk to Scott."

It warmed my heart, but I also felt like a charity case. "I don't want him doing anything just because you told him to."

"I'm sure he'd love to spend some time with you." She pushed out of her chair, carrying her plate to the sink. "For what it's worth, Jace, I'm glad you talked to me about it."

Since that conversation, I realized the value of communication. Maybe that's why I told Blu how I felt. There were so many things she kept hidden, so many secrets she wanted to bury. If she wanted a friendship with me (as much as I wanted one with her), we had to be open and honest, even a little. How else was I supposed to get to know her?

"Jace?" Scott's voice pulled me out of my head. "Wednesday sound good?"

"Yes, yeah. Absolutely," I responded with lightning speed, as if the invitation was going to fly away and I wouldn't be able to catch it. "Looking forward to it."

The sound of Sabrina's voice rang through the line. "Hi Jace!"

"Hey Sab," I smiled, feeling a little more included in my brother's life addressing his girlfriend.

"I'll text you Wednesday. Pick a place and meet me downtown for eight?"

"I will, see you Scott."

The line cut off and I immediately called Blu back.

She answered in two rings. "Hey again."

"Hi," I smiled. "Have I ever told you about my brothers?"

"Oh, um – No, never."

The surprise in her voice made me smile. I felt like I was on top of the world.

"Can I tell you about them?"

She listened while I spoke for over half an hour, opening up to someone who I knew wanted to listen. Even if she didn't experience the same things I did, I felt like I could trust her. The biggest part of me knew she was a good person, the smallest part of me felt like she cared. Maybe one day those small parts would amount to something larger than they were.

"I'm sorry you feel this way," Blu said. There was sincerity in her voice.

"My mom said the same thing."

"At least he asked you to go to dinner, right? That'll be fun."

"Yeah, yeah it will be."

There was a level of silence that followed, a silence that was no longer awkward or deafening. It was comfortable being in contact without saying a word. I felt okay.

"Tell me something about yourself."

She laughed. "Like what?"

"I don't know, I feel like I know nothing about you."

"On the contrary, I'd say you know quite a bit."

"You've never come out and told me anything, though."

She exhaled. I pictured where she was right now. What she was doing. Why she was devoting her time to talk to me, but then I let go of all those inhibitions and remained present on our call.

"Tell me something that's happened to you. Something that hurt you."

"That's um," she paused, "That's a loaded question."

I didn't speak further. I knew she'd eventually give in. My voice was strained enough. Hers was all I wanted to hear.

She told me a story about how she had been in a five year relationship, from thirteen to nineteen. How he physically abused her, mentally drained her and stained the idea of love she used to have.

A Hue of Blu　　　　　　　　Marie-France Leger

At first, I couldn't fathom how deep the conversation got in such a short period of time. I listened to all the stories she told me, about how he threw her anniversary gift (a gold watch) at her face, how he cheated numerous times that she gave up counting and turned people against her.

"It blows my mind how some guys can do that to the girl they're with, the girl they say they love." I was angry, hurt for her. Blu didn't deserve that. No one did.

"He never loved me."

"No, he didn't." He couldn't. "But that has nothing to do with you."

"I was part of the problem," she sighed. She did that far too many times in this conversation. I wanted to take her pain away.

"Do you still think you are?"

She was quiet, so I asked another question. "Is that why you didn't want to tell me anything? You thought I'd judge you?"

I could feel her nodding. "A bit, yeah. I didn't want to scare you."

Blu Henderson.

The fiery girl I'd met over two months ago, was scared. She was frightened to allow people in. She didn't want anyone to get to know her because she thought they'd leave.

"I'm not going to hurt you," I swore.

For the first time, I truly believed it.

But sometimes, belief isn't enough.

And ~~sometimes~~, all the time, I wish I were a better man to have kept my promises.

Chapter Thirty-Seven
Blu

Year Four/Week Eleven – Present

I spent an extra ten minutes in the bathroom fixing my hair.

Honestly, it was a bit embarrassing, trying this hard to impress someone but I had to do it. He needed to see that I was more than just a broken shell.

Ever since our phone call, I felt weird. A part of me was happy that he knew more about me, but the biggest part felt intolerable. I never anticipated that Jace would learn anything below surface level stuff, but when he asked, I couldn't deny him.

I walked in five minutes before class and saw him sitting in the second row, like usual, more dressed up... Huh. *Unusual.*

"Going to an event?" I guessed, sliding into the chair next to him.

He smiled, brighter than ever this time. It actually lifted me up.

"I'm meeting my brother for dinner tonight."

"Oh, right! That's tonight. Have fun."

"I will." His grin was permanently plastered on his face. I felt the joy bursting through him and I basked in it.

My eyes surveyed his outfit, immediately catching on a watch around his left wrist with a sage green strap. He always wore a silver bracelet, but it was tucked beneath the sleeve of his beige sweater. A silver-gold chain sat polished around his neck, a little heart charm attached to it.

"My mom gave it to me," he'd said when I asked.

"Your earrings are different."

He felt the red heart studs on his ears and nodded. "Just got 'em too."

Everything about this made my heart flutter. In that moment, I realized how much family mattered to Jace. I wanted to ask about everything and learn all the ins and outs of his life.

Seeing how he dressed up to go to dinner with his brother was the cutest thing in the world. It was precious, wholesome, perfect. I felt all the harsh parts of me melting because I'd never gotten the chance to impress a family member – only men. No one else cared to see me. No one else was around.

A wave of envy infiltrated my veins but slowly dissipated when Jace nudged my arm.

"Smile more, Blu. You have a nice smile."

Never in my life did I want to hug someone so bad, to hold them and erase the horrible parts of their past. If he was happy, I was happy. When he laughed, I wanted to be the one who caused it.

But then the voices hit.

No, no, no, Blu. Don't do this again. Don't fall in too deep with someone you barely know.

I wanted to block them out but they kept coming.

He's only saying these things to get a reaction.

He's only complimenting you because he's in a good mood.

You're nothing special, don't ever fucking think you are.

I wanted to scream, to shut my mind off, to burn the thoughts that made me anxious. But I couldn't. I spiralled. I constantly worried. No reassurance in the world could settle my nerves.

I glanced over at Jace, the ocean in his eyes that pulled me to shore, and I wondered, were they yanking me to safety, or leading me to a storm?

An itch formed between my fingers, tingles trailing to my wrist and forearm. This man, smiling beside me, could break my heart any day.

And I'd let him.

That was the problem.

Wherever his eyes would lead me, storm or shore, I'd follow.

Chapter Thirty-Eight
Jace

Year Four/Week Eleven – Present

Scott let me pick the restaurant tonight so I chose Terroni.

"In the mood for Italian tonight, eh Jace?" he asked, choosing a bottle of red for the table. "The Malbec, please."

Our waitress nodded and sauntered away, leaving me alone with my brother. Fuck, that felt weird to say.

"It's been a while since we had dinner together," Scott said, folding his grey cufflinks. I'm glad he dressed up too. It made me feel important.

"Yeah, how's Sab doing?"

"Good, good." He leaned in, whispering as if he wanted no one but me to hear his next words. "Between us, I'm thinking of proposing soon."

My jaw dropped. "Shut the fuck up, no way."

"No way, good? Or no way, bad?"

I was awestruck. "No way, good, are you kidding? Scott that's awesome, I'm happy for you."

My brother relaxed into his chair as the wine arrived. The waitress poured two glasses but I couldn't concentrate on anything except my brother's happiness.

I loved Sab. They'd been together for over four years now and she always treated me and everyone around her like gold. It was a trait I admired and often times, I imagined that's why Scott was always the kindest to me.

Baxter and Will were go-go-go. They'd had a string of relationships and never really settled. With their lifestyles, I doubted they even wanted to. But there was something peaceful about a solid commitment.

Hookups weren't fulfilling, not to me anyways. Giving away a part of myself to someone who knew nothing at all held no place in my mind. I mean, no girl really did. No girl except…

"Any marriage material you been seeing?" Scott asked. "Will told me you were talking to someone, but I forget her name."

I figured. He probably told her she was some art freak and chewed ground up cigarettes. "What do you know about her?"

"Ah, so there is a girl."

"I really don't know how to explain the relationship." And that was the truth.

Blu and I were just friends. If anything, I wanted to save her from the circumstances she refused to tell me about. Did I like her? I really couldn't say. Did I enjoy spending time with her? Yeah, a lot. But feelings were never black and white. They never stuck with me. I was picky and the last girl I wanted didn't choose me. It wouldn't be fair to choose Blu if I wasn't one hundred percent certain.

"Just having fun with her then?"

I sipped my wine, licking the residue off my bottom lip. "We haven't done anything. I really don't know if I see her that way, honestly."

He watched me curiously, elbows on the table, glass stem in hand. It made me feel good, like he wanted me to continue, like he cared about what I had to say.

Truthfully, I was tired of talking about Blu. But if he asked the question, I wanted to answer. We hadn't talked like this in ages.

"I like flirting with her. I know she likes me and she makes me feel good about myself." Releasing those words made me sound like a total jackass, but I could always be honest with my brothers. They were family, after all.

"Hm. Well, you got all the time in the world, Jace. You're young."

There it was.

The comment I was dreading. The insult that every single fucking person in my family hung over my head like a goddamn pacifier.

You're young. You got time.

"We all have time, don't we?" I said through gritted teeth.

"Jace."

His voice was distant. I kept staring at the wine in my glass. I didn't want to look up.

"Jace," he tapped the top of my hand, demanding my attention. "Mom told me a bit about how you were feeling. If there's anything you want to say, just say it."

That was an opportune moment to address my emotions. I mean, I had the chance, he'd given it to me. But instead, I tipped my glass to him and forced away the annoyance.

"Nothing to say. Just happy to be here." My smile was a lie. My response was a lie. But how would my brother react if I failed to control my feelings?

Fitting for a child, he'd say. *Can't stop whining.*

So for the rest of dinner, I lived in the present hearing about my brother's proposal ideas, his work and life plans. Equally, he asked about my direction, the paths I considered taking and the places I wanted to go.

It was a success, you see. I did the right thing. Had I opened up, things would've been awkward. He'd view me as weak, no doubt. But I was strong now. I got to have an earnest conversation with him because I hid what needed to be concealed.

There was no space for insecurity, doubt or blame. I was too mature for that.

I was.

Scott needed to believe that.

Otherwise he'd see right through me.

Chapter Thirty-Nine
Blu

Year Four/Week Twelve – Present

"Do you think Carter will be mad if we don't invite him?" I directed to Fawn, spooning some chicken noodle soup into two bowls.

"No, I think he'd be relieved not having to fifth wheel," she answered, licking brownie batter off a spatula.

Fawn had the bright idea of booking a ski trip to Winter's Lodge after exams were finished, which happened to be Friday. She invited me, Bryce and of course, Jace.

"You said that y'all were getting along. Why wouldn't I invite him?" That was her argument. That's all it took.

It seemed simple. We had opened up to each other a lot over the last week. He seemed more comfortable telling me things which I enjoyed. But even still, I couldn't bring myself to go into detail about my past. After I'd told him about Zac, my traumatizing first relationship, I decided to take a break from spilling all the dark corners of my life. Would he end up holding it against me? Could I even trust him?

He never pressed about my past, which counted for something. It seemed as though there were invisible boundaries set, and he never crossed the line. It was almost like a friendship. *Almost.*

"Did you talk to Jace about it?" Fawn asked.

"No, I assumed Bryce would."

"And he hasn't even brought it up?"

I shook my head, blowing on my soup. "Nope."

"Call him, see if he's coming. I'm going to bring this to my room," she picked up her bowl, "and talk to Bryce."

I laughed as she kicked the door shut behind her, leaving me with an empty kitchen and a disaster of a sink. Fawn loved to cook but hated cleaning up. Probably why she left me alone to do the dishes. Little rat.

Every time the chance to talk to Jace arose, I got butterflies. We were friends. Surely I could call him randomly and it wouldn't be weird. Yet, I caught myself overthinking everything I was saying. Would he judge me for talking too fast? Too slow? Not enough? Too much?

I opened FaceTime and decided to bite the bullet, clicking his name. I'd never Facetimed him before but it wasn't any different, was it? I'd seen him plenty of times in person. There was no way I'd trip up –

He answered laying down with a cut-off tank, a red bandana pushing his hair back and a jaw like fucking stone. I was salivating. I was. I –

Wow.

His dimple was the first to make an appearance as his smile grew. "Hey Blu."

"Am I interrupting your workout?" I could tell I was. His face was red and splotchy, a barbell was tucked in the corner of the screen and his shoulder muscles were practically popping out of frame.

"No, no," he lifted himself off the ground, adjusting his bandana. "You're good. What's up?"

It should be illegal to look like that. Why the fuck was I saying that in my head? I started off the relationship bold; I didn't need to hide that.

"You're flustering me, Jace, I may need to look away." I grabbed a sponge and turned on the tap, propping my phone up against the paper towel holder.

He laughed with his whole face, the laugh I loved to see. "Been a while since I flustered you."

Oh, if you only knew.

I rinsed out the pot as I spoke. "I was just wondering if you were coming to the lodge this weekend?"

"Oh, right, Bryce mentioned that." He scratched the sharp edges of his jaw. "Are you going?"

"Yeah," I nodded. "It would be nice to not third wheel."

He chuckled. "Fawn and Bryce seem to be having fun together."

"And my fear is that they'll have too much fun without me, and I'll be forced to ride the ski lift alone."

"So that's all I am to you? A riding buddy?"

I rolled my eyes, separating the washed and unwashed dishes. "Obviously. What other use do I have for your existence?"

As soon as I released the words, I knew I'd set him up for something. And what he said definitely didn't fall short from what crossed my mind.

"I can think of other ways I may be useful."

"Cut it out," I teased. What I really meant was *keep going.*

"Ha-ha, I'll be there. You aren't going to class this week, right?"

"No, I don't think there's a need, I –"

Fawn's laugh shifted my attention to her closed bedroom door. Only during these past couple weeks did I hear her laugh like that. It made me happy. Maybe her and Bryce were the start of something good.

"Sorry, Fawn's talking to Bryce."

He scrunched his eyebrows. "I can't imagine what's so funny. Bryce has an atrocious sense of humour."

Now we both laughed in unison, and my nerves eased aside.

"But yeah, I'm skipping class this week. I have to catch up on work before exams so I can just relax at the lodge."

"I'll do the same," he agreed. "No point in going if you aren't there."

I stopped cleaning, staring at the sink, unable to meet his gaze. My smile was out in the open, I didn't try and hide that. But still, looking at him, in this moment, felt too intimate.

"Who do you go to class for?" I repeated the question he'd asked me once before, my eyes softening as he responded, "You."

"I got to go, Blu, but I'm glad I could fluster you two times tonight."

He ended the call abruptly and my phone lit up with a notification a few seconds later.

9:02pm – Jace Boland: Imagine the things I could do in person.

If my hands weren't gripping the counter, I would've fallen to my knees. He'd never said anything so bold before, so *Blu*. It took me a second to register what he was referring to, but when it did, I died.

It's insane where the dynamic of a new relationship could take you. When I met Jace, I had no idea that he'd end up living rent free in my head. Had I known, maybe I would've avoided the connection entirely.

But looking back at the past three months, seeing how quickly time sped by with him around, it didn't matter if our pain and comfort held hands.

As long as they were interconnected.

Chapter Forty
Jace

Year Four/Week Thirteen – Present

"You pack like a chick," I griped, shoving the rest of my shit into a duffle bag.

Bryce had crashed at my place since we were carpooling to Winter's Lodge together. He had an irrational fear of forgetting something everywhere we went, so triple checking his belongings became a regular thing.

"I bought Fawn an early birthday present," his fingers combed through sweaters and pants, "Just making sure I have it."

"When's her birthday?"

"Two weeks, the twelfth of December."

My eyes narrowed. "Why the hell did you buy her something now? You don't think you're going to be together by then?"

He stopped rummaging, darting a shifty gaze my way. "You can be a real ass sometimes, man."

"It was an honest question." It was. Truly.

After Riley, I learned my lesson that doing the most for someone would never be enough. I'd bought her flowers every date, her favourite candy when I went to the store – Everything, *everything* I did, I thought of her.

And still, I never satisfied an inch of what she wanted.

I never satisfied her.

You could be the greatest person, perform the grandest gestures, but if that someone never valued the love you showed them in the first place, they never would.

"I just don't want you to get hurt, you know, if things don't work out."

Bryce let out a laugh, and I knew exactly why he was laughing. Of all the people to give relationship advice, I was the worst. I never knew what I wanted, never even began to understand how I felt about anyone, and here I was, preaching to the most solid friend I'd ever had about what he bought a girl.

"I know Fawn and I haven't been talking long, but she makes me really happy." He took a pause, folding a grey shirt back into place. "I wanted to do something nice, that's all."

I swallowed hard, nodding in respect. "I'm glad everything's going well, really."

He deserved it. Some people just did.

"It still baffles me how Blu is her best friend, though. I mean, what are the odds." He tossed me a protein bar, but I set it aside.

"Crazy coincidence," was all I had to say. Because it was. Everything about Blu and I was.

There were multiple times throughout the past week where I tried to deny a connection, anything with Blu in general. But the more I fought it, the more I wanted her.

Connections didn't just happen. I'd met a string of girls that were beautiful, more aesthetic than Blu, prettier than fucking Riley, and they were just… Boring. Sad to say, but a gorgeous face only got you so far. I learned that the hard way.

That's what pissed me off about the situation. I didn't want to feel anything, I didn't expect to. Flirting with her came naturally, like the words slipped off my tongue before I could register what I was saying.

I texted her something risky after our Facetime call. She responded by hearting my message, and we hadn't talked since.

It bothered me. It bothered me so fucking much.

She wanted the last word in every text conversation, I'd noticed. Probably because over the phone she could regulate what was being said, not blurt things out. I was calculated face-to-face. She was calculated over the phone.

"What are you thinking about?" Bryce asked.

Nonsense. Sheer fucking nonsense.

"Nothing."

His cell rang and it had to have been Fawn. Her voice, one that I'd become familiar with over the last few weeks, spoke sweetly.

I tried to tune out their calls, but sometimes it was hard. After I figured out that her and Blu were friends, a part of me always listened in to see if she was there, if she'd said something about me.

"We'll pick you up in fifteen," he promised. "See you soon," and hung up the call.

"What? No 'I love you, baby'?" I joked, grabbing the Honda keys from my desk.

Mom came in clutch by letting me use the car for the weekend. Maybe she really did feel bad for me. Perks of opening up, I suppose.

"Unlike you, I don't abuse terms of endearments to rile up women." He zipped up his bag and kicked my ankle. "*Darling*."

I shrugged, scooping up my duffel and scanned my room for anything I could've missed.

"There was a time where you were jealous of me, you know."

He exhaled. "Jealousy and admiration are two different things, man. I always wanted the best for you."

Jealousy and admiration.

Two different things.

Somehow, that never clicked to me, never registered.

Did I admire Morris? Danny? Max?

Or was I always pining for what they had, envious of the things they possessed when I didn't possess them?

Did that make me a better man, that I became what they were? Or a worse one?

Jealousy and admiration.

Huh.

Something to think about.

Chapter Forty-One
Blu

Year Four/Week Thirteen – Present

I'd never seen Jace drive before.

What a sight.

Maybe I was the type to romanticize every little thing, but Jace, wearing his black ballcap and a dark thermal, his long, slender fingers wrapped around the wheel... I just about melted.

Winter's Lodge was roughly an hour drive away, far enough that conversation was a necessity, but close enough that it could be superficial.

I wanted none of those things.

I wanted Jace to prove what he said in that message.

Imagine the things I could do in person, he'd typed.

One thing I hated about men was how they were all bark and no bite. The ballsiest promises could be made over text, but face-to-face, no moves were made.

If Jace was like that...

His fingers scratched my knee, slow and calculated, before he removed his hand. "Warm enough?"

I blushed, staring at his angular side profile.

Jace was definitely not all talk.

Pushing my legs closer together, I shook my head. "I could be warmer."

He picked up my insinuation almost immediately and shot me a lazy smile, cranking up the heat setting to three.

"Is this your car, Jace?" Fawn asked from the backseat.

"No darling, it's his mom's," Bryce answered for him.

"Darling?" Jace laughed, taking a left turn. "Stealing my lines now?"

Darling.

The way Jace said it felt like smooth velvet. Only he could make a word sound so alluring, so sultry.

Maybe that's how Fawn saw it with Bryce. After all, when you liked someone, everything they did became attractive. Nothing could put you off, nothing could shift the pedestal you placed them on.

That was the problem.

That was always *my* problem.

I took a sip of my water just as Fawn released, "You know Jace, you and Blu would look good together."

My face burned with fire. He chuckled, his gaze fixed on me for a moment before turning to the road. I didn't want to look at him. Instead, I stared at Fawn in the rear-view mirror, glaring with daggers.

"Oh yeah?" Was Jace's response. Diplomatic, per usual.

"What do you think, Blu?" His hand was on my knee again, squeezing once before retracting. "Do you think we'd look good together?"

Stop it, I wanted to say. *Don't start something if you have no intention of finishing it.*

"Dye your hair blue and then we'll talk." My joke was the only thing that could straighten out my senses. I didn't know where we stood.

"You want to match?" he asked.

"Why not? We could be like The Smurfs."

"I don't think I'd look good with blue hair, darling."

You'd look good with anything. "No, you really wouldn't."

It was shameful, how good I was at lying to him; how much I could conceal to save desperation. Every part of me wanted to beg for a sliver of emotion, to acquire a secure answer that would never make me question. But I had no right to look at things this introspectively.

Jace wasn't mine.

And if he wanted to be, he would be.

"Can I connect my music?" I asked, removing my phone from my pocket.

"Yeah," he nudged his head forward, "Just turn off my Bluetooth."

Clicking open his lock screen, I caught a glimpse of an unanswered text. A girl. Tara.

I wasn't going to say anything, shutting off his Bluetooth and connecting mine, but the curiosity was baiting me. I opened my mouth.

"Someone messaged you." My voice was nonchalant, but my thoughts were buzzing with insecurity.

He reached for his phone and clicked it open, reading the name with a straight face before placing it back in the cupholder.

"Just a girl from school. I'll answer later."

My nails bit into the creases of my palm. "Which girl?"

"Uh, she's got long brown hair. The one who sits near the front in Flowers' class."

Girl-next-door.

A Hue of Blu   Marie-France Leger

Girl-next-door.

My mind raced like a fucking stallion. My jealousy tipping between sanity and insanity. Why would she be texting him? Why would *he* be texting *her*? I'd never even seen them talk, not once. Not fucking once. When did this happen?

The rest of the way, I didn't say anything. I didn't trust myself to be centered, calm. My alternative music played as Bryce and Jace talked about the World Cup and whatever the hell else boys talked about. Fawn saw my anger through the mirror. She texted me not too long after that.

    12:11pm – Fawny: You okay babe?

    12:12pm – Blu: Remember the girl who kept looking at Jace in class? The girl-next-door I was telling you about?

    12:12pm – Fawny: Oh no. She was the one who texted him?

    12:13pm – Blu: Yep.

    12:14pm – Fawny: Ugh that's so annoying. Did you see the message?

    12: 14pm – Blu: Nope. I'm so annoyed right now Fawn.

"Fast texter," Jace poked my knee. This time, I moved away. He probably realized. I didn't care.

"Something going on?"

"Just talking to my mom," I lied.

I hadn't told Jace anything pertaining to my family so it was a solid excuse. Mom probably didn't even have my number saved. He didn't need to know that.

At this point, did I even want him to discover those parts of me? If I was so insignificant, why should I care to prove my position in his life? Why should he get the opportunity to know me?

After another half an hour of gruelling silence, we arrived at Winter's Lodge. Garland lights hung around the neatly trimmed hedges and cascaded down the rooftops like loose ribbon.

"Beautiful, right?" Fawn beamed, making her way to my side as the boys retrieved the bags from the trunk.

"It is," Jace added. "Thanks for inviting us."

She waved him off and linked her arm with mine, pushing me towards the entrance. "We're going to the bar tonight," she winked.

I knew her reasoning behind telling me that. I knew what she wanted me to do.

"There are so many cute guys at the lodge, Blu. If Jace is texting other girls, flirt with other guys. It's fair game."

But that's the thing – I didn't want to play games. For once, I just wanted something normal, something easy. At twenty-three, it didn't seem appropriate anymore. But that little voice kept coming back. The voice that told me I was nothing but an option of convenience to Jace.

After seeing Tara's message on his phone, all I wanted to do was infuriate him. I needed to know he cared.

I needed to know I was desirable.

"Did you bring any dresses for me?"

She grinned, nodding fast. "Blu Henderson, only the best for you."

I glanced back to find Jace on his phone, probably responding to girl-next-door.

The fury returned. The cord snapped.

If this was how it had to be, then *game on*.

Chapter Forty-Two
Jace

Year Four/Week Thirteen – Present

After the girls unpacked, they spent the rest of the day out while Bryce and I hiked a trail.

Fawn's cabin was modern and sleek, with cherrywood flooring and high glass windows. A small kitchen was stationed in the corner with a forest green theme to match the living room.

When it came to the sleeping situation, I found out there were two bedrooms. One for Fawn and Bryce, I could only assume, and the other for Blu and me.

"You're really pushing this couple thing," I told him, laying my slacks and dress shirt out on the bed. My bed. With Blu.

"What? You want to sleep with me?" he poked, collapsing on the loveseat next to the window.

"Fuck no. I just don't want to make her feel uncomfortable."

"You can take the living room couch."

I contemplated it the second I found out about the number of bedrooms, but I was a selfish man. Even if I slept on the goddamn floor, I'd want to be in Blu's vicinity.

"No."

"I'm sure she'll be fine," Bryce reassured, painting a smiley face on the frosted glass window. "She's into you."

That much, I could gather. I wasn't an idiot. The reason why she went into quiet mode was because she saw Tara's text. Personally, I thought I did a good job of acting like it was nothing.

Because it was nothing.

She'd sat next to me the week Blu had skipped class and asked for my number to compare notes if need be. Her message had been a question about the final essay, nothing else.

But Blu didn't strike me as the type to forget something like that. I wished she would, but it wasn't my responsibility to change her brain chemistry.

"Where do you stand with her?" Bryce's voice was laced with curiosity, like always.

I shrugged. "She's a great girl. I like spending time with her, but I don't know."

That was the truth.

I never knew.

"I think I want her to like me more than I like her," my admission froze me in place but the words flowed out. "It's flattering."

Bryce stopped drawing on the frosted glass and turned to look at me. "You like Blu because she flatters you? Come on, man. Do you hear yourself?"

Loud and clear, and that's why I shut the fuck up most of the time.

Our hike was mostly in silence. I knew Bryce was disappointed in what I had to say, but I'd never been known to be a liar. Other people were. Who I became, what I became, was years in the making.

Years of disappointment.

Years of shame.

Years of never feeling good enough.

If Bryce didn't understand why flattery was so important to me, then I wasn't about to draw it in sand.

It was only at the canteen that Bryce spoke up again, saying, "You should tell her you aren't interested."

Sheer annoyance bubbled inside of me as I ordered a frozen yogurt, never ice cream – dairy made me break out and the sugar was poison.

"Why do you care so much? You guys aren't even friends."

"No," he practically spat. "But I'm friends with you. And I care about who my friends are and their fucking morals."

"You're questioning my morals? Because I don't know if I like a girl? What is this, some favour you feel like you owe Fawn to get laid?"

As soon as it came out of my mouth, I bit my tongue. It was too late though, because Bryce stomped off, tossing the fresh cookie dough cup he bought in the trash.

I'd been in enough fights with him to know he needed time alone. I'd been in enough fights to know that I was always the one who caused it.

He was so levelled, so calm. It bothered me. I wanted a reaction. I wanted him to say something, anything to prove that I wasn't insane for feeling the way I always did.

Useless. Tethered to a burning desire of proving I was worth it.

And seeing Bryce walk towards the cabin alone, hands in his pockets with his head hung low, I realized I wasn't worth it.

Not even a little bit.

Chapter Forty-Three
Jace

Year Four/Week Thirteen — Present

Bryce and I met at the bar around 8:30.

We needed to talk; I needed to apologize.

He'd actually gone through another trail before he came home, and I sat like a desperate ex waiting for him in his room.

He hadn't showed.

And when he did, he hit the shower and I got the message loud and clear.

Space Jace, he practically screamed. *I still need space.*

I threw on a black button down, cuffed the sleeves and stepped into my dress pants. The cross earring I always wore was secure in one ear, a pearl in the other, before I started my walk to the restaurant.

The lobby was massive, so I explored some amenities for the first hour. But the guilt weighed on me too much, and only one thing could fix it.

Alone, I sat at the bar for a couple hours, contemplating the string of words I'd use before Bryce showed up and pulled out the seat next to me.

"Where are the girls?" I asked. I didn't bother texting Blu at all while she was out for the day. I felt like a dick as it was.

"They just got back an hour ago. They'll probably be here soon."

His voice was clipped, but not hostile. I hailed down the bartender and ordered two rum and cokes.

"Sorry about earlier." That was it. My grandiose apology. When would my pride settle? When would I mean the words that left my lips?

He didn't look at me, his jaw tight as he said, "You're not, but thanks anyways."

"Look man, I am. I feel like shit. I didn't mean –"

"You feel like shit because I feel like shit, Jace. Nothing affects you unless it affects how other people see you."

Before I could react, he flicked up his wrist to check his watch. "Let's get a table. The girls will want to actually make conversation, not side-eye us at the bar while we drink."

And he was up, flagging a waitress to seat us next to the window. They were floor to ceiling with a gorgeous view of snow covered mountains and ski-lifts.

I couldn't appreciate any of it.

I didn't deserve to.

But I sat down all the same and admired the view. Because somehow, life was as cynical as I was. Life rewarded bad behaviour.

Maybe that's why I became who I became.

Because nice people never got very far.

And once upon a time, I was too nice, and life never rewarded me.

It spat in my face.

***

She walked in wearing a chrome dress with bright blue heels, not quite the colour of her hair – more vibrant.

I barely noticed Fawn, but I didn't blame myself. Next to Blu, everyone would blur into nothing.

They didn't come to the table right away; something else caught their attention. *Someone* else.

My eyes trailed the girls as they walked towards two men dressed in tailored suits with gelled hair.

I looked to Bryce who shared an equally annoyed sentiment, jaw tight with sharp eyes. He said nothing.

These guys were older than me, older than Bryce. One of them had a line of scruff while the other had a full beard. I was cleanly shaven. It suited me better. But did Blu prefer that? I could only wonder.

She started laughing, her smile bright as she placed a soft hand on his shoulder – the guy dressed in dark grey. Fawn kept to herself. That was the better choice.

The double rum and coke sat coolly in my hands, but I melted the glass with my palm, at least that's what it felt like.

"Do they know them?" I demanded, feeling the buzz take over whatever rational side of me was left.

I didn't care if Bryce was still mad from earlier. My thoughts were self-invested. Luckily, he didn't seem to be, noticing the advances that were being made upon his woman.

Upon *my* woman.

That feeling didn't scare me. A part of me wanted to claim her as my own. A part of me wanted to give it a rest and let her find shelter in a man more suitable for her.

But not tonight.

Tonight, she was with me.

I calmly pushed my chair back, taking one last sip of liquor before making my way towards the bar. Bryce made no objections as he followed behind me. He was right to.

On my arrival, I caught glimpse of Blu's arms, for once, uncovered. Various tattoos lined her pale skin, stamping in mismatched patterns, painting her like a canvas.

The dress she wore glittered beneath the dimmed restaurant lights, a contrast between the blue waves cascading down her face.

She looked like a shooting star.

She looked gorgeous.

She looked mine.

"I hope I'm not interrupting," I drawled, sliding a hand around Blu's waist.

It was the first time I'd touched her since Halloween, held her close to me just to feel her affection. A part of me was worried she'd slip out my grasp, but the biggest part of me knew she wouldn't.

She liked being in my arms. Almost as much as I enjoyed holding her there.

The next room attached to Winter's bar had a clubbier vibe, and as the moonlight poured in past the mountain tops, more and more people made their way to the disco-lit floor.

"Dance with me," I whispered in her ear, keeping my hand firm on her skin.

"This is Derek," she said, looking me dead in the face. "Fawn and I met him at the gift shop earlier."

I barely turned my head to meet him, my eyes still fixated on her rosy cheeks and plump lips.

"Derek," was all I responded in acknowledgment.

Fawn and Bryce had already backed away, retreating to our table. Blu remained, stubborn and unmoving.

"Have anything to drink tonight?" the suit-fuck asked.

My buzz intensified. "Plenty," I eyed my blue-haired raven, "And plenty more."

"What are you staring at?" she practically barked.

A smile spread across my face. "Something that belongs to me."

Her cheeks heated and I wasted no time to repeat, "Dance with me."

"And what if I say no?"

This.

This is what I loved about her.

The push and pull. She took it and gave it.

Fire.

That fucking fire.

I took her hand, lacing our fingers together and led her away from the threat. "It's never good to tell lies, darling."

One head nod was all it took for Bryce to understand where I was taking her, what I wanted to do. He was mad, sure, but he wouldn't stay mad. As well, he was smart enough to realize I was a grown man and could make mistakes and screw ups, but I'd never hurt Blu. Not intentionally.

The dance floor was packed with sweaty bodies and melding people, twirling one another with blissful glee. My buzz never heightened to a point where I couldn't control myself and I was glad. That way, I could enjoy the company I possessed with a clear head.

I could savour Blu's body as I grasped it tightly, pulling her towards my chest and felt her bare arms in my palms.

"How do I look?" she fished, allowing herself to sway against me.

"Too good," was my response, staring at her lips.

She kept some space between us as she threw an arm over my shoulder. "I haven't even had a drink yet."

"Do you want one?"

"Obviously," she laughed, "We're at a bar."

I led her back to the table, making a conscious effort to avoid the two meatheads nesting at the stools. If they were watching her, I didn't care. She was watching me. That's all that mattered.

"Short lived dance, I'd say," Bryce joked. I met his eyes and he gave me a look that said, *"We're okay."*

I pulled out Blu's chair for her and slid the remainder of my drink to her position. "It was too crowded. Couldn't see what I wanted to see."

For a split second, her and I were the only two people in the room. For a split second, everything was right and uncomplicated. But only for a split second, because nothing good lasted forever. I knew that.

"What is this?" she asked.

"Try it and find out."

Her eyes narrowed. "Sketchy, Jace. Sketchy."

"If you want to talk sketchy, your Derek might have the conversation you're looking for." Jealousy wasn't my strong suit. But it was a better suit than the one Derek wore.

She rolled her brown eyes. "Not *my* Derek."

"A shame." I grabbed Bryce's drink and downed it in one gulp, signaling the bar for another round.

"I wasn't thirsty anyway," he glared at me.

"Good, alcohol is horrible for your body. Make better choices."

He couldn't help the smile, couldn't hold back the fact he loved me. Bryce was a day one. He'd never stay upset.

When I glanced at Blu, the corner of her lips was tugged up behind the rim of the glass. I lowered it for her.

"Don't hide your smile, darling."

That familiar scarlet hue rose to her cheeks. "You're chipper tonight."

And as the evening progressed, I realized I had been. Getting to know Fawn was rather pleasant, since she was dating my best friend, it was essential that I liked her. Blu, well, her presence was promising enough. She didn't say much, but she laughed a lot.

Her laugh was the only discourse I needed.

The jealousy faded into peaceful oblivion – my world orbited around the three people sitting at this table. In this moment, they were what mattered.

After a few more drinks, I called it quits and helped Blu to her feet.

"Come with me," I insisted, taking her delicate hand in mine.

"I don't feel like dancing," she groaned, but kept my pace regardless. "Where are we going?"

The thought hit me the second she walked in the room, dressed like starlight, reflecting like the moon.

"There's a view as beautiful as Blu that I'd like to take you to," the sweet words slipped off my tongue easily. *Too* easily.

She let out a playful giggle. "Okay Dr. Seuss, lead the way."

And as we walked past the imperial staircase and carpeted floors, my tipsy mind began listing words that rhymed with Blu.

True.
Clue.
Flew.
Hue.

Chapter Forty-Four
Blu

Year Four/Week Thirteen — Present

Jace led me to a rooftop terrace, encased by a glass dome.

There was a clear view of the mountains, the onyx sky painted with stars. The dome must have been heated because I didn't shiver, or maybe it was the alcohol. But as Jace approached the railing I now stood behind, his body hovering inches from my back, I realized it was his proximity keeping me warm.

"How'd you find this place?" I shifted aside, making room for him to stand next to me.

He leaned over the metal bar, staring out into the open plain of dusted snow and evergreen trees.

"I had some time to kill earlier, so I took a map from the front desk and found myself here."

"You and Bryce, you mean?"

His face hardened. "No, just me."

"But, weren't you two together today? On the trails?"

His throat bobbed, his jaw clenching. "We got into a bit of a fight."

I didn't want to pry, but... Oh, who was I kidding? *I really, really wanted to pry.*

As if he could see the intrigue on my face, he turned to me with accepting eyes. "You can ask, it's fine."

"Only if you want to talk about it."

Luckily, he did, because he cleared his throat and shifted closer. The smell of his cologne wafted from his clothes; citrus and woodsy.

"It was actually about you," he began, and this piqued my interest tenfold. "He asked how I felt about you and I said I didn't know."

Like a knife wound to the heart, my excitement vanished as quickly as it came. I didn't speak. He had more to say. Mind you, I didn't know that I wanted to hear it.

Those blue-green eyes sparkled like snow, turning to me with care. "I don't want you to be hurt, Blu. I don't want you to make assumptions on how I think, and I definitely don't want you to overthink my feelings."

Frustration boiled my blood. "You don't want me to make assumptions about how you feel, but you're doing that to me right now."

"What do you mean?"

"You think I like you."

"Don't you?"

"Oh my God," I shook my head, pulling back my bottom lip. "Even if I did, I don't read into how you feel about me." It was a lie, but he didn't need to know that. "I know there's nothing between us."

With this, he took a step forward, squaring his shoulders. "Now that, I didn't say."

I swallowed hard, trying my best to meet his stare. I wasn't backing down. I couldn't let him see how much it pained me.

"You said you didn't know how you felt about me," my nails dug into my palms, "So how could there possibly be something between us?"

"Because you confuse me enough that I question having feelings in the first place." He took another step forward, forcing the curve of my back to hug the rail. "You confuse me enough that I think about you throughout the day, wonder where you are and who you're talking to."

My heart hammered in my chest as he placed both arms on either side of my body, leaning down to hear me breathe. His eyes roamed my face, searching for a reaction, willing me to cave.

"You confuse me enough," his eyelids softened as he licked his lips, "That I've thought about kissing you more times tonight than I care to admit."

With tentative movements, I slid a shaky palm up his chest, feeling his muscles tense beneath the cotton material of his shirt.

"Admit it," I whispered, though it came out more like a plea.

He was so close to me now, too close, and I welcomed his scent and heat. There was a point where I thought Jace was too tall to accommodate my shorter height, but in this moment...

We were perfect. We fit.

"If I admit it, what then?" He never moved from his stance. I stood frozen in mine.

"Say it and find out," I challenged.

His jaw tightened as he looked from my eyes, to my nose, and settled his gaze on my lips – a cherry red, I wore, just for him to notice.

"I want to kiss you, Blu," he confessed, his tone laced with need. "I have to kiss you."

Any remark I could have made died in my throat as I tugged the back of his collar and pressed my lips to his.

His arms enveloped me like angel wings, sealing my body between his and the railing. A sinful shudder swam through my body as he planted gentle kisses across my jaw, down my neck and behind my ear.

"*Blu*," he released, gripping the bottom of my dress, balling his fist into my hair.

The way he said my name sounded desperate, a plea for me to sweep my tongue into his mouth and feel the hardened length of him against my stomach.

His lips claimed mine, solidifying what I knew to be true –

We longed for each other. Denying that was useless.

In that moment, we felt unified, entangled in a web of passion. All the anger and pain I felt, the pining and the chasing I'd done, it blurred into nothing but a distant memory.

He chose me.
He kissed me.
He desired me.
That's all that mattered.

He pulled back slowly, nipping my bottom lip once before brushing strands of frenzied hair from my face.

"I think this should be our make-out spot for the weekend," he chuckled, guiding me off the ledge and onto the cold cement.

Instantly, I regretted not getting one more kiss in. I regretted not holding on a little longer. I regretted so many things, because what if that was the last time I got to kiss him? What if this was just an intoxicating setting in our inebriation?

What if –

His fingers found mine as a group of people strode through the rooftop doors, chatting and yelling amongst one another.

We walked down the staircase in silence, hand-in-hand, a smile stamped on our lips. There were no need for words, just touches and glances that held all our emotions in one.

Before entering our cabin, Jace drew me in for another tight embrace, one that calmed the rushing anxiety of losing our shared moment forever.

"You kissed me," I breathed, as if saying the word would demand a promise for one more.

He smiled, his thumb brushing against my cheek and pressed his lips to mine, hearing the silent promise I'd hoped for.

"And you taste even better than I imagined."

Chapter Forty-Five
Blu

Year Four/Week Thirteen – Present

Fawn had texted me saying she and Bryce were enjoying their time alone, and that I should as well.

I responded with the devil emoji and shut my phone off for the night. After all, the only person I wanted to speak to was standing in the confines of these four bedroom walls.

The sleeping situation may have bothered me earlier; everything had. After Fawn and I unpacked, we hit the nearest town to get our hair and nails done. As it turned out, the salon also had a makeup studio attached to it, so we took the leisure of beautifying every part of ourselves.

"Jace is going to combust when he sees you," she'd said to me, perched like a baby bird in the stylists' rolling chair.

That was the goal. Tara's text pissed me off, and we had a plan to grind his gears. It just so happened that the universe rewarded me because while Fawn and I browsed the gift shop, a handsome stranger [Derek] approached with wondering eyes.

We invited him to the bar, told him to bring a friend because we, too, were meeting our own. I made a promise that I'd spend time with them, but I'd broken so many before that one insignificant one meant very little to me.

I knew Jace would see me speaking with him. But what I wasn't prepared for was the sheer jealousy he'd depicted.

He cared about me.

His annoyance solidified that.

The thought of Tara hitting up Jace's line dissipated. Especially after that kiss – the kiss of dreams, that I'd seen only in my sleep, experienced only in my head.

The light was dim in the room as I stared at Jace undoing the cuffs from his dress shirt.

"I'll take the floor," he said, running a hand through his hair.

The hands that had just been in mine moments ago.

Disappointment drowned me. "You want to sleep on the floor?"

Even through the lack of light, I could see his bluish eyes twinkle. "The bed is my second choice Blu, but your comfort is my first."

I…

I opened my mouth to say something, anything, but no words came out.

The flashbacks of Kyle came through, touching me against my will when he'd had too much to drink, Zac pounding his fist near my face when he got upset. Tyler, my oh-so-lousy hookup Tyler, who critiqued my appearance and fucked me in the dark.

None of those men, those *boys,* were Jace.

Where my confidence came from, I had no idea. I'd been a lying, deceitful girl for far too long, basking in arrogance and masks to prevent vulnerability.

I swallowed hard, staring at Jace with intent as I pushed my dress strap off my shoulder, followed by the other until it was a pool of fabric around my feet.

Never in my life had I felt comfortable standing naked in front of someone, not my boyfriends of years or hookups of months. But the way Jace looked at me, nude and bare and willing, I would've bottled his gaze and kept it forever.

He didn't move, not for a few seconds which sent my brain into a spiralling whirlpool.

Had I gone too far?

Could he see my stretch marks?

Is he not turned on?

Oh my fucking God, what a fool. *I'm a fucking fool.*

My cheeks heated as I took a step back, covering my breasts with an arm but then he said one word – one word that halted my movements immediately.

"Don't."

The clap of his footsteps creaked atop the flooring as he made his way over, my eyes still glued to the ground, my chest covered by my arm.

I spied the points of his oxfords slide beneath my silver dress as he cupped my chin, demanding attention.

His gaze made my spine shiver and my insides dance. Carefully, he peeled back my arm and massaged my wrist, leaving me exposed for him to see.

Though his eyes didn't drop down once as he flipped over my forearms, holding them out for me to inspect.

"What do these mean?" he asked, choosing his words carefully.

He knew. He knew there were scars beneath the black ink. That's why he questioned. He knew.

"Tell me." His voice was kind, trusting. I would have spilled twenty-three years' worth of secrets to him right then and there.

"My dad died when I was thirteen," I began, feeling the tears burn with no emotion attached.

It was me who I mourned for. My sadness.

"He was an alcoholic and my mom… Um, she's one too. I don't talk to her much," my throat suddenly felt sore, but I powered through.

It felt good telling someone who knew nothing. Like a release. A release from my permanent pain.

"I used to…" *Fuck*. "I used to think there was no cure for losing a parent, one you thought you knew. I wanted to feel something, so I –"

He kissed my cheek, right where a tear had fallen, pulling me closer. "You don't need to say it."

Only then did I realize how shattered I'd become, when salty liquid hit my lips and I whispered, "They're underneath my tattoos. The memories of wanting to feel something other than sorrow."

My mouth was taken by his, and in one swift movement, I was sitting on his lap as he settled on the soft duvet.

My body trembled. My mind ached. My flesh, the skin I wore, was covered in markings that represented me.

A broken shell.

A damaged past.

Unlovable, reckless, Beatrice Louise Henderson.

My anxiety, my panic and pain, they became one and taunted me with shame. The sobs never stopped, the storm-cloud of emotions never settled, and I remained, a lifeless corpse in the arms of Jace Boland.

Minutes passed, maybe hours. I felt lighter, freer; maybe I'd lost weight while crying. One could only hope.

But Jace's features were rock solid. He hadn't let go of his grip, his eyes stalking my every flinch, my every breath, my every exhale.

As reality set in, I grew painfully aware of the fact I was naked aside from my underwear, cocooned in his grasp while he said nothing.

"I'm sorry," I murmured into his shoulder. "I'm sorry I unloaded that on you. I'm so sorry."

"Blu…" I could feel tension, the hesitation, as he yanked the throw from the edge of the bed and wrapped it around my body.

"Sleep," he released, carefully lying me down on my back and tucking me between warm sheets. "I'll be on the couch if you need me."

What…

What –

What!

"Jace, Jace… No, no – I, I'm sorry, I didn't mean to –" My breaths were ragged, bleeding like an open wound. "Jace, please don't leave."

"I'm not leaving you, Blu," he kissed my forehead, but it felt forced. "I just think you need space."

"Space?" My bones hurt, my brain screamed. "I just opened up to you and you think I need space? Right now? In my fucking state?"

He moved towards the door just as Fawn broke in. "What's happening? Blu?" She moved towards me in an instant as Bryce filled the doorway.

Her soft palms caressed my face, forcing my head to meet her. "Blu, sleep in my room tonight."

Space.
Space.
Space.
That's all anyone ever gave me.
That's all anyone knew how to give.
An excuse to leave, an excuse to run.
No one stayed.
No one cared.

Any ounce of love within me died, but it was justified. How could anyone love a fractured soul? A sad girl who couldn't control the carnage of emotions that lived within her?

"Jace, let's go." Bryce's words were distant. I didn't dare look away from Fawn's kind eyes. They were the only thing keeping me afloat.

I heard two sets of footsteps exit the room and the door locked.

It was then that I collapsed into Fawn's arms.

It was then that I allowed her to soothe my aching heart.

It was then that I realized the comfort I thought I'd felt with Jace was an illusion; a trick of my mind attaching itself to the potential of someone, rather than who they were.

Carter was right.

Fawn was right.

I knew nothing about Jace Boland, other than the truth I knew about everyone else.

They'd always leave.

Chapter Forty-Six
Jace

Year Four/Week Seventeen — Present

I hadn't heard from Blu since Winter's Lodge.

After Bryce talked to Fawn, she said it would be in my best interest to leave the following morning. Her and Blu got a ride back somehow. I didn't know how. I couldn't ask.

She was safe, Bryce told me. She was doing better since that night. That's all that mattered.

Christmas came and went, the first snowfall and the tiresome nights.

Nothing could shake me from the guilt, the utter torment I'd felt day-in, day-out since Blu opened up to me.

There were scars beneath those tattoos that I could've asked about, could've cared for.

There were questions I wanted to know about her father, about her mother, about her childhood.

There were things I should've done.

Things I didn't do.

Baxter bought me a camera, hoping I'd leap on to his photography business and rethink modelling.

I didn't touch it.

Will bought me a new cologne, Dior Sauvage, and instructed me to wear it on dates.

I never went on one.

And Scott, he asked me to stay the weekend at his place while Sab was visiting her parents in Florida. He was the only brother who saw that I needed someone.

That was the only Christmas gift I appreciated.

We were on his couch watching some stupid horror movie when he asked, "School start back up next week?"

I simply nodded, staring at the mediocre gore FX.

"Excited to be done? It's your last semester of university ever."

Yeah.

And then what?

What would I do with my life?

Who would I amount to?

I'd hurt enough people, been wrecked and scrambled. I wasn't good enough for the only dream I'd ever chased, I wasn't good enough to be sought after and I couldn't even help my damn friend – Couldn't even text her because I'd been a fucking coward and a self-invested prick.

I only lost.

With all the trouble I'd put myself through…

I only lost.

"Jace?" Scott's voice was concerned. I didn't deserve it.

"Sorry," was all I could muster up.

Sorry.

The words that rang through my head on a constant loop.

Blu was sorry that she opened up to me, sorry that she burdened me, when all I could see when I looked into those brown eyes was a girl who wanted to be loved.

I couldn't love her.

I didn't know how to love myself.

"She's better off," I said aloud. I needed to. Even if Scott had no idea what the fuck I was talking about.

But he did, and more surprising he asked, "What happened at Winter's Lodge?"

My walls were down; I felt no need to lie to him. "I asked her to open up and had no idea how to handle it when she did."

Scott didn't know the *her* I was referring to, didn't know her name, knew nothing. But even still, he tried and said, "Do you want to talk about it?"

I did.

I really fucking did.

And so I spent the next thirty minutes detailing the events that transpired that night, minus a few intimate details that required no spotlight.

He stared at me for a long while, as if assessing me. Then finally, he let out, "You care about her but you don't know how to."

I nodded, swallowing the defeat. "I thought I had everything under control. I thought," *Goddamn fucking idiot,* "I thought that if I held her or kissed her she'd be okay. And she just broke even more and I didn't want her to latch on to me when I knew I couldn't –"

I stopped to take a breath, burying my face in my palms. "When I couldn't be what she needed."

Maybe what she wanted.

Not what she deserved.

"Jace, if you're this confused, take yourself out of the equation. Quit going back, hurting this poor girl and fucking up again."

"You're saying I fucked up."

His jaw hardened. "You said it yourself."

I couldn't even be offended that someone recognized the fault. Honestly, what was I expecting? That Scott would side with me when I didn't even side with my own actions?

I was in the wrong.

Jace, my brain hammered, *You're in the wrong.*

But that singular thought, the idea of me not speaking to Blu anymore, avoiding her because I wasn't right for her... It pained me.

Somehow, I got used to her company, used to her pursuits. I wanted her around. I craved that attention. It made me feel worth it, desired —

Lovable.

Mel's words banged against my skull. *"You two seem so similar but don't want to admit it. That maybe, you both orbit around each other — a hue of something."*

Was that possible? Could she be a hue of me? Was I a hue of Blu?

Did we compliment each other? Or tear each other apart?

The latter. It had to be the latter.

And yet, I couldn't let it go. I couldn't let her go.

"You've known this girl how long?" Scott asked.

"About four months." Felt like eternity and seconds all at once.

"That's not a long time, Jace." He leaned back, analyzing me with a narrow stare. "Have I ever told you about Delilah?"

I furrowed my brows, shaking my head. There was a lot I didn't know about my brothers, a lot they hadn't told me.

Probably because I was too young and naïve; a product of Will's beliefs.

"Delilah and I met when I was around your age. I was walking downtown after a night out and we crossed paths," he let out a laugh, "man, I thought she was the most gorgeous thing I'd ever seen.

"We instantly clicked, texted every single day, hung out constantly. It's like we existed because of each other, you know? That type of connection. And as the days progressed, I realized we'd only known each other for two months before I felt this urge to make her my fucking wife."

I opened my mouth to interject but he cut me off.

"What I'm saying is, Jace sometimes you meet someone and you don't understand the tie you two have. Sometimes you fall for the wrong reasons and sometimes the right ones. In this case, I think you saw a girl who needed saving… And you wanted to fix her broken heart so you didn't need to mend your own.

"I can't speak for her, but you're my brother. And if you want to know the truth, I think you guys have passion but not stability. And that passion always dies out as quickly as it comes in."

I eyed Scott for a long while, as if staring at his face was the only thing that kept me centred and alive.

He was right. Everything he said was right.

When I met Blu at the beginning of term, I didn't know how to feel. And now, months later, I remained stuck in the same position.

The only thing I was sure of was that I was wrong. That I had hurt her. That I had acted on a prior instinct to win and receive over being a decent human being. If I didn't let go of her, if I didn't sever this connection between us, what would become of her? What would become of me?

Karma was a mirror, not a bitch. It reflected the mistakes within me, the mistakes I draped over Blu. I'd led her to believe there was something.

I fucking kissed her.

Why had I kissed her?

Because I was fucking horny.

I was fucking horny and she looked fantastic and the primal part of me wanted to shove it in that bastard Derek's face before he could be inches from hers.

I hated the thought of it, I couldn't stomach it. I hated what had happened to her in the past, and hated that I was too fucked up to be the one to heal her.

She deserved something good, someone good, and I couldn't be that. I couldn't.

But the way she made me feel... The way she lifted me up, showered me in the attention Riley hadn't, Morris, or Danny or Connor. My own brothers made me feel pathetic.

My own fucking brothers.

Blu, she was the only one who saw me. Who saw me and cared. I couldn't give that up. She mattered too much. Her presence, anyway.

"What are you thinking about?" Scott asked.

I lifted my chin. "That I'm going to right a wrong."

He tapped my shoulder and resumed the movie, blissfully unaware of the fact I lied to his face.

I lied to my brother, who for the first time, tried to be there for me.

That was all I ever wanted for years, and I lied to him.

Because Karma would come after me, that much I knew –

Whether I let her go of her or not, she'd always be my Blu.

Chapter Forty-Seven
Blu

Year Four/Week Eighteen – Present

A month of no contact.

    A month of repair.

    I thought I'd be more hurt, thought the next time I saw him my heart would rip out of my chest.

    It was embarrassing what happened between us. Utterly fucking embarrassing.

    Spilling my secrets, my life story to someone who didn't care. God, I was an idiot.

    But over Winter break, I learned three valuable things:

1) Time heals everything.
2) What you think other people think about you is really what you think about yourself.
3) One man is not all men.

    The last one I was still trying to work on, but slowly and surely, I would get to where I needed to be.

    Jace was sitting in the second row when I walked in; his hair freshly cut, a new earring in place of the cross he'd always wore.

    Memories of that night flashed in my brain; me standing naked, stripped of all my defenses and his pleas to leave me alone. That face of pure guilt when he heard me open my mouth and realized he couldn't help me.

    No one could.

    But no one mattered.

For Christmas, Fawn bought me a polaroid and some film. *Try and get back into old hobbies*, she'd said, and dragged me to festive markets and holiday events.

I'd taken over one hundred photos over the break, seven of which I adored. That beat me up at first, thinking I wasn't even good enough to handle a camera. But seven was better than six, and six was better than none.

We purchased some fairy lights with clothespins and strung the polaroid photos across my wall, reminding me that I had memories to look back on, and moments to look forward to.

Each day after that, I vowed to take one photo a day, and purchased a disposable camera to fit in my purse.

It felt surreal, seeing life through a different lens; coffee shops became romantic, public parks felt magical, tiny neighbourhoods carried more mystery than I could ever fathom.

All because I started to love life again.

Loving life wasn't the same as loving myself, mind you. But I'd come to realize that taking space from Jace made me feel better about myself, not worse.

The pressure I carried to be the girl he wanted was overwhelming and unattainable. I'd broken every part of me trying to fit into that pretty, perfect mold. I'd lost sight of who I was just so he could glance in my direction for one second – because that one second was my heroin. And he watched me overdose.

I planted myself right beside him, something I knew he wouldn't expect, and smiled. "How was your break?"

Like nothing. Ever. Happened.

I got this. I can handle this. I'm better without him.

His eyes flickered, as if he was in utter disbelief. I figured as much, but the words that came out of his mouth threw me for in a spiral.

"You're supposed to hate me," he said, barely a whisper.

No.

Fuck. No, no, no.

I can't feel anything. I can't.

"You don't hate me," he stated like a question.

Yes, I do! I wanted to shout. *You ruined me!*

"I don't hate you."

I hated myself.

"Blu…"

I turned to face forward as Prof. Granger pranced in, a jolly glee trailing her aura. "Hopefully you all had time to do the Marshall McLuhan readings over break."

A series of groans and sighs filled up the classroom as she commenced her lecture, replacing the tension hovering between Jace and me.

His stares pierced my side throughout the entire seminar, but I couldn't face him. Luckily, she decided to shelve the break and compensate by ending class early which allowed me to slip through the doors and dart towards the exit.

But Jace caught up with me, and called my name.

"Blu."

I'll be damned if I turn around.

"Blu, please."

I turned around.

"What?" I demanded, sharp, guarded. *There goes my attempt at healing.*

He wore a sad expression, almost hurt. Why was he hurt? What did *I* do to him?

"I can't even explain to you how sorry I am," he shook his head, pulling me away from the crowd of people leaving the building.

"I've thought about texting you so many times, but there was absolutely no way I could convey what needed to be said in person. Please," he begged. "Please hear me out."

It took everything in me to say, "I'm standing here, aren't I?"

A small grin formed at the corner of his mouth, so slight I would've missed it had I not spent the last four months paying attention to all his mannerisms.

"That you are."

"Get on with it, Jace." This wasn't me. I wasn't cruel. He was. I had to remember that.

He swallowed before he spoke, softly and collected. "I'm not good with feelings; I don't know how to navigate them and I'm sorry that you were on the other side of that. I care –" He reached out to touch me, but I moved away.

"I care about you, Blu. I care about your life and your past and everything that you've been through. I want to hear about it, I want to be your friend. I want…"

There was hesitation, but my reaction remained still. No part of me wanted to show any more emotion, even if he had.

"What do you want, Jace?"

His throat bobbed. "I want to do it right this time. You and me."

You and me.

He wanted us.

He wanted this.

Fuck. Fuck. Fuck.

I'd spent months thinking about this moment, contemplating my reaction if he finally gave me what I wanted?

This past month away from him allowed my heart to rest. Why was I ready to get hurt again? Why did I want to?

When he reached out to hold my hand, I let him. I fucking let him. Like a breathing girl who claimed her casket, he *killed* me in all the pleasant ways.

His eyes were so kind, so warm and forgiving; a calm sea surrounded by blades of pointed grass. That's who Jace Boland was.

A delicate man with sharp edges – one who possessed a good heart, but needed someone to teach him how to use it.

Could I be that someone?

Have I not suffered enough?

My mind wailed at me, warning me to walk away no matter how bad it hurt. To never turn back even if he called after me. To run, to run and escape the chains of loving someone who couldn't love themselves.

I knew all these things.

I chose to ignore it.

I chose to butcher my heart.

A Hue of Blu
Marie-France Leger

    My hand crawled up his sweater, wrapping around the base of his neck as I pulled him down to hear me say, "You and me."
    And kissed him.

Chapter Forty-Eight
Blu

Year Four/Week Eighteen to Twenty-Four – Present

And so it began.

Blu and I spent every chance we could get making out in empty classrooms and flustering each other in seminar.

Just last week we'd been watching a media documentary and she placed her hand on my leg, inching up and up until I couldn't take it anymore and squeezed her fingers.

"Behave darling," I'd whispered in the way she liked. "We have an audience."

There was a one-stall washroom we quickly sought out after Professor Granger's class and made it our own playground. It was unsanitary, disgusting and always stank of rum.

If a drunk student was having fun in there, we were too.

As the weeks went by, my feelings for her grew into a frenzy of lustful passion – I couldn't keep my fucking hands off her. Scott's warning of becoming too invested in each other suddenly seemed like a prophecy.

When I told Blu I wanted to do things right, I didn't know what I meant. At first, I was set on the idea of us just being friends. But the second she pressed her lips to mine it was game over.

She was too good, too sweet, too interested.

I needed it and her and the affection.

Maybe we used each other, maybe we helped each other. Semantics. It was all the same.

She was the fix I needed to stop worrying about what my brothers were doing, what direction I was taking and who had or had not noticed me.

I was the intensity she craved, the buzz she sought, the man she challenged and won over.

I never saw it that way, though.

We fit perfectly when we needed to. Everything was right.

Until it wasn't.

Blu had come over for our last reading week ever, and I introduced her to my mom. Dad wasn't there. He never was. He wouldn't have given a single shit either.

"Hi sweetheart," Mom said, as if she hadn't been crying over my absent dad for the past couple months.

Blu shook her hand and beamed. "So nice to meet you."

That was it. A cordial exchange. I took her to my room shortly after that and began taking her clothes off.

"I'll never get tired of this," she released in between kisses, unzipping my pants and pushing me onto the bed.

Her bra was off in seconds and my fingers dove deep inside her, willing her moans.

"*Fuck*," her breathing was ragged and high-pitched. I covered her mouth.

My dick was the next thing to enter, slow and gentle, then filling her all at once. She grinded her hips against me, my fingers coated in *her* slipped between her lips.

"I love when you do that," I said, increasing my rhythm.

We stayed a tangled mess of sweat and sex until I released on her stomach, quickly grabbing a tissue to wipe her clean.

She began to talk but I silenced her, rotating my thumb on her clit while she squirmed beneath my touch.

There was no better feeling than this, seeing her cave to me, crumble beneath my hand. I did this. I was good enough. No one could take that way from me.

After a few minutes, she half-whispered half-moaned, "I'm coming."

I kneeled beneath her and pressed my mouth to her entrance, licking and nipping at her sweet spot until she climaxed onto my tongue.

She kissed me, tasting herself, and let out a satisfied breath. "You're too good."

I brought her to my chest, curling her body into mine and slid beneath the sheets.

"We're pretty healthy now," I teased, drawing invisible hearts on her bare shoulder. "Who would've thought?"

She laughed sweetly. "Not me."

There was silence for a few moments, but it wasn't uncomfortable. Just a shared appreciation for the girl I held, and the man she desired.

"How did we get here?" she asked.

"I couldn't tell you." That was the truth. I had no idea, but I was glad.

"Do you think we moved too fast?"

I shifted my gaze from the ceiling to her eyes. "Sometimes, yeah."

She pressed her lips together. "Then I'm not going to say what I was about to say."

"Alright, you can't just say that and not tell me."

"I don't want to."

"And I didn't want to pose in a checkered tuxedo for Baxter's photoshoot but adjustments needed to be made."

She chuckled, turning her body to face me completely and poked my cheek.

"Come with me to Paris."

At first, I wanted to laugh. She had to be kidding, I mean. She'd told me a few weeks back that she wanted to live in France for a year or two and travel, but I was under the impression she wanted to do that alone.

Not with me.

"When?" I swallowed, forcing a smile.

"After we graduate. I want to..." she paused, her brown eyes bleeding into mine. "I want to go with you."

Scott's words.

They held a different meaning now.

Too intense, too much – the warning bells in my head alarmed like sirens.

"We graduate in a little over a month and I thought it would be a fun trip. I don't know, I don't – "

That's when she realized; when my best efforts couldn't hide what my mind was thinking.

Immediately she shot up, scrambling for her shirt, her pants, her fucking everything – *Jesus Christ* –

"Blu, stop," I reached out a hand but I didn't know what the fuck to do with it. "Blu."

"*Blu* what, Jace? What do you want to say?"

My brain hurt trying to find the right words. But any word was better than none right now.

"You asked if I thought we moved too fast," my jaw tensed as I gritted my bottom teeth, "This, *this* is too fast for me. A trip? Across the world? You said you wanted to live there –"

"Forget I said anything."

Somehow, her clothes were on within the matter of a minute and she was already darting for my door.

I couldn't even get a breath out before she turned to me with tears in her eyes saying, "It's a fling, whatever's between us. It's not real. I don't –" she squeezed the bridge of her nose, "I can't afford to fall for temporary anymore, Jace. We're finished, whatever this is, we're finished."

And so I watched her go, because that's what I should've done the second I hurt her. Over and over and over, I hurt this girl. How invested was she in me? In us? How invested was I?

We had a few more weeks left with each other. What, was she just going to avoid me? She couldn't. We'd talk this over. We'd be fine in a few days.

My head readjusted to the soft indent of my pillow as I relaxed, realizing that she just needed to blow off steam and it was another pointless argument that required no resolution but time.

A knock sounded at my door. "Blu?" I asked.

But it was my mom who entered.

"Back away for a second, Mom, I have to get dressed."

It probably would have been weird had my mom not given me "the talk" when I was barely a pre-teen, but her and I were always so close. She respected my privacy, I respected hers. Even if I knew that her "privacy" equated to loneliness, and it wasn't privacy she wanted at all, but my father's attention.

I threw on my sweats and a tee, opening the door for her enough to enter.

"Why was that girl crying?" she questioned, crossing her arms. Very motherly of her to do; it was a nice act.

"She's a bit emotional right now."

"Why? What happened?"

"Don't pry, Mom. It's being handled." That was that.

My PS5 controller was in my hands, the new Call of Duty game booting up, but she was relentless with her curiosity.

"Are you two dating?"

"No," I responded flatly.

"Friends with benefits or something?"

"*Mom –*" I warned. "It's being handled."

She huffed, running shaky fingers through her blonde locks. "You said that already."

So I didn't respond, at least not for a few minutes while she hovered near the door, staring into my soul.

"Anything else, Mom? Or can I play my game?"

"I don't want you hurting anyone, Jace. I raised you better than that."

At this, I paused the T.V. and threw my controller behind me. "I'm not hurting anyone. She's hurting herself by asking ridiculous questions."

"What sort of questions?"

Holy. Fuck. "She just expects a lot more out of this and I guess…" Saying it out loud was nuts, considering I spent the past few weeks with her non-stop. "I guess we're just not on the same page."

She tilted her head, eyeing me with suspicion. Didn't have a clue what she thought she'd find, but I let her watch. Her choice.

"Does she know that?"

"Clearly not," my voice was strained but I laughed anyway. I didn't understand how girls worked, what they got mad over, what they cared about.

The more I sat on it, the more I realized how the crazed obsession I often felt with her dissipated the second she left. Maybe it was because I knew I'd see her again, knew she'd be there.

It was probably a good thing she left. She wasn't the only one who needed time to think.

I knew I cared about her, I did. When she finally opened up to me about the trauma of her past, my knuckles were white with rage. The shit she'd gone through, the people in her life – Fuck, *fuck*.

Still, a part of me always felt like she was holding something back, like she didn't fully trust me. That bothered me.

Maybe I didn't fully trust her either.

I'd been so deep in thought that I hadn't realized Mom already left my room, probably pissed that I didn't give her more information on why Blu had run off. Justifiable, I suppose. But I owed no one anything.

It was a courtesy text that I sent Blu, even though this situation was beyond my level of comprehension.

6:31pm – Jace: I hope you're doing okay. Give me a call when you feel up for it. See you Wednesday.

Honestly, I didn't expect a text back, but when her named flashed on my phone seconds later, I wasn't shocked.

6:32pm – Blu Henderson: I'm not going. And I meant what I said. We're done.

The good guy in me wanted to demand why, wanted to wipe away the stress and anxiety she clearly felt. But the biggest part of me knew how ludicrous the argument was.
I understood liking someone, hell liking someone a damn lot made you do insane things sometimes. But her wish for me to accompany her to Paris? Come on. She couldn't be serious. She probably didn't even want that.
My guess, it was after sex, she was riding a high (like she always did) and got sentimental. Didn't blame her for that. In a few days, she'd know what she asked of me and come to terms with my reaction herself.
In the meantime…
Morris and Bryce hopped in the C.O.D lobby, bringing my attention back to the game.
"Where'd you go, Boland?" He said my name like he did in high school.
Once, it was a nail gun to my ears, now it was a salute to being an equal. We were on the same playing field, him and I. No one was better than the other.
I definitely was. But he didn't need to know that.

"Mom was nagging me, sorry boys," My voice travelled through the mic as I picked out a camo skin for my gun.

I could practically feel Morris rolling his eyes when he released, "Women."

Paris.

Fucking *Paris*.

I shook my head. "Tell me about it."

Chapter Forty-Nine
Blu

Year Four/Week Twenty-Seven — Present

"You seriously skipped the last two weeks of school?" Carter's eyes were wide, sipping on a Belgian Moon.

"Yeah."

"For a boy, Blu. You skipped because you didn't want to see a boy."

My response was tired. "For a boy."

He might as well have patted my head and handed me a binky. "You're acting like a kid."

"The most intelligent minds bloom late," I jibed, sinking my teeth into a breadstick.

Ordering food was never a standard for me at bars. Honestly, it was kind of embarrassing. The thought of people watching me eat, surveying the way I took bites and judging me for it... Despicable. Heinous.

But over the last fourteen days, I consumed maybe eight-hundred calories per day. I'd lost a noticeable enough amount of weight that my own mother asked if something was wrong.

"If you only knew," I wanted to say.

"No," was what I told her.

Carter cleared his throat. "What ever happened to that guy Vince? Maybe you should start talking to him again, you know, get your mind off all this Jace shit."

Ah, Vince.

After our one anti-climactic hang out, I deduced that the only use he'd be to me was for in-class entertainment.

I thought he was interested. Maybe he was. But interest wasn't enough to keep something steady.

Choices were.

Hard work, strong will and fucking choices.

So many marriages failed because of lazy choices. It was easier to leave than it was to work things out.

I wondered sometimes, if I would be the one to exit or the person who would try. Sometimes, I was both of those people – sometimes I was neither.

"It fizzled out." I hid my mouth behind a napkin as I took in a mouthful of carbs. It was a big bite – one that screamed I was emaciated beyond belief but didn't want to show it.

"Why don't you give therapy a go?"

I halted mid-bite.

"Maybe you'll find out the cause behind all this," he used two fingers to air-quote, "*Fizzling out.*"

My fingers dropped the breadstick. "What the hell is a therapist going to tell me, Carter? I could literally sit in front of a fucking mirror, Google-search therapist questions and ask them to my damn self."

"I'm in therapy."

"And look how you turned out."

His eyes narrowed. "Watch yourself, Blu. I'm just trying to help."

My cheeks heated. I took in a breath.

Exhale. Inhale.

Exhale. Inhale.

"I'm sorry." I was constantly apologizing to the people I cared about.

When would they see through it?

When would they decide they'd had enough?

He leaned back into the chair, running his fingers through his blonde curls.

Carter was sort of beautiful, in a way that I'd never admit out loud. He ran in yearly marathons for charity, worked a six-figure marketing job in the heart of downtown and most importantly, he was loyal.

Loyal to me.

Even when I was a dick to him.

I reached out for his hand. "I don't deserve you."

He snorted, patting my fingers gently. "On the contrary, I think I'm exactly what you deserve and more."

"Then why won't you date me?"

He almost choked on his beer. "Whoa."

I knew the question was out of pocket but I wanted to hear his response anyway.

"Why?" I pried. "We've known each other for so long now. We're great friends. I find you attractive, you find me attractive." The last part was an assumption, one I was hoping he'd agree with.

"Blu," he laughed in discomfort. "Don't start."

"I want to start."

"And this is precisely why you need to talk to someone."

"Because I'm not normal?" My fingers slipped on the sweat of my palm as I picked for skin, scraped for flesh. "Because I need help?"

"Damnit, Blu!" If we'd been alone, it would've been a shout, or something of the sorts. But it was a warning.

He'd had enough.

I'd pushed him.

"Are you going to leave?"

"Keep talking the way you are and I just might."

Tears burned my eyes. "I can't believe you just said that."

"I'd be right around the fucking corner and you know it. But Christ, Blu –" His throat bobbed as he strained for words, but I knew even before he opened his mouth that I wouldn't be able to hold the sadness in.

"Your dad died when you were thirteen. Your mom barely looks in your direction and if she does, it's because you didn't clean a mess that *she* fucking made! You were in the worst relationships with the worst fucking people who treated you like trash from day one and you stayed –

"You stayed and you toughed it out for pieces of shit who never deserved you, broke you and you stayed because a part of you wants to feel like you did something right. That you made something work. That you tried. Because if nothing redeemable came out of your commitment, then you burned for nothing.

"You want a relationship with the only parent alive to have one, but she's an alcoholic just like your dad and a part of you wants to keep distance because if you got closer, you'd lose her just like you lost your father."

"Carter –" My throat was dry. I shut my eyes to prevent the sting.

"And you chase these men, these unavailable men because a part of you hopes they'll assign value to you and then, only then, you'd feel worth it."

I buried my face in my hands, pushing back the plate of food, thanking the Gods above that we were one of three tables occupied in the whole restaurant.

Carter removed one of my hands, placing it steady in his palm. "Show me your emotion, please. Show me the real you. I don't think you show her enough."

And so I did.

I cried, holding Carter's stare.

I cried, letting his words cascade over my body and touch the parts of my soul that struggled for air.

I cried, letting myself cry, knowing that crying was a solution and not a sign of weakness.

I'd been weak for too long.

I'd never move forward if I stayed stuck in the past.

After ten minutes of silence, Carter brushed his thumb over my skin and passed me a scratchy brown napkin. The tears dried on my face.

"Who needs a therapist when I have you?" I chuckled, blowing my nose.

He rolled his eyes. "I'm not licensed."

I pulled back the plate of breadsticks, not caring if anyone saw me eating, and crunched the crusty layer.

"I think it would be a good career path for you. I'll be patient zero."

He shook his head, clinking his glass against mine and said, "Eat your damn breadstick."

Chapter Fifty
Jace

Year Four/Week Twenty-Eight – Present

She sat across the room.
>She didn't sit with me.
>I stared at her.
>She saw me staring, she would've had to. I made it obvious.
>Then, seminar was over.
>She left.
>Only her eyes said goodbye.
>Oh Blu…
>*What have I done?*

Chapter Fifty-One
Blu

Year Four/Week Twenty-Nine – Present

One last class until the year was over.

One last class that I had to pretend Jace didn't exist.

Had to pretend he wasn't inside me.

Had to pretend his touch didn't linger on my skin for days after he'd held me.

Had to pretend he meant nothing –

When he meant *everything*.

There had been no contact in weeks.

It felt like months.

His presence was overwhelming.

As soon as Prof. Flowers announced that class was over, the twenty-some peers I'd never gotten to know cried out in joy.

It was a feeling I often envied, seeing as I never quite experienced it in the way I knew I should.

A young girl, who was now free of responsibilities with her deceased father's inheritance fully loaded in her bank account – and yet, *nothing*.

I was finally going to Paris.

Nothing.

I didn't need to worry about school.

Nothing.

Jace and I were never going to see each other again.

Everything.

I exited room one-sixteen, silently saying one last goodbye to the building I'd never step foot in again when someone grabbed my arm.

I knew it was him before I even turned around.

I'd sought out the pleasure of his grasp one too many times.

"This is getting a tad dramatic, don't you think?" His words came out sharp and cold, but the undertones were vulnerable and desperate; a last resort to mend damaged goods.

I mustered up enough courage to say, "I told you we were done."

"We've been done a million times and you never avoided me for weeks like this."

His eyes flashed with sincerity, a silent plea for me to make a move. But I was tired of making moves. I was tired of doing everything, saying everything.

It was exhausting to chase after someone who never wanted you from the start.

It was even more exhausting to pretend that there was a chance in hell you could change their mind.

"Honestly Jace…" *How real was I getting?*
Screw it.

"You fucked *me* over," I started, bleeding into the pain I felt for months. "You fucked *me* up. And yet, you come back every time. Why? Why do you insist on doing this to me?"

His response may have been the most honest thing he's ever said, and that terrified me.

In one breath, he shattered my soul. "You let me."

I don't think he realized the impact of his words until I'd walked away, refusing to turn back, refusing to ever speak to him again.

You let me.

I was already crying when I reached the washroom, locking the door behind me just in case he decided my need for space wasn't apparent enough.

The bathroom floor was covered in scraps of toilet paper, tampon holders and unidentifiable wet spots, but I sunk down anyway and sobbed.

He could've been standing outside the door or thirty hours away in the middle of a desolate forest and I wouldn't have cared.

You let me.

I allowed him to hurt me.

I allowed him to think there was a chance.

You let me.

It was all my fault.

The way I'd been feeling this entire term was my fault.

We finished quicker than we started. We barely got time to explore what we could become.

You let me.

It was all because of me.

I should apologize.

My phone vibrated in my pocket: **Jace Boland**.

"No, no, no," I whispered through sobs, throwing my phone against the stall. "No, fuck! No more of this."

But I scrambled for my phone, a large crack denting the screen protector and answered anyway.

"Leave me alone," I spat, crunching my hair into a ball. "I don't want to talk to you."

He sighed. "You dropped your bus pass."

Of course I did.

Of fucking course.

I ended the call, pulling myself up off the ground and opened the door. Lo and behold, he was leaning against the side wall with my transit card in his hand.

His jaw clenched as he looped it between his fingers, staring at the ground.

I extended an open palm, patting away wet mascara fibers. "My bus pass, please."

Languidly, he handed it over, his tall posture sagging low.

"I paid attention, you know," he whispered, unable to meet my eyes.

"What?"

Now he looked up, a deep blue sea swimming within his irises. "I paid attention to everything."

My heart pulsed, battling the bars I placed around it. "What do you mean?"

"You never ate a thing, and at first I didn't think much of it. You kept your arms covered, I chalked it up to you maybe being anemic or something. But after a while, I caught on. I broke through your persona."

I felt the need to hide myself from him once again, to build a wall between us but I knew – I knew he'd break the barrier.

He already had.

"I saw you," he said, pointing to my chest. "The real you. The you that you don't show anyone and I felt like I'd won something."

He grimaced, as if he'd known his words were a burning knife.

I didn't speak.

I couldn't speak.

"Instead of trying to be your friend Blu, I tried to be something else, something *more*. I don't know —" he shook his head, "I don't know if loving you properly would've changed the trajectory of our friendship, but I'm sorry that I couldn't have been better."

"Loving me?" The words tumbled out of my lips before my brain could register what he was saying. All the other sentences were gibberish, inconsequential to that one word.

Love.

His cheeks flushed. His throat bobbed. I wanted to scream.

"I don't know what to call it, I —"

"You don't know a lot of things," I licked my lips, my eyes wide with hope.

Hope.

The thing that killed me.

The thing that cost me everything.

He ran long fingers through his hair, eyeing me carefully, as if his gaze could cradle me through the rubble.

"I'm sure a part of me loves you or cares for you. I've known you long enough."

"You think love is determined by a length of time?"

"*No*, fuck — Blu, I'm not good with this shit."

"And what if," I swallowed, taking a step forward. "What if I loved you back?"

"Blu —"

One more step towards hope. "What if we could work?"

He grabbed my shoulders, halting my motions. A cold hand caressed my cheek, his thumb brushing over the corner of my lip.

I knew then that he was about to reject me for the fiftieth time. And yet, I stayed in place because his touch melted the frost beneath my skin, replacing it with hot lava and molten sunlight.

My comfort and my pain.

"There are so many guys out there…"

Don't say it.

"So many guys that will treat you right, who will deserve you."

He spoke as if he were a hundred miles away, not rubbing my cheek and keeping me still.

I couldn't hold back the tears. They came as easy as breathing.

"Why…" My fingers found his knuckles, then grasped at his wrist. "Why couldn't it be you?"

In his eyes I saw sadness, regret, guilt. It was at that point that I knew, even if he stayed, if he tried to love me, he wouldn't be able to.

Jace was incapable of it.

Jace only knew how to twist that burning knife he held onto so tightly.

That was his defense.

And he was okay with letting me go.

"I can't be that person for you, Blu," he let out, squeezing my fingers. "Try as I might, I can't. I want to be your friend, I want to help you and —"

"Help me?" I stepped back. "You kissed me, you *fucked* me and you want to be my *friend*?"

His eyes went wide. He took a step forward, but this time I took two back. "I care about you —"

"Please, for the love of fuck get a grip Jace."
My heart was racing but I felt it. The fire. The anger. The hurt.

All my emotions banded together and pushed me to realize that in one week, I'd be graduated.

In one week, this torment would be over.

I no longer needed to subject myself to Jace or this pain I couldn't seem to suppress.

By begging for a man who couldn't be what I needed, I devalued my worth, my self-respect.

All my life, people had an easy time doing that for me.

Mom.
Zac.
Kyle.
Tyler.
Jace.
Jace. Jace. Jace.
And me.

I'd done it every minute of every day.

It had to end somewhere.

So the calm took over. The anger subsided just enough to steady the point I needed to make.

"You want to know what I think?"

He didn't respond. I said it anyway.

"I think you lie to yourself about who you are, Jace."

His eyes that were once avoidant now faced me with a longing I couldn't gauge.

A piece of my heart broke with each word. But he'd been breaking mine for far too long.

"One day you're the mysterious Jace Boland, the next you couldn't care less who's watching. One day you're happy, one day you're too prideful for your own good and another day you're sharp and callous.

"Somewhere," I wiped a tear from my waterline, "Somewhere between those days I fell for you. And I think you expected me to love you when you never, not once, showed me the parts of you I could love. You've never even shown yourself."

His jaw twitched as he opened his mouth to speak, but no sound came out. He just stared at me, stuck in his position; stuck and unable to move forward. A metaphor of some sorts.

I willed my foot to move towards him, step by step, proving that I was able to make a jump – I could progress.

"You don't understand how hard I fought for you to see me as someone other than any of the prospects who threw themselves in your direction. I wanted to be the one you fell for, but instead I fell for you."

A tear broke out but I wore it proudly. Sometimes it was better to show someone the hurt they brought upon you.

Sometimes people were visual learners.

"I fell for you," I repeated, though he seemed to look through me. "And I kept falling and you wouldn't even lend a hand. You couldn't handle it."

We stared at each other for a few moments, though the quiet seemed to be more than enough sound. There were silent conversations going on between us, though I couldn't yet decipher the words. Maybe there were none. Maybe that was enough.

I turned to walk away but he grabbed my hand. I was shocked to find that I wasn't the only one who'd been crying.

"I promised to love you, Blu."

His hand slipped to my fingers, but I couldn't feel it. I realized then that I never really have.

"You promised to love me," I stated, as if it was the most ridiculous thing I'd ever heard.

It was.

He seemed to believe it when he nodded, "When you told me about your father, your scars, *everything* – I promised to love you and protect you. I promised myself that I wouldn't hurt you like this."

In that moment, I pitied him. I pitied the sadness he concealed behind his eyes. He said he knew me, saw through me and maybe, maybe he did. It was never a competition, but to Jace, it always was.

He'd told me about his high school friends – Morris, Danny, Connor and them. When he spoke of their stories, I realized he wasn't telling me them to reminisce, he was proving to himself that he belonged to the stories he told.

This was no different.

I saw you, Blu, he'd said. *I felt like I won something.*

My fingers entangled from his grasp as his words drilled a hole in my skull.

I was a prize to be won.

Carter said I thought of Jace the same way.

He was wrong.

For months I doubted if I was good enough for him. I let my infatuation, my intrigue and my ego fill up the insecurities that settled in my brain. It worked for a time, until I realized that every romantic moment, every kiss, every fuck had been a projection of what I wanted from Jace, not who he truly was.

But me?

I was no better than a giant teddy bear on the top shelf of a carnival game.

Each step towards the exit was the win I needed. One step away from him. One step towards my new life.

It stung unlike anything I'd ever experienced.

It burned me harder than most heartbreaks.

I couldn't explain why, what it was about him.

I mourned the loss of losing him before he was even gone.

All the impulsive parts of me that'd ruled my brain for years and years begged me to turn around, to run into his arms and dissect his meaning of love.

But instead I wrapped my fingers around the cold handle and met his eyes one final time. "Promises never meant much to you, Jace."

Chapter Fifty-Two
Jace

Year Four/Week Thirty – Present

I sat beside Baxter at his studio, wiping off the nail polish he'd asked me to wear for his photoshoot.

"It looks good," he said in passing, carrying his tripod to the center of the room. "I don't know why you always take it off."

"I don't know why you insist on me putting it on," I extended my fingers. "It always leaves a black residue."

He laughed with his chest. "Beauty is pain."

I grumbled something inaudible and glanced at the paperwork on the table next to me. A long list of names coated the pages, all having to do with potential buyers for Baxter's photos.

I grabbed the notes, scanning for people I recognized. Mel had a bunch of friends in the modelling industry; sometimes she'd paint their portrait and sell it to Carson, the owner of Prix's Art Gallery and her family friend.

The art gallery Blu and I went to.

I shook off the thought, remembering the moment like it was just yesterday.

All those months ago, when I hadn't so much as touched her, but felt her skin so innocently with one trail of my finger.

At the time, I'd done it for a reaction. To this day, I still wonder if that was my intention. Maybe I'd always liked her, maybe I never did. Either way, I was thinking of those memories with a sad fondness in my mind.

Things changed [and escalated] after Winter's Lodge. It's like all the softer sentiments I had, the ones untouched by desires and lust faded into the fucking wind and I was left with this surging obsession to feel her skin, not anything beneath it.

I guess I hated myself for it, because I had no reason to go back to her. What we had… Was it really that deep? Was love too simple a word to throw around the way I did, only because I felt like she wanted to hear it? As if that one, four-letter word would magically erase all the bad parts of us?

It didn't feel like the end, even though her last words sliced a wound so deep I'd sat on it for days. Bryce and Fawn were on the rocks, probably because Blu gave her the rundown of our situation.

I imagine the conversation went like, "How can you still be friends with him?" to Bryce defending me by saying, "They weren't together, darling."

He'd always steal my lines. Even if he wasn't good at it.

But even my confidence was gone. My jokes were gone. *She* was gone.

Everything Blu said was correct – sad, but correct. I spoke to Scott about it, expecting him to take my side, but it was wrong of me to assume my brothers would do that.

He merely agreed. So in the end, I was the walking, living, breathing piece of shit that broke a girl who was already broken.

And I had no right to feel sorry for it.

Isn't that fucked? Even a little bit? That I couldn't hurt because she was hurting, because I caused her pain?

Did people forget that I was a human being with feelings, too? That I had *something* with this girl, *something* beyond a friendship?

"Get your hands off my contacts," Baxter swatted the paper from my grip. I didn't realize I was still holding it.

"Sorry," I muttered. "Any luck with selling your prints?"

He ran two stressed palms down his face, messing up his bushy eyebrows. "Sadly no. I'm trying, though. Can't give up."

I admired his work ethic, but I knew from Mom (because Bax would never care to tell me) that he'd been in a dry spell for a few months now.

"Why don't you try something different?"

His eyes narrowed. He hated taking suggestions, but I knew he was desperate for something.

"What do you mean?"

I cleared my throat, taking a glance at the scattered grey photos all over the walls. "Your shots are all of people sitting against plain white walls."

"Great observation." I could feel the disinterest slipping by the second. "What's your point?"

"My point is they're good, but do you not get kind of tired shooting the same shit?"

"You're my model, Jace. You aren't supposed to have an opinion."

"Holy fuck," I laughed because it was so ridiculous. I was a model, a toddler, a fucking stranger – not a brother, no, never a brother to my own flesh and blood. Everything but.

Everything fucking but.

"What?" he griped, sharp and irritated.

I had every right to be just that. Not him.

"Your photos are fucking boring, Baxter. They're fucking boring and I'm sick and tired of you treating me like I don't have a say in shit when all I want to do is help you."

He stared at me with piercing blue eyes, dark like Dad's, and dropped his tripod like it weighed bricks.

"What did you just say?"

I had enough. I finally had enough.

"You treat me like a kid," I spat. "You treat me like a fucking kid and you don't listen to anyone but Will because he works in finance but he got a business degree, Bax! That's the difference between you two.

"I get you love art and making all this shit, but you don't know anything about marketing it, or at least contacting the people who could help you, not just buy your prints."

"Oh, and you know so much?" He let out a sarcastic laugh. It boiled my blood. "You don't have a fucking car, you live with Mom, you're twenty-one with no job, no girlfriend and no fucking direction!"

At this, I stood up, my anger bursting out of me like untameable embers. "Are you that proud, to not even hear me out, to listen to someone other than yourself? Do you not see that you've been unsuccessful doing the same damn fucking thing every single day and getting no results?"

"Unsuccessful," he scoffed, and I knew his words were about to burn. "You couldn't even play pro because you were whining about the loss of your ex-girlfriend, Jace."

And I was right.

The one thing he knew would kill me, would fracture every corner of my confidence – he knew. And he used it against me.

I kicked the chair back and stepped up to his face. We were eye to eye when I said, "Fuck you," and walked out of his studio.

The walk home was tiring even though it was five minutes away. My bones felt broken, my body was wrecked and I just wanted one second of peace. Every thought in my brain screamed, retreating back to the comfortable corners of old Jace. The Jace who got nothing – who had nothing –

Who was nothing.

Couldn't keep a girl? *Check.*

Wasn't good enough for my soccer career? *What fucking career?*

Wasn't good enough –

Wasn't good enough –

I WILL NEVER BE GOOD ENOUGH.

Mom was in the kitchen with Dad talking about their fucking relationship like they were kids in school. I couldn't care less.

"Hi baby, how was –"

I ignored her and jogged up the stairs, slamming my door before throwing my face into a pillow. If I cried, the liquid would get soaked up by the cotton material. If I screamed, no one would hear me. No one could care.

So I yelled and I thought of everything, everyone who was better than me – everyone I disappointed – everyone who disappointed me.

I thought about Scott trying to help me, feeling like he owed me just that.

He didn't.

I thought about Riley cheating on me, feeling as if I deserved it.

I did.

Then Blu –

Blu. Blu. Blu.

My Blu, who I hurt, who I broke and shattered and it was me – *Me* who deserved it. Not her. My Blu…

God, my poor fucking Blu.

After ten minutes of suffocating my screams, I flipped over and stared at my phone, unable to flip it over because if I did, Blu would be the first one I'd call.

I couldn't do that to her.

But even still, I couldn't stop looking at the iPhone screen, wishing I could send her a message through my mind – wishing there was no proof of my feelings, that a private bubble existed around my conversations with her – only her.

Just Blu.

Just me and Blu.

The only two that mattered.

My hue.

Chapter Fifty-Three
Blu

Graduation – Present

"All I'm saying is I missed you." Fawn curled her hair, facing me in the bathroom mirror. "We barely hang out anymore."

I snorted in feigned amusement. "And why do you think that is?"

She placed the iron on the counter and turned to me. "You can't blame me for hanging out with my boyfriend."

"I don't blame you, I just hate the fact that your boyfriend is also Jace's best friend."

"But what does that have to do with us?"

Did she not get it? "I don't want to be associated with anyone involving Jace Boland."

Heat radiated off her body. "I AM NOT ASSOCIATED WITH HIM," she practically yelled, "We barely speak!"

This, I knew for a fact, was true. Bryce made it a point to have date nights with Fawn and guy nights with Jace separately. Mind you, I don't know why you would couple those things together, but I guess Jace enjoyed bringing girls around Bryce. Probably another one of those ego games he liked to play. Wouldn't surprise me.

"Blu, when you and Jace were fucking around I never said anything because you seemed happy. A little obsessed, but happy."

Ah yes, the short-lived time period where we fucked in empty classrooms, made-out in campus bathrooms and riled each other up during seminar.

The first time Jace and I had sex was at his house when his parents were both gone (he'd told me his dad was always gone so not to worry). It was raining that day, the first time I went over, and we sat on his bed staring out the window.

I remember saying, "I could watch this all day." The rain always calmed me.

He was staring at me already, a hand on my knee when he responded, "Me too."

If I wasn't already enamoured by his sharp jaw, blue-green gaze and handsome face I would've thought that comment was cringey. But the second his lips touched mine, I knew I was a goner.

We fucked twice in two hours. At the time, it was euphoric. Now, I felt stained. But even still, if he kissed me, I don't know that I'd be capable of saying no. I don't know that I'd want to. Because him inside me felt like the most intimate thing in the world. Every touch, every kiss, every look after that was not nearly enough.

Him being inside me wasn't even enough.

I craved his closeness, his attention, his affection. Every other guy was erased from my brain; a blank slate replaced by Jace.

Jace. Jace. Jace.

He was all I saw.

Fawn snapped her fingers, calling my attention. "Helloooo?"

I picked up the straightener again, flattening the frizz. "I don't think I was ever happy with Jace."

"Weren't you?"

"No," I shook my head. "My happiness was unhealthy. I don't think that's happiness. Like, I neglected everyone but Jace. Not that there were many people to neglect."

Who did I have besides Fawn and Carter?

My own mother was happy to hand over my dad's money because she received five times more than I did. My own mother looked down on my wealth because she suddenly had more. It wasn't even her fucking own. Did she not realize that? Did she not realize her husband had to die to feed her alcohol supply?

The thing that killed her, made her feel alive.
She and I had that in common.

Only my bottle of bourbon was a 6'3 painting of a man who split my heart in two.

Fawn rubbed my shoulder. "I should've been there more."

"I should've let you."

A few minutes of silence passed between us. Both her and I had things to think about, we knew that.

"You leave for Paris next Tuesday," Fawn stated, avoiding my eyes.

I nodded. "Yeah."

"Are you excited?"

In the beginning of fourth year, the thought of walking the cobblestones in front of the Eiffel Tower, inhaling the scent of Parisian croissants and shopping in too-expensive boutiques was my joy-fuel. Now, it wasn't so much of excitement but an escape.

I wasn't going to Paris for enjoyment.

I was going to run away.

I guess a part of me always wanted to take shelter somewhere foreign, only now I had different reasons to hide.

A Hue of Blu

"Yeah, I'm going to miss you though." I was. But Fawn had studied abroad before dropping out of York to pursue her freelance writing career. We were apart for six months and Facetime was our saving grace. We could do it again.

She pulled me in for a hug, wrapping her arms tightly around me. "I hope you find what you're looking for out there."

"Me too," I whispered in her hair.

Me too.

***

The ceremony was an epic drag.

People cheered, cried, laughed. It was personal to them, this momentous occasion that felt like a blur to me.

I sat with Fawn and her family since my mom was "working." Convenient that, she was always so productive every time I needed her.

Maybe I didn't need her to see me graduate.

But I wanted her to.

Carter showed up a few minutes after we arrived, calling in sick to work just so that I'd have company.

That's what Mom should've done.

That's what she didn't do.

Fawn grabbed my hand, tipping her cap to me. "We did it, Blu. We made it."

She turned away but I continued to stare at her; her brown eyes that twinkled with light, her manicured fingers that applauded everyone – especially the people she didn't know.

I always envied her, but maybe it wasn't from a place of jealousy. No, it came from a world of adoration, of love.

She was incredibly kind, soft-spoken and talented. Her parents had wealth, but she always worked for her success. A talented writer, an even better friend —

The single lifeline I had that kept me afloat.

Carter sat by my left side, nudging my shoulder. "Congratulations, Blu."

I leaned down to kiss his cheek, then did the same for Fawn. No words could describe the way I felt sitting between two people who cared for me. The only two people I never doubted.

It was a peaceful thing. The feeling of not feeling. Knowing that the person beside you loved you, flaws and all. I never had to try and pretend to be lovable, not with them — I just was.

Amidst the crowded auditorium, in the corner of my eye, I recognized Jace's mother. I didn't expect any less, seeing as the universe loved to taunt me with his presence and the presence of those around him.

Beside her was an older man from what I could tell. Probably his father. And to his father's right were three other men — Jace's brothers.

I remember him telling me how he wished he could have a closer relationship with him. A part of me wanted to go up to him, hug him and say, "They came for you."

But it wasn't my place to be happy for him.

It was my place to be happy for me.

So when my name was called to go on stage and collect my diploma, I mimicked the sentiments of everyone around me.

I did this.

I should be proud.

"Beatrice Henderson, class of 2022, Bachelor of Communications degree."

The auditorium burst with delight, not because they knew who I was, but because it was the proper thing to do.

At a point, maybe that would have mattered to me. But the important people sat by my side, tapping my back before I made my way across the stage, waving at a bright light that allowed the crowd to blend into black. I grabbed my diploma from the college president and shook his hand.

I made it.

I did it.

I should be proud.

I –

Jace's eyes met mine, standing in a row of graduates I hadn't spoken to before, hadn't seen. He never heard my actual name; I never told him. That explained the shock of wonder on his face.

"My name's not really Blu, dumbass," I wanted to say. But instead I smiled.

Because today, just today, I was Beatrice Henderson, the name my father gave me. The name he left me with.

I took my place beside a boy with golden hair, acknowledging him with a cordial nod and stepped out of Jace's view.

Deep in the crowd, I pretended everyone was gone. The only two lights that remained were Fawn and Carter. My mom didn't want to be there, so she didn't deserve to be. But somewhere, somewhere far away my father came to cheer me on.

Somewhere, he was proud that they called on Beatrice instead of Blu.

Somewhere, he was alive and breathing and healthy.

And I wanted to be too.

After the ceremony, the graduates filed off stage and hugged one another. Fawn embraced me, then Bryce.

I knew Jace wasn't too far behind, so when he emerged from a group of huddled peers, I was prepared.

"Happy graduation," he smiled, but it didn't meet his eyes.

Snarky remarks tried to pry its way out, but it was a happy day for most people… Why couldn't it be a happy day for me?

"Same to you," I said. I forced tenderness. I tried.

"When do you leave for France?"

Screaming and whistling echoed through the hall, so I pulled Jace aside to a quieter area next to a trophy case.

"Tuesday."

His jaw clenched, those uncertain eyes shifting from the ground to my face. "You must be excited. I've always wanted to go."

I wanted to scream at him, reiterate the fact that we ended for the precise reason of me asking him to come, and him rejecting my invitation.

But instead, I played it off. I was exhausted of him. *He* exhausted *me*.

"You never told me that."

He shrugged. "There's a lot of things I haven't told you."

And now, we'd never get the chance.

"Why did you choose Paris of all places?" he asked.

"Honestly, I just think it's the atmos —"

"Atmosphere," he interjected at the same time as me.

We did that often enough; finished each others sentences. It was odd. We were odd.

If I thought about it too much, I would've read into it. Anything is a sign if you look hard enough. I couldn't do that to myself anymore. My heart's had enough.

"Have you thought about what you want to do after all this?" I waved my hand, directing it to the happy graduates and golden streamers.

He removed his cap, trailing the square edges with his finger. "No idea."

"You'll figure it out."

"Yeah," he chuckled sarcastically. "I'm sure."

The noise quieted as people began exiting the hall, leaving me in a private bubble alone with Jace. "What are your interests?"

He leaned his body against the glass trophy casing. "Soccer. It's always been soccer. I guess I just never had time to think about who I was without it, even though I had years to decide," he shook his head, "It just never felt like I was on a time crunch, you know? That my life had to start somewhere after I failed."

"You didn't fail."

"You didn't see me play."

"I would've liked to." My cheeks heated, but it was a sincere desire. Innocent. If we would've had the time, maybe we would've been normal.

Maybe.

The corner of his lip twitched into a half-smile. "I would've liked that."

"It's weird," I started, "I feel like we never talked about the normal things when we were…" *Together? Fooling around? Something? Nothing?* I didn't know how to label it, label us. We always jumped in head-first.

A soft chuckle. "We were too busy arguing or jumping each other's bones to talk about anything."

"We did it wrong," I admitted out loud, before I could tie my words back and shove it in a net.

His gaze softened as he whispered, "But at least we did it."

Fawn and Bryce approached, hand-in-hand, with happy smiles. A pleasant contrast between Jace and I, who looked as if something died in our presence.

Something did.

Maybe he felt it too.

"My parents are waiting to take us to celebratory brunch, babe," Fawn said, chipper. She ignored Jace's existence like always. The purest friend I could have ever asked for.

Only I didn't want to ignore him. Not with the moment we just shared. But if I didn't, I would've danced in this merry-go-round again and again until remnants of me were all that remained.

This was a new chapter.

I vowed that to myself.

So I grabbed Fawn's hand, said a swift goodbye to Bryce and hugged him tightly. "Take care."

"You too, Blu. Have fun in Paris." He smiled kindly. "Take lots of pictures."

I nodded, dreading the last moment I knew I had with Jace. The last moment I'd see those sparkly bluish eyes, that sharp jaw and sunken dimples. Hear his laugh; that laugh that filled my chest with something other than solitude.

But the time had come to bid farewell to all his attributes, all his being.

No more late night calls.
No more fighting.
No more kissing, fucking, nothing –
No more going back.
No more hue.
No more hue.

I had tears in my eyes when I turned to Jace for the final time, refusing to see if my sadness mirrored his.

"Are we saying goodbye?" I asked softly, staring at the grey-tiled floor covered in glitter.

With his final touch, his fingers gently lifted my chin to face him – forcing me to see that he was crushed, crushed like me.

His voice broke as he said, "Maybe next time."

He turned around before I could respond, pushing through the exit doors without so much as a glance back. Bryce shot me a look of apology, trailing after him as my eyes remained glued to the spot in front of me – where he'd been before he took the executioners blow to my heart.

I didn't cry.
I felt breathless.
But I didn't cry.

I cried too much in my lifetime to cry again —
to cry over someone who couldn't even say goodbye
to me after all we'd been through.

"He's not worth it," Fawn insisted, scrunching her fingers against my shoulder.

"No," I exhaled. "He's not."

As we walked to meet her family, I looked back at the exit doors where he fled, picturing him standing there waving to me.

I couldn't figure out which outcome was worse.

The one where he didn't care, or the one where he cared too much.

Either way he wasn't worth it.

He's not worth it.
He's not worth it.
He's not worth it.

But you know who was?

Me.

I was worth it.

I was worth it.

I am worth it.

And maybe that's exactly what I'd find in Paris. Maybe that's the belief I'd search for.

That from this day forward, no one would take my worth away from me again.

You are worth it, Blu Henderson.

Love, Beatrice.

Part Two
EVERY YEAR AFTER

*"The **blue** seems eternal."*

Virginia Woolf

Age 25
Blu

Present

"Thank you for coming today, Beatrice," my psychologist released, shaking my hand.

One year.

One year I'd been gone.

Five months I'd lived in Paris, four months in Italy, and three months in Dublin.

My style was different, my hair was longer – still a rich blue, that would never change – my French accent polished and my Italian... well, a work in progress.

I spent my twenty-fourth birthday in an Airbnb in Rome, with Fawn on Facetime and my new friend Claire (who I met in Paris) sipping wine next to me.

She was the type of girl I was once intimidated by; bright blonde hair, striking green eyes and puckered, rosy lips. Jace's profile type, I thought at first. The woman he'd pursue.

But Jace's memory became a thing of the past as months flew by and Claire showed me cities and streets, flower gardens and museums.

I met her upon arriving in Paris; a map in one hand and a baguette in the other. Yeah, I was *that* girl.

She reminded me a little of Fawn due to the fact the first time she saw me, she laughed and said, "You're a tourist, I'm not speaking French."

Her long, manicured fingers extended to mine, but before I could reciprocate the handshake, she'd already taken the bread from my hand and threw it in the trash.

"Let's get you an actual meal, *oui?*"

I decided right then and there that I could make a joke. That we'd be friends. That this solo trip was the best idea I could have had.

"I thought you weren't speaking French?"

"Aha! So you do understand the language," she teased. "I was testing you."

"What for?"

Her eyes beamed with excitement as she mouthed, "Fun."

I learned a lot of things about Claire on our travels. One, she was relentless and would not take no for an answer. Two, she preferred to be called "eclair" *comme le dessert* [like the dessert], she'd said. And three, she lived off her parents' wealth (kind of like me, only no one had to die for her inheritance).

That was the defining factor between my friendship with her and my friendship with Fawn. Claire was fun, exactly what she wanted me to think, but Fawn was reasonable. She could be a bitch, but she told me things straight up. Claire never wanted to press my buttons, only the ones that led to partying or drinking.

After Italy, I said my goodbyes to her and left for Dublin. I knew it was the last stop I wanted to explore before going home.

Paris was a dream, but that's all it was to me. I thought I could find a purpose there, something equivalent to a lost and found. Instead I found ten pounds of chocolate croissants, handsome French men who knew their way around the sack, and a lot, I mean *A LOT,* of tourists.

I thought the weight gain would bother me more since for the last twenty-some years of my life I'd been obsessed with my appearance, but something about being in a foreign place with no one who knew who you were... It was freeing.

I guess that's what Paris taught me.

That I was free.

It was in Italy that I met a couple – Hunter and Marley Lane, their names were. The day after my birthday, I'd been too hungover to function and crossed the street to a café called "Tazza."

It wasn't my finest moment, but I lazily walked up to their table and asked what the pretty woman with brown eyes was having, as my Italian was terrible and I didn't want to make a fool of myself.

"Oh, we're actually from America," she laughed. Her smile was bright, like Fawn's. "Nebraska."

"Oh." My mouth made a physical 'O' as I turned on my heel and prepared to flee. "Sorry."

"No, no –" she'd said sweetly. "Stay." She turned to her partner, a handsome man with blonde hair and blue eyes. "I'm not going to finish all the food you ordered, Hunt."

"Your name is Hunt?" I pried. Genuine curiosity always got the best of me. "That's actually a really cool name."

"It's Hunter, actually." He extended his hand to shake mine. "You are?"

I shook it proudly, feeling a calloused palm against my own. "Blu."

"Blu? Now that's a cool name," he smiled.

So I made my decision to stay and chat with a random couple I'd never met before. Lo and behold, it was some of the most engaging conversation I'd ever had.

Marley and I had a lot in common, more so than I realized. She was a city girl who quite literally adapted her lifestyle to the country after losing everything. She didn't go into much detail about her family life, but I knew it was bad.

I could relate.

I felt comfortable enough opening up to them about some of my experiences, but it was never forced upon me. If anything, I was the curious cat that begged to know everything about this beautiful couple. There was something priceless about the looks shared between two people who fit so perfectly.

I longed for someone to look at me that way.

"So what brings you to Italy, Blu?" Marley asked, sipping on a hot tea.

I'd been so honest up until that point. Why not dish it all out? "I just needed to escape my old life."

She clinked my cup of water and looked to Hunter. "She sounds like me when we first met."

He laughed, a husky, rough laugh fit him perfectly. I swear some laughs were just made for certain people. It made me smile.

"I got you to stick around though, sweetheart," he winked at her, making my insides bubble with envy.

This.

This was normal.

This was love.

Everything I had with all of those men... those boys – that wasn't love.

Maybe this is my quest, I thought at the time. Finding that. Maybe my solo trip was about falling in love with myself, the world, the people in it... Maybe it was my destiny.

In Dublin I sat near the water every day with Fawn's camera. The sights were beautiful, the greenery unmatched. Everything was a picture-perfect painting and I longed to soak it in.

Eventually when I got home, I'd rent a bachelor apartment and start looking for jobs, start the real life bullshit I knew I couldn't avoid. But for now, I thought of the way I'd decorate my living room, covering my walls with photos of my travels.

That was a form of love, wasn't it? Loving my surroundings so much that I wanted to bottle it up and cherish the memories forever?

One day, I sat on a cement block, taking photos of the sunset above waves when a man came and sat right next to me.

That was the one thing I discovered about my travels; anyone could approach you and have no reason to do so, simply because they wanted to spark up a conversation with someone interesting.

I guess many people found me intriguing because I wasn't short of contacts on my trip.

It felt nice, to be noticed.

This man, Jeremy Hysac, worked at a bar in Riverside. He said a corny line like, "Haven't seen you here before" even though Dublin had a population of like, five-hundred-thousand.

Anyway, we got to talking and he wanted to see some of my photos – said his good friend worked for a company in need of a travel writer. Fawn would've jumped at the chance, but I was no writer.

"I only take photos," I explained, a tad disappointed that I couldn't do more. That feeling of uselessness slowly started to creep back in.

At first I didn't think he heard me; his eyes were glued to my camera screen as he clicked through the shots I'd taken across months of travel.

"These are amazing," he eventually responded in a cute little accent.

I blushed. He recognized my talent. "Seriously?"

He nodded multiple times. I thought he'd snap his neck. "Here, take his card. He may have a spot for you."

I read the red-stitched name on a white square: **Hamish Cartwright**. Below it was an address listed in Chicago.

"He works in the states?" I asked. "And he's *your* friend?"

"Yes?" He laughed like I had ants crawling up my nose. "Why?"

"I don't know Jeremy," I handed back the business card, "I'm doubting the legitimacy of this offer."

He rolled his eyes. "Look up Cartwright Blogs under Vakehale Press."

So I plugged all this information into Google and clicked the first website I saw, widening my eyes. "Vakehale Press is a section under Chicago-Sun Times? He works for a newspaper?"

I continued to click and click until I found a face of a man in his late thirties, his credentials underneath the portrait: **Hamish Cartwright, Senior Editor of Cartwright Blogs.**

"No bullshit here, love," Jeremy said, pulling out a cigarette. "Puff?"

I shook my head, waving the smoke fumes away as I wildly searched through articles and columns he'd written.

His main focus seemed to be documenting resorts and "Places to Go Before You Die." He travelled himself, but never took the photos for it. Jeremy told me they were all Googleable shots that he'd placed within the article to add some life, but he wanted to make his journals more personable.

"That's where you come in," he stated.

"I have no experience with professional photography. I don't even know where to begin."

He slapped my knee, crushing the half-finished cigarette underneath his boot. "As long as you begin, you're one step closer to being where you belong."

And he walked away. No wave. No goodbye. Just his friend's business card sitting next to me on a cement block, and a burning cigarette on the ground beneath my shoe.

That was the moment I realized the entire duration of my trip, I was waiting – *anticipating* for something bad to happen. But all the people I met, the events that'd taken place… It reminded me of all the kindness in the world.

The kindness outside the torment of my mind.

And that kindness brought me to this moment here.

The now.

Sitting across Dr. Hemline, spilling all my life secrets to a random stranger because I wanted to heal.

I wanted to be kind. I wanted to be the person someone met on a solo trip and never forgot about. In order to do that, I had to do this. For my sanity. For my self-discovery.

For me.

"Why are you here today, Beatrice?" she asked, pulling out a notepad.

When I first returned back home two months ago, I was jumping back and forth between Fawn and Carter's apartments. Mom sold the house and dipped to God knows where. She only texted on holidays to let me know she was safe.

It didn't matter if I was. Just that she was.

Maybe in her own way, that's how she showed love. I had to accept that. It was the best she could do.

One thing I had to learn was getting comfortable with the unknown. In some situations, I'd never have closure and I had to be okay with that. Sometimes it was better for you to assign your own before letting that open wound fester.

Fawn and Bryce had ended four months into me leaving town. Apparently it was a mutual breakup, and they wanted different things.

"I still have so much love for him," she'd explained, "But at least now you don't need to worry about running into Jace."

Jace.

It was the first time I heard his name aloud since I last saw him at graduation.

A part of me wanted to know everything about his life, but the biggest part of me wanted absolutely nothing to do with it.

So I never addressed that part, just consoled her hurting heart.

I felt comfortable enough to stay with Fawn now that she was single when I got back, but only for a few weeks before I needed my own space – my own home to go back to.

While I was apartment hunting, Carter let me crash in his spare room, visiting potential places with me on the weekends when he had the time.

Eventually I found a respectable studio near York and fully moved in a week and three days later.

After unpacking and relaxing, Fawn asked for a girls' night. I was all for it since I'd been so go-go-go for weeks trying to find a place to live.

But of course, life couldn't give me a break.

The first bar we went to was dead, so we sat on the street and contemplated our next move.

"Want to try Deaks?" she suggested.

It was a sports bar, and I knew there was some massive football game happening so I wasn't sure we'd get seats but I said fuck it anyway and we went.

We shouldn't have gone.

Maybe I wouldn't be sitting across Stacy fucking Hemline right now if we hadn't.

Jace, Bryce, and a random guy I'd never seen before were sitting at the curve of the bar, right near the entrance.

He saw me before I saw him. He would've had to. Another one of life's jokes, I guess.

"Oh for the love of –" I started but Bryce cut me off by prancing over with a beer in hand, clearly wasted.

"Fawny?" he uttered, gaping at her like she was a goddess incarnate. "*Ohhmyygoddd*, Fawn!"

A Hue of Blu

Marie-France Leger

He embraced her as if they hadn't broken up ten months prior, shocked that she didn't reciprocate the same affection.

"Hi Bryce," she responded, tapping his back respectfully. "Nice to see you."

"Been way too long!" He wiped his mouth with the back of his hand and gasped, "Blu? Blu Henderson? Do my eyes deceive me?"

"Yes," I said, shifting behind Fawn. "Yes they do."

"C'mere," he gestured for me to stop hiding, "Give me a hug."

But a hand pulled him back just as he stepped forward. A hand I recognized just by his rings alone.

"Down boy," Jace released, squeezing Bryce's shoulder.

I could feel his piercing stare as the other man I didn't recognize approached our group. "Want another round? Jean's asking."

"Not now, Morris," Jace addressed him.

Morris.

The guy Jace went to high school with. The one on his soccer team. The one he was jealous of.

God no. All those memories – I didn't want them anymore. I didn't want to remember any conversation we had last year; I barely wanted to remember him.

But here he was. A silly trick life played again, dangling the man I fought so hard for, and fought so hard to forget, right in front of me.

The air between us changed as I looked into those blue-green eyes for the first time in over a year, his angular, chiseled face, and those lips that spilled broken promises.

Fawn snapped her fingers, placing an arm around Bryce's shoulder. "Let's get you some water, shall we?"

She gave me a look as she led him to the bar where Morris sat, and I could hear Bryce slur, "*You've always taken such good care of me, Fawny…*"

And just like that, I was transported back to every memory, every feeling and every circumstance where I felt trapped inside the web of Jace Boland.

He adjusted the chain of his necklace before closing the distance between us. Even still, he left breathing room. It was for the best, we both knew that.

"Hi Jace," I said. A year later and I was still the one making the first move. *Classic.*

His throat bobbed, his jaw tensed. "You're…" He shook his head, searching for the right words. I recognized the mannerisms all too well.

It seemed like the perfect time to make a joke, to shield the weight that had been pressing on my chest since I arrived. "Dashing," I smirked, "Dazzling, radiant —"

"Mine," he whispered, cutting me off completely.

The words in my throat died, the smile on my face fading into nothing. I almost wanted to correct him on his mistake, to laugh in hysterics but then — then I would've played off the situation. Then, I would've made his comment non-existent.

I wanted it to exist.

I remembered what it was like to be his.

"Mine," he repeated, as if he read my thoughts.

Was he as wasted as Bryce? "How much have you had to drink?" I teased, though my cheeks were stained with blush.

His features were inscrutable, void of happiness. He seemed pained, *hurt* almost. I felt the sudden urge to ease his sorrow – whatever that entailed.

"Yeah," he nodded a few times, blinking like he couldn't believe I was standing before him. "Yeah, that's it."

"*That's it* what?" I laughed, twisting my lips into a genuine smile. "I asked how much you've had to drink."

"Enough that this is a little too real."

"What's too real?"

"Jace!" Bryce yelled from across the bar. "Jace you're missing second half!"

I turned to his direction but Jace grabbed my hand, ignoring Bryce, and squeezed my fingers gently. "Let's go for a walk."

It was early July, the night's breeze blowing through my blue hair. Claire convinced me to get layers in Paris, and ever since then that became my go-to hairstyle. Only I wish the wispy locks didn't poke my eyeballs every time the wind blew.

"Are you cold?" he asked, his eyes raking down my tank top.

While living in Dublin I got seven more tattoos, making my patchwork sleeve on both arms almost entirely complete. In other words, my scars were entirely invisible. Sometimes, *sometimes,* I almost forgot they were there. It was nice.

I rubbed my biceps, my fingers running over the tight skin where my cuts had been. Only they were fully concealed now — no one needed to know they existed but me.

Jace knew, but maybe he was too drunk to remember.

I'd never be too drunk to forget.

"It's humid, so no," I replied, throwing a half-smile his way. "How've you been?"

He continued to watch me, as if I was a creature at the zoo or the most majestic thing to roam the earth. It had to be the former. He'd always seen me as a burden.

"You seem different," he let out. "I don't know what it is, but you just… Sorry, I keep staring at you — Sorry."

"It's fine." It wasn't. I didn't want him to look at me, to dissect who I'd become once again. That's how he ripped me open and tore out my heart. By seeing through me.

"I mean," I started, "It's been over a year. I'd hope that I changed even a little."

"Paris treated you well," he stated, flicking his eyes to mine.

Fuck.

Fuck him.

Fuck his stupid black tee that constricted his lean muscles, his navy blue pants and his muted grey ballcap.

Fuck the way he looked, the way he spoke, his fucking smile and eyes and walk and voice.

I hated it all.

I hated it all because I didn't want to admit that I loved every part of it. That it was so easy to pull me back in. That he could yank the cord and I'd run back willingly.

I hated that a year later, I could sink into my old feelings by just one glance from Jace Boland, like I'd never even left at all.

"How was it?" he asked. "The trip."

I cleared my throat, creating a gap between our steps. "Good, really good. I actually only stayed in Paris for five months, then moved on to Italy and Dublin."

"Oh shit, seriously? Tell me about that."

So I did, freely and openly. It felt like a breath of fresh air, a sense of normalcy between us. He asked questions with genuine interest, his glossy eyes wide with sparkle. He... He cared.

He cared.

That was the fucking problem.

His laugh carried two streets over when I told him about me getting thrown out of the Louvre for taking photos of Van Gogh's painting.

"It was an honest mistake," I defended, placing a wounded hand over my heart. "How was I supposed to know I couldn't take a photo of a photo?"

"A painting isn't a photo, Blu," he wiped a teary eye, snorting in amusement. "It's art."

"A photo can't be art?"

"A painting and a photograph are different."

"Oh don't even," I challenged. "Weren't you the one who told me that beauty is all around, if you only looked for it?"

His eyes softened. "How'd you remember that?"

I decided to ignore that comment. I knew it would lead to something more sincere, and I was quite enjoying our witty banter for once.

"Well I personally think my own photograph of Van Gogh's painting to be beautiful," I jested, crossing my arms. "It might even be better than the original."

"So, you've been taking photos then?"

I nodded. "Tons," then pulled out the digital camera from my purse. "Do you want to see them?"

His smile widened. "I really do."

We crossed the park and sat on a picnic bench. I had no idea how far we were from Deaks, but I didn't care. Being with Jace filled a vacant hole inside of me; I began to think that would never change.

Several minutes passed of Jace looking through my camera, commenting on the scenery of plains in Dublin, the streets of Paris and different foods I tested on my travels.

We laughed at my embarrassing selfies (luckily there were only a few), and he grilled me by saying, "Why didn't you just use your phone like a regular person?"

"Why would I use my phone when I had a legit camera?"

His hand tapped my knee, sending a shock of pleasure up my spine for a single moment. "Classic, stubborn Blu."

"I think I looked quite pretty," I beamed, allowing a smidgen of confidence to shine through.

He stopped pressing the advance arrow and held my camera still, chancing a glance my way. "You always look pretty, darling."

Darling.

Darling.

$\mathcal{D\ A\ R\ L\ I\ N\ G}.$

God, I could hear it in every language, every fucking accent, but the way it rolled off of Jace's tongue would never compare to anything else.

He owned that word, I remember thinking last year. *He still does.*

His phone rang, Bryce's caller ID announced aloud, but he didn't budge, his eyes glued to me.

"Are you not going to answer?"

"Absolutely not," he released sternly. "Not with you right in front of me."

"Got something to hide?"

He shook his head, dropping it low. "Not in the ways you think."

I pushed his shoulder playfully. "Always so cryptic, you."

But before I could retract my arm, he grabbed my hand, placing it in his.

I remained frozen, unable to move as he circled his thumb against my palm, weeding his fingers through mine and letting out a long exhale.

"Please hold my hand," he whispered, almost breathless.

My voice was shaky. My pulse erratic. "Why?"

A quiet sniffle escaped his nose as he intertwined our fingers, placing his left hand over the bundle of ours.

"Because —" he began, his voice breaking. He wouldn't look at me.

My body willed a movement, but succumbed to paralysis. I didn't know what to say, didn't know what was happening. But his emotions bled onto me, whatever they were, and stopped me from breathing.

"Because if you touch me, I'll be okay. I'll know you're still in there — that…" He turned to me, his eyes bloodshot and glazed, "That one year later, you still have love for me."

    I stared at him, my heart pumping out of my chest, begging to mend his own. Out of all the things he could've said, all the emotions he could have felt… This, this I could not predict.

    I remember Blu Henderson, the broken shell of a girl I used to be over one year ago, crying in her room over this very boy who grabbed hold of my hand currently.

    I remember her sobbing in the arms of Fawn because Jace couldn't embrace me – couldn't embrace me because he was the one who caused my pain.

    There were moments of utter heartbreak that tormented me through my travels, moments that found me in my sleep. Promises he made never to hurt me, but bled me dry until the very end.

    He didn't say goodbye.

    He didn't contact me.

    He abandoned me, and now –

    Now, he wished for me to have love for him.

    I wanted to scream in his face, to wipe away his tears and plaster them all over my cheeks because that is where they belonged.

    I loved him viciously, my entire being stripped raw by his essence. I would've done anything for him; he knew that. He took advantage of that.

    And he still continued to do so. To play on my emotions. To see if I would run back all to boost his ego.

    One.

    Year.

    Later.

A Hue of Blu

Marie-France Leger

I released my hold on his, swallowing the truth and spitting out the lie. "I don't."

His hand opened and closed a few times, as if feeling the loss of my absence.

How does it feel, Jace?
How does it fucking feel?

"Then pretend," he whispered through a cracking pitch. "Pretend for me, Blu."

Pretend.

Pretend.

It was all fucking pretend.

Nothing was ever real, and he was okay with that.

As long as I was pretending.

Pretending to love him, to need him, to want him –

Just as he did.

I shook my head, moving away from the bench, forcing myself to my feet and ran.

I fucking ran rogue.

I ran even though I knew he wasn't chasing me, because he never would.

It would always be me.

Days, months, years later –

It would always be me.

The wind howled in my ears, a chill frosting my bones. Not because of the cold, but because I let him in. Somehow, someway, he tugged on my vulnerability once again and swallowed me whole. He opened me up, allowed me to feel, and it wasn't real.

It was pretend.

I rang Fawn once I cleared the open street, hiding behind an alley wall next to a pharmacy.

"Hello? Blu?"

"I'm near Adelaide, by a Subway and barber shop. Can you come meet me?"

I could hear Bryce's groans through the phone. "Yes, yes I'm coming. Are you coming, Bryce?"

"Yes!" He shouted at the same time as I said, "No!"

Fawn respected my wishes and hung up the call, asking me to turn on my phone location.

When she reached me I hugged her tight, explaining everything that happened, then called Carter before Ubering home.

Now we were back to this moment.

Present day.

Sitting on a velvet sofa across a middle-aged woman with chestnut hair and bronzed skin.

"Why am I here?" I reiterated my psychologist's question, blinking away the flashbacks of Jace from last week. The panic attack I had on my bathroom floor. The cuts I almost made.

Almost.

She nodded for me to begin, leaning back into her loveseat.

"Because I thought I healed," I admitted, turning away from the mirror to my left.

My thoughts unintentionally wavered to *him*.

My comfort.

My pain.

"Honestly, Stacy…" I exhaled, cursing the reality of my life. How I'd travelled to three different places across the world and still wound up back in the same position that I was last year.

Fake growth.

Fake healing.

I'd wasted three-hundred and sixty-five days chasing a fake dream of being fake happy.

Fake. **Fake**. *Fake.*

"Yes, Beatrice?" she provoked, her voice soothing and levelled.

I wished so badly that I could mirror her solid exterior, her calm demeanour and straight posture.

But instead I released a cynical goddamn laugh and declared the truth. "I'm still really fucking fucked up."

Age 23
Jace

Present

My mom always told me never to let success get to my head, and failure to my heart.

Well, I'd been failing too much to succeed. My heart wasn't capable of success.

Over the past year, I worked two jobs. One was at a contracting company that ran me dry for too little pay, the other was at a coffee shop and every regular cursed me for being too slow.

Too fucking slow.

Imagine how many orders you got per minute, a long criteria of ingredients that needed to be stirred and whipped within twenty seconds and I —

Was too —

FUCKING SLOW.

If I learned anything this year it was that people really loved to judge what they didn't understand.

I guess I was one of those people, because when Blu ran away from me four months ago, I failed to make the connection that she was no longer the same girl I'd fucked with before graduation.

People did change, of course they did.

But how?

At what point did your brain and heart overlap and come to that conclusion — that you needed fixing, that you needed help?

After graduation [and Blu left the country], I sort of checked out. Grades weren't an issue for me

A Hue of Blu — Marie-France Leger

anymore, so there was nothing tying me to responsibility.

I didn't have a job, no, just got the occasional winning from soccer bets and still lived at home. *Where was the responsibility, Jace?*

Where was the ambition?

Three months of nothing went by. I stalked Blu's socials ever so often, repeating to myself that she was finally happy [without me] and I had to let her move on in peace.

Will tried to land me an internship at his company but that didn't pan out because I had zero fucking experience and all jobs ever wanted was a shiny golden star on your resume that read: *"HEY! LOOK AT ME! I WORK ON WALL STREET AND OWN THREE RENTAL PROPERTIES AT THE AGE OF TWENTY-TWO!"*

Impossible. Unrealistic. But it was the world we lived in.

Experience = Success.

There was little room to grow because you were expected to be *grown*, to be mature – to erase any part of you that was incompetent.

But imagine that's all you ever felt; day in day out, you hated the person you became so much you never felt worthy of stepping out of the shadows.

You were just one with them.

Lost, grey, mute.

It was almost better that way, having loneliness on my side. Silence became my friend. Silence never blamed me for the people I'd hurt.

My birthday was three weeks after graduation.

I think I was depressed.

Scott told me I should let out my feelings, but I couldn't even place them. Numbness was kind to me, and paralyzing.

So very paralyzing.

The worst part was I didn't even know what was truly wrong. It's like every horrible emotion I'd ever felt metastasized into a fucking cancer that attacked my brain, probing my insides every second I was awake.

I spent my birthday combing through job sites, hoping that someone would miraculously come across the resume Will crafted for me. It was the only good thing he'd done in years.

Probably cause I was depressed and couldn't do it myself.

As I slipped through the cracks, trudging my way through life every second of every day, my brothers became more prevalent players in my life.

Funny that, that when you stopped giving too much of a fuck, the fuck crawled to you. No finger lifting needed. So why bother trying?

That was the mentality that got me fired from the coffee shop. That was the mentality that pushed me to quit the contracting job.

That was the mentality that cost me Blu.

She was always so accepting of the affection I gave, *the lack of it,* rather.

God, that fucking trip to Winter's Lodge. It still messed with my head every time I thought about her stripping down, begging for company, hoping for someone to listen – not just someone, but *me*. Me. She wanted ME.

And I didn't give that to her.

I left her there, just like I did at graduation.

A Hue of Blu

Marie-France Leger

I couldn't say goodbye, I just couldn't. She'd grown on me too much to lose. So if I didn't say goodbye, I didn't lose her. No. She'd still be around, accessible… Ready.

The closure was tough, because there was none. When you see someone on a regular basis, they start to become a habitual part of your existence. Like, drinking coffee every morning or sleeping at night.

She was just there. And if she wasn't, something was missing.

I never liked to lose things.

I obsessed over what was gone, even if never really mattered much to begin with.

So I went to Mel, told her that a part of me felt empty when Blu left, and she set me up with her friend Lily.

I'd never heard of Lily before; apparently Mel had met her over New Years at an art show. She was a petite blonde with bright blue eyes and a vibrant smile. As soon as I saw her picture, I knew she'd be a good distraction.

But that's all that anything ever amounted to - a pleasant pastime.

Lily and I went on a few dates, but she was just kind of… boring? I guess? Fuck, everyone was so disinteresting nowadays.

Everyone except Blu.

It was a breath of fresh air when she approached me, when she peeked inside my brain and extracted elements that I never dared show.

I didn't compare anyone to Blu because no two people were the same.

[I didn't compare anyone to Blu because she was incomparable].

It became apparent to me that my tastes had changed, that they catered to Blu's essence more than anything else when I asked Lily what she did for a living.

"I'm a model," she gloated, a wide grin stretched across her face. "I was at the art show as Victor Chaffron's muse."

A muse.

Imagine being interesting enough, valued enough, beautiful enough to be that important to an artist.

One can only wish.

And that's all I ever did while spending my time with her.

I wished that I could be up to standard physically. Some may say I was.

I say I wasn't.

I wished that I could attend the art shows and stare at portraits of the beautiful Lily Kaiser.

I couldn't.

Because she was the muse, the model, the mold of perfection. Front row, glimmering like a star.

But I wanted the moon, the night sky and everything Blu[e].

The artist behind the scene; the talented mind that created the muse. I wanted the director, the designer, the *painter* – not the bloody fucking canvas.

Blu made people feel important, made people feel confident.

I didn't want the end result, I wanted the rough draft, the outlines, the Blu[e]prints.

For once, just once, I wanted something real. Someone to make me feel. Someone who understood what it felt like to be a jester, not a king. Someone who wore a coat of armour when underneath, they were as brittle as an apple seed.

So when I saw Blu four months ago, wasted out of my mind at Deaks, I caved. I fucking caved because I *craved* every inch of the feeling that she gave me once, and I thought that if there was still love left in her, we could do it again.

We could do us again.
But she ran.
And I died.
Four months later –
I was still dying.

***

One Week Later

After Bryce told me he'd been talking to Fawn again, the world rerouted itself to the past. I couldn't *not* ask about her.

"How is Blu doing?"

He shrugged, increasing the weight on his squat set. "How should I know?"

I took a sip of water, ignoring the groans and moans of the meatheads at the gym.

"You're fucking Fawn again, aren't you?"

"What the hell gave you that idea?"

"You said you were talking," I secured the clamps against the plates, "So I assumed."

He settled on the bench and curved his fingers around the silver rod. "We're talking as friends, Jace. She isn't interested anymore."

"Bullshit."

"Dude, I'm not either."

I laughed out loud. "Bullshit times two."

"Why is that so hard to believe?" He began his bench press as I spotted him, wondering why he was lying to my face right now.

"How is it possible that you go from liking each other, to dating, to not speaking, to now being friends?"

He didn't say anything as his arms shook, grunting in response.

"I mean, can you even go back to normal after that? I don't think you can."

After a few more reps, he released the bar and let out a long exhale, slapping a hand on his chest. "You can if you're mature," he let out two more tired breaths, "Why do you care about how Blu's doing anyway?"

I gritted my teeth. "I can't care about someone I had history with?"

"No, I mean, sure. But you guys didn't even date and you were kind of an asshole to her."

"Asshole how?"

I knew how. I knew all the ways how. But I wanted to hear my best friend say it. I couldn't help it. Rubbing salt in my wounds became my favourite hobby.

He narrowed his eyes. "You know how."

Can't blame a guy for trying.

"I think she's talking to someone, I don't know –"

"*What?*" I snapped. "Who?"

Damn.

I did not expect to get that heated so quickly.

My jealously escalated to a burning point even before he continued his sentence. Scattered images of men I saw her associate with in passing, in the halls,

A Hue of Blu

Marie-France Leger

on her Instagram stories, all flashed in my brain as I filed a list of potential partners that she could be interested in.

"Who is it?" I pushed, curling my fingers around the cold metal bar.

"Again," he rested on his back once more, preparing for his final set, "How am I supposed to know?"

"Well how do you know she's talking to someone?"

"Christ Jace, you're sounding like a crazy ex right now."

"I've got to make a call," I said, storming away from the gym mats and into the locker room.

I could hear Bryce yell after me, "*I need you to spot me!*" But I ignored him and dialled Blu.

"*Please be the same number, please be the same number*," I muttered just as she picked up within two rings.

"Hello?"

I'll be damned. "Hey," I rubbed my forehead, pacing back and forth, "Hey Blu."

"Um," her voice cracked. She knew it was me. "Who is this?"

Her and her games.

I fucking missed it.

"Jace," I replied, biting back the smile.

Just as I opened my mouth to say something else, the line went dead.

She hung up on me.

She –

Blu hung up on me.

I gripped my case, staring at her contact name in my phone with a hung jaw, blinking in disbelief.

Blu. Hung. Up. On. Me.

But then my cell began to vibrate and her caller ID filled the screen, pushing me to answer in one ring.

"I'm sorry, that was rude," she apologized, clearing her throat.

"I…" *How the fuck am I supposed to navigate this?* "I probably deserved that."

"You think?"

"Can we please not –" I began, but stopped myself before she could end the call once more. "Can we just start over? I want to catch up. Coffee?"

A moment of silence. "We caught up already."

"When?"

"Four months ago."

"Hm?"

"At the park," she huffed in clear exasperation. "Do you not recall or?"

I caught myself smiling and for the life of me, I couldn't understand why. She was pissed I was calling. Probably pissed that she even answered herself. But she couldn't stay away. Meaning that night, when she said she didn't have love for me anymore, she lied.

We were both such good liars.

"Honestly, I've got a pretty foggy memory," I softened my tone, "If you want to recount the events that transpired I'd be more than happy to listen over coffee."

I knew she was trying hard to stay mad at me. Her seconds of silence were a tell-tale sign of that. But I was an expert at breaking down those walls. It was my second favourite hobby.

"I still hate coffee," she deadpanned, "But where?"

My brain screamed in victory. "Aroma at York, say, an hour?"

"See you then," and the line went dead.

But this time, I wasn't mad about it.

This time, I had something to look forward to.

This time –

The locker room door burst open and in walked Bryce, his forehead red as a fucking cranberry.

"What the hell happen –"

He grabbed my shirt, pointing to an evident injury. *Ohhhh.*

Shit.

Laughter bubbled in my throat as he released his grip, scolding me.

"I told you I needed a fucking spot."

Age 25
Blu

Present

"Please give me one good reason why you're meeting with him again."

Carter's annoyance reverberated through me, instantly dampening my mood. But he was right. He was always right.

After I finally settled into my new place, I decided to give Hamish Cartwright a call. Even if Jeremy, my momentary Irish lad, was lying about a potential job position. What did I have to lose?

As it turned out, the job really was legit but the position had been filled a few weeks before I decided to call. It was disappointing, but he asked me to send over some photos as Jeremy ended up telling him about our little encounter.

I did exactly that, and Hamish ended up loving them. So much so that he set me up with one of his Canadian colleagues who was local to the area, and got me an interview with Toronto Pix magazine travel blog.

Parker Mickelson, the head journalist under "TTC Travels" called me in a month ago to tour the streets with him, taking photos of things I deemed relevant to the public.

"My opinion actually matters?" I queried, curious about the objectivity when it came to press articles.

"Hun, your opinion is irrelevant. It's us journalists that can't document bias." He seemed to survey my blue hair as he said, "Photos are not a problem. Now go snap some shots while I order us lattes."

God, what was with everyone and coffee?

But I did exactly that and by the grace of some celestial fucking being, I landed a position under Denise and Courtney, two of the lead photographers at TTC Travels.

If I was being honest, my job thus far had just been beverage runs and organizing camera equipment, but I had my own desk – and my own desk meant I had a job – and having a job meant I had a purpose and I wasn't just cruising through life abusing my dead dad's inheritance.

What a fucking sentence.

But despite all the loss, my psychologist pushed me to work on appreciation.

"You have so many things to be grateful for," she'd told me.

I rolled my eyes. What a birthday card thing to say.

"My dad's dead, my mom might as well be, I spent the past year of my life travelling and ended up back in the same spot I used to be in, Stacy. In love with a boy who reminded me that I was hard to love."

"Why do you think that is?" she asked.

A stupid. Fucking. Question.

"Aren't you supposed to tell me that? Is that not what I pay you for?"

… Yeah. I was a bit of a bitch in the beginning, I could admit. But wasn't everyone who needed healing? Did we all not find confessing our problems to some stranger not the least bit odd?

"There's a lot to unpack in what you just said," Stacy sipped her tea, eyeing me like a baby bird.

I scoffed. "Try living with the trauma."

"Try facing it, Beatrice."

She wiped the smug smile right off my face with that comment. A bit of me was taken aback at her words; as if she knew the only way that I'd finally listen was if she put me in my place.

Maybe therapy wasn't so bad after all.

So I continued to attend the weekly sessions, but she never said anything like that again.

Two weeks ago, I asked her why she used that tone with me. "And why did you never use it again?"

She simply replied, "Because you enjoyed it."

"And you're depriving me of what I enjoy? Are you not supposed to help me?"

"Precisely why I refuse to speak with you in that manner again."

"Why?"

She leaned forward, her palms pressing against her grey pleated pants. "Beatrice, you're used to getting what you want, not what you need. Because you don't chase after kindness, you chase after challenges."

"So you challenged me," I glared, a bit wounded. I felt like an experiment.

She shook her head calmly, fishing for a paper in her black folder. When she handed it, my eyes scanned over the long questionnaire that had no heading or title, just...

"What is this?" I asked, crumpling the sheet.

"Homework."

"I'm not in school anymore."

"No, but you've taken on some responsibility by coming here, by choosing growth. I'd like to learn a little more about you since you don't seem too keen on telling me much right now."

I opened my mouth to combat her, but she was honestly right. Trusting anyone, regardless of their professional status, was tough for me. I'm sure I wasn't the only person on this planet who remained sewn shut during therapy sessions.

So I took the paper and shoved it in my coat pocket, forgetting about it until now as I threw on my beige trench and fished it out.

"You didn't answer me," Carter said over Facetime. I completely forgot he was still there.

I silently skimmed over the list of questions, typed out in neat font. It was too much work for me now; I'd get to it later.

"What did you ask again?"

His tone was laced with irritation. "Why are you meeting up with Jace again? Do you seriously want to rewrite what happened last year?"

"I'm not a writer," I jibed, then tapped my phone screen. "I got to go, Carter. I'll update you."

"Don't," he practically barked, ending the call.

"Well goodbye to you too," I grimaced, speaking to air.

His exit stung, but I couldn't blame him. My relationship with Jace had been a rollercoaster ride from the beginning. If someone asked me to list a timeline of events that occurred between us, I'd truly blank. Because everything that happened blurred into one thing and one thing only –

Trouble.

As I walked out my front door, sliding my key into the lock and turning it sideways, I realized that I had a thirst for trouble.

I mean, why else would I be walking to Aroma at 4:47pm meeting up with the man who put me in a goddamn psychologist's chair?

A thirst for trouble? Maybe.

An unquenchable thirst for Jace Boland? Definitely.

***

"I went ahead and ordered you my usual."

Jace was already sitting down, his hair a tad shorter than when I'd last seen him; trimmed neatly on the sides, but generously wispy.

He wore a black long sleeve, his muscles stretching against the fabric and black button earrings to match.

Memories of us at the campus coffee shop flashed in my brain; a time when we were just getting to know each other.

A time that felt much easier than this.

Who knew he'd ever be this important?

I wondered then, as I slid into the wooden chair across him, if he still lacked that sense of importance within his family. He hadn't spoken about them at all in our last encounter, mind you he was wasted and I – well, I was trying to prove that he didn't mean much anymore.

A pity, being so deceiving to even my own brain. *Such a hypocrite,* I thought. *Such a liar.*

My eyes travelled to the dark liquid in the white cup. "Isn't your usual order two shots of espresso?"

He chuckled. "No, it's a latte with oat milk."

I ran my finger along the curve of the drink, pinching the plastic lid. "Interesting."

"You could say thank you," he suggested, pushing the cup closer to me. "I think that's the polite thing to do."

I didn't ask for this, I wanted to say. "You're right, thank you."

God, would I always harbour such resentment towards him? It was my choice to be here, *my* fucking decision. I *wanted* to be here. Why did I act like I didn't?

"I wasn't sure if you wanted something to eat but," he pulled out a rice-crispy treat from his pocket, "I got you this anyway."

"Oh." His hand touched mine as he pressed it into my palm. The warmth burned. "That was kind."

"Yeah," he smiled.

"Yeah." I didn't. I placed the treat down.

He cleared his throat. "Look, Blu, I don't want things to be awkward between us."

I pushed my shoulders forward, biting back the attitude. But it was no use. It was bound to come out regardless.

"You always say that after something awkward happens between us."

"What happened between us?"

"What didn't?" I combatted, already feeling the tipping point of anger approaching.

"Alright," he began unwrapping the rice-crispy, splitting its gooey texture in half. "I've come to the realization that every time we talk about us, we end up fighting. So let's talk about anything but," he offered me the torn piece, and surprisingly, I took it.

"Cheers," I said, nipping at the crunchy coating.

For thirty minutes, he caught me up on his year; all his work troubles, his lack of motivation, *Lily*.

"When did you guys end?" I sipped on the latte, not quite enjoying the nutty taste, but it was bearable.

He snorted in amusement. "Of course you'd pick out that part from everything."

"You were in a relationship," I reminded him. He seemed to forget that. "That's a big deal."

"Is it?"

"I mean, kind of."

"Aren't you talking to someone right now?"

How did he know that? My cheeks heated. *How did I forget to mention that?*

Kade was a junior editor at TTC Travels, working underneath Parker. A week and a half ago, we'd bumped into each other while I carried boxes of film tape out into the hall.

"My bad, I wasn't looking," he'd said, like every start to a rom-com movie ever.

"Clearly."

My hostility apparently turned him on, because two days later he kept "accidently bumping into me" on purpose.

"Have dinner with me tonight," he persisted. "I'm not taking no for an answer."

It was the fact that he had a decent career with room to grow, some facial hair [that Jace lacked] and an endearing smile that pushed me to agree. He wasn't ugly, he was safe.

That's what I needed, right? Stability?

Needed.

Not wanted.

Stacy's observation battered my skull.

While we chatted over wine and Italian, I realized I was relatively calm and non-threatened by the fact we were on a date. It wasn't something I was used to; boys asking me out because they wanted to get to know me, not just sleep with me.

But Kade Clement was a twenty-six year old man with his shit together. He held every door open, picked me up from my apartment, and never insisted on getting too fresh while leaning in close.

We kissed one time, *one time*, and I was the one who initiated it.

That was three days ago in the break room. He still had peppermint tea lingering on his tongue.

Although the kiss was swift, I decided to tell Fawn about it, blanking on the fact she'd recently rekindled her friendship with Bryce.

In that moment, I put the pieces together.

"I'm assuming Bryce told you that," I guessed, though he solidified my assumption with a nod.

"Figured."

He stared at me narrowly. "Does it bother you?"

"Does what bother me?"

"That I know you're talking to someone."

"Why would that bother me?"

He shrugged, "You can talk to me about other guys. It's not weird for me."

I scoffed, "Thank you for your permission, but it's nothing to ride home about."

"So it's not serious?" His eyes flickered with emotion; whether he was pleased or displeased, I couldn't tell.

"No, I mean, we've been hanging out at work and stuff but it's not really anything."

"Work," he released, "Tell me about that. You didn't have a job last time we spoke."

And just like before, I let the words tumble out of my mouth because it felt good to talk to him, to show him that I was capable of moving forward with my life.

Maybe a part of me wanted to prove that to myself and I was using Jace as a mirror. *Look at me doing shadow-work.* Something Stacy would be proud of.

Jace was relatively interested, but I could tell something was wrong. He didn't ask nearly as many questions as he did when I divulged about my photography and travels four months ago.

"What's on your mind?" I prodded. "You seem off."

His gaze was fixated on his hands, stretching out his fingers and flexing his knuckles. "That obvious, huh?"

I felt the urge to touch him, comfort him, soothe his pain. But every time that feeling bubbled inside of me, I'd acted on it, and that never ended well.

"You just seem so set in life," he shook his head, lifting his eyes to mine. "I can't even relate to you anymore."

"Set in life?" I could've laughed. "I'm in fucking therapy because I have no idea what I'm doing."

This time, I did chuckle. But it was only when I watched his gaze soften that I realized what I'd revealed.

Weakness.

Frailty.

The incapability to cope with my own emotions.

"Why is being in therapy a bad thing?" he questioned, but the tone of his voice already threw my sanity into a spiral.

"Let's talk about something else." He opened his mouth to contend but I interjected.

"You said you can't relate to me anymore, but clearly you can. I'm still the same."

He nodded, pressing his lips together in acceptance of the fact I didn't want to address therapy. I appreciated that.

"You look different, Blu. You've lived a lot more than I have in the last year."

"You could've too."

"I didn't know what to live for," he released, immediately clipping his mouth closed.

Oh.

Oh.

My back hit the ladder of the wooden chair as I stared at him, unable to look away now that he'd admitted his struggle.

I'd been so wrapped up in my own world, my own thoughts, my own everything that I failed to see his existence beyond me. He had a life of his own. A life that was completely disconnected from mine, and entirely connected to his.

Had I been this blind to his own pain because I refused to see a human underneath it? Did I deem my own problems more important than his?

Distractions are what saved me.

But we were different people.

Maybe what healed me, hurt him.

Maybe what killed me, strengthened him.

"You didn't tell me that," I whispered, swallowing the bitter taste of my own selfishness.

The corner of his lip lifted into a half-smile, but it didn't wipe away the sadness that lingered.

"That isn't something you usually start a conversation with," he said, "But um, yeah. Yeah, I've just been kind of lost."

I leaned forward, intertwining my fingers. "I wouldn't have guessed."

He scrunched his eyebrows, crossing his arms. "How come?"

"I don't know," I shrugged, "You're always so calm. You always seem to know what to say and when you don't, you just kind of… You just, remain silent."

"Sometimes silence is the best form of conversation."

This.

This right here is why I fell for Jace Boland.

That one sentence alone.

The way he understood me, the way he read my mind. His deep introspection, the reservation of expression.

He didn't desire for anyone to figure him out, he liked it that way. Whether it was calculated or not, he was the epitome of everything I could have ever wanted –

Not needed.

Wanted.

Maybe I liked the fact that he didn't explode with emotions every five seconds, or at least the fact he kept it controlled.

Maybe that's why I begged for reactions, greedy for something more than he delivered because silence was sometimes the conversation he preferred.

I was the firecracker. He lit the spark.

I was the puppet. He was the puppeteer.

A Hue of Blu

Marie-France Leger

I was the colour. He was the hue.
He was the hue.
My fucking hue.

My fingers travelled to his side of the table. I opened a palm and allowed him to rest his atop mine.

A transference of emotions passed between us as we looked into each other's eyes. That's what he needed right now. No words.

Just my company.

"Do you want to have a silent conversation with me somewhere else?" I asked, braving the potential rejection.

But he didn't say no.

In fact, he pushed out of his chair and met my side, tangling his fingers in mine before we left the café.

You could probably guess where we went, what we did.

The lingering kisses and almost dates.

The fighting fueled by too much emotion [on my end], and the lack thereof [on Jace's].

The blissful months that repaired my brokenness.

The pathetic months that shattered it.

Because whatever fire we had –

It always turned to ash.

And I realized since the day I met Jace, we found our way into each other's bodies, but not each other's hearts. For a while, it melted the ice that lodged there, but it was never enough to keep me warm.

And it never would be.

No matter how much I shivered and begged –

Some things were just doomed from the start.

Age 25
Blu

Present

I ended things with Kade three weeks after Jace and I hooked up again.

There wasn't much to end, honestly, but there was a time where I would've continued seeing Kade and loving Jace all to woo my ego.

With Jace, my world orbited around his.

No one could penetrate it.

Not even the nicest of guys, the kindest of hearts, the best for me.

I was addicted to hurting myself being with him, pushing aside all the things that made me whole and healthy.

I lost weight while we were together because who would want to be with someone heavier than them?

I stopped seeing Stacy because I couldn't face the confrontation she'd give me, knowing I crawled back to the pain that put me there to begin with.

Carter and I were on the rocks since I decided to meet Jace for coffee again. It was his breaking point I think. I gave him every reason to break.

Fawn stuck by me, but she wasn't happy. Like every good friend, even if they didn't approve of your decisions, they wouldn't leave you.

I would've left me.

I think the best parts of me did.

The irony, that the people you cared about most were always the ones to leave you in pieces.

A colleague from work, Marcus, was Kade's proof-reader, and we'd gotten to know each other over the course of a couple weeks. Because he only had to work when Kade submitted his edits, he did some of the servant work like me sometimes.

On a coffee run, he'd asked me, "What went wrong between you two?"

The hot cups burned my palm. "I didn't realize you two were so close."

"I've been assisting Kade for months, Bee."

Everyone at work knew me as Beatrice (or Bee). Blu only existed if Jace's name followed suit.

I guess I morphed into someone new wherever I went, but that didn't change who I was to the core. Not while Blu still lived inside of me.

"I got back with my…" *Ex?* He wasn't my ex, we never dated. Even in the times that we spent with each other, we were never really together. To this day, I still had no idea what to call him, so I was grateful when Marcus interrupted my thought.

"Gotcha. Can't compete with a good ex nowadays."

But was Jace considered good? Did he treat me right? Or was I just patiently waiting for the day that he would?

"It's not like that," I added before I could shut my trap. "It's complicated."

"Well for what it's worth, thank you for not bringing that complication to Kade. He's a good guy."

"Why don't you date him?"

He snorted in amusement. "Believe me, Bee, I've tried."

After that conversation, I decided to approach Kade with a sincere apology. Never in my life did I feel like I had to do that, but hurting people became uncomfortable. Maybe because I was hurting, and I knew how it felt. No one deserved to be the second option.

I wish I realized that sooner.

"Can we be friends?" I suggested, though I knew it was a long shot. His answer was just as I expected.

"We weren't serious, Bee. It's okay." He even chuckled. "No hard feelings."

No hard feelings.

Meaning no feelings.

Because how could there not be hard feelings if he didn't fall hard?

That conversation led me to one with Jace, where I sat on his lap after he'd fucked me senseless, and whispered, "Do you think there were hard feelings between us when we ended the first time?"

He furrowed his brows. "What do you mean?"

"Like, were you upset or…"

"I mean," he raked his fingers through sweaty hair, "Yeah. For a bit. Nothing I couldn't get over, though."

Nothing I couldn't get over.

Because he was capable of getting over me.

I took a few days of space from that conversation, but over the duration of a few weeks, we'd been getting into more and more arguments just like that one.

I don't think I was happy.

I don't think I ever was.

But if I made him care about me, then I did something right.

A Hue of Blu — Marie-France Leger

We'd been apart for over a year and he still came back. That counted for something.

I wasn't forgettable.

I was worthy.

But over time, I realized that maybe, I was just a pawn in his life that he had complete control over. That every other person he seemed to care about – his cocky friends, his brothers, his dad – they all shelved him for rainy days.

Maybe I was his rainy day.

And that hurt.

That really fucking hurt.

Because where I carried clouds and wind and precipitation, he carried the sun, the stars and the sky.

Yeah, that's what he was.

My sun.

And I was his rain.

I was his fucking rain.

Age 23
Jace

Present

When Blu and I were good, we were really fucking good. But when we weren't...

Drag me to Hell.

That's what the last four months of our life had been, how it'd felt like.

On and off, on and off –

Up and down, up and down.

I was turning twenty-four in a little over a month and I had no intention of continuing this vicious cycle, one I knew I should've cut off the night we first slept together again, but I was thinking with my dick.

Just like I'd done the first time around.

I blamed it on my inability to change, but that just wasn't true.

The games were fun. Winning each other back was euphoric. Our relationship fed on my jealousy, my ego and sadly, my pride.

In a way, I loved Blu.

The thought of her being with someone else, the thought of *losing* her sliced a cord somewhere deep in my heart.

One night, she really was prepared to cut things off. I saw it in her eyes. The exhaustion, the hurt. I caused some of it, I knew that. I wanted to repair the damage.

"Kade wouldn't do this," she shook and cried, "He wouldn't keep placing doubts in my head, not like you."

We were out at the bowling alley and I bumped into a girl who Blu felt clearly threatened by. I don't think I intentionally made her jealous, but the fact Kade's presence loomed over our relationship was enough to warrant a flirt.

"I can't do this anymore," she snapped, picking up her phone. Her finger hovered over Kade's contact name.

My walls fell apart right in front of her. My mind spiralled.

"Don't," I released, pleaded.

"Don't what?"

I thought of losing my brothers to age, to maturity and differences that were out of my control; losing my father to something I clearly could not provide – a bond that was broken [or never really there].

A tear fell down my cheek. Crying was easier when you didn't think about the act of it. The weakness it represented.

"Don't fall in love with him, Blu," I wrapped her in my arms, feeling the weight of past burdens building up in my chest. "Please don't fall for anyone but me, please."

"Jace," she pulled back to look at me, her brown eyes gleaming with empathy.

My soft girl.

My Blu.

I pressed my lips featherlight against hers, allowing the cool tear to stamp her cheek as well as mine. "I'm selfishly in love with you."

After my admission [and plea], she cut things off with the editor guy Kade. I thought we had a real shot, I did, thought she was serious.

But she wasn't.

And maybe I wasn't either.

Time after time, she just kept getting mad at me over little things and I was sick of feeling like I wasn't good enough to please her.

Some days I went to bed wondering what I did wrong, and other days I was just too exasperated to deal with it.

Maybe I wasn't the best lover, but I'd done what I could. She needed to work things out on her own, so I ended it.

I fucking ended it.

Actually…

I'd done that a few times.

But I always kept running back; always felt like something was missing without her.

I think she felt the same way, that's why she let me in even if I didn't deserve it.

We were almost worse than we were before. She quite literally said, "I hate you" when we were fucking.

She told me she hated me.

While I was inside of her.

Next level shit, man. Next level shit.

I convinced her to revisit her psychologist, since she'd ghosted her for months when we got together again. For the life of me, I couldn't understand why. Doctors were supposed to help. It's like she didn't want that while she was with me, as if she deemed our connection unsalvageable from the start.

Eventually Blu filled out that questionnaire assigned to her months back and sent it to Stacy. She wasn't ready to face her yet, so she just emailed the results.

"I have no idea what this is even for," she'd told me. I just glanced at her and shrugged, letting her twirl her fingers anxiously in my bed.

A few days later Stacy had emailed her back and told her to make an appointment. Apparently it was serious.

But we'd gotten into a fight just two days before her appointment. That was last week.

I hadn't spoken to her since.

"Should I text her?" I asked Mel.

We were walking through Prix since Mel had another art showing, admiring the new portraits on display. Well, she was anyway. I was typing out a message to Blu.

Mel snagged my phone and shoved it in her tits. "Enough."

"If I were a worse man, I'd grab it back," I scolded, accepting my defeat.

"Even the best of men would kill for an opportunity to grab my boobs," she teased, but there was only bite to her tone.

"I shouldn't text her then."

"No, leave her alone." She waved at a couple who entered the gallery, hand in hand, and offered two flutes of champagne. "Hi, nice to see you Earl. Tina."

They left and I laughed. "You aren't a fucking server, why do you keep pawning off champagne?"

"It's hospitable."

"This gallery isn't your home," I contended.

"It will be," she said, dragging me away from the crowd. "Carson's retiring."

"What?" I couldn't conceal my surprise, my eyes growing by the second. "Since when? He's only, what, fifty-four?"

She squared her shoulders. "He makes enough money with his artists' commission pieces. He said he wants to pass the gallery torch to me since I make him the most money."

"Oh yeah?" I smirked, knowing she said that to boost her self-esteem. "Not because you're family friends or anything?"

"Of course not, why would it be that?" But her lips lifted in amusement. "This is big, Jace. I could be a business owner. I need people to like me."

I placed a gentle hand against her arm. "Everyone likes you, Mel."

"Well, aren't you just the sweetest –" Her attention immediately switched to someone behind me as she swatted my touch away. "Get your paws off me, I have to mingle – Hi! Bella, hi, *how are…*"

Her voice faded into the background noise of everyone else's chatter. I snagged a champagne glass from the marble table and did another round of the gallery, halting my pace in front of the "Controlling Chaos" painting I'd seen so long ago with Blu. *Surprised it's still here,* I thought. *Simpler times.*

I squinted at the intersecting circles, the lines that represented the turbulence of life and the untouched soul in the middle of it all, protected by a hue.

The more I looked at the tiny dot in the middle of chaos, the more I resonated with it.

A Hue of Blu

Marie-France Leger

Art was never really my thing, but I could understand why people thought deeply when looking at paintings.

They signified stories, memories, chapters in people's lives that made no sense to anyone else but the muse.

So maybe if I identified with this muse, I'd become it.

All the lines furthest away from the middle dot, the black ones, that represented my high school friends – Morris, Danny, the lot of them. I tried to become them, tried to fit in. Maybe those lines were my insecurities.

The charcoal lines which represented the grey area of happiness, the mundane life that provided something of relevance was my family.

Don't get me wrong, things weren't awful. Dad was starting to come around more, Mom seemed happier. Baxter surprisingly took my advice and started branching out to different concepts, and Will, well… we golfed on occasion.

Scott was the one who really stepped up. He proposed to Sab last year with a ring hidden in her birthday cupcake. She almost choked on it. Hilarious way to go, honestly.

But their wedding was coming up in just a couple weeks, and I was supposed to bring Blu.

Supposed to, being the keyword.

That's it, I had to call her.

But just as I reached for my phone, it vibrated with a text.

9:42pm – BLUberry: I'm sorry. I need you. Can I see you?

She read my mind. She always did.

And so I went over.

She was already two glasses of Chardonnay down when I walked through the door, weeping quietly in the corner of her couch.

"What happened, darling?" I rushed over to her spot, caressing her back.

Mascara had streamed down her face, dripping onto her lips. "I have BPD."

"What?"

She moved away from me, swatting a form in my direction.

"The questionnaire that Stacy made me fill out, yeah," she rubbed her nose raw, "It was to test for borderline personality disorder."

Borderline personality disorder.

"Borderline personality disorder," I repeated aloud.

I'd heard about it before, but never did I know anyone to have it around me, let alone someone I was involved with.

"Don't look at me like that." She buried her face in her knees, wrapping her arms around herself in protection.

I didn't even realize I was staring. I felt like I was seeing her through a different lens.

"Come here," I whispered, pulling her warmth into my arms. "What does BPD entail?"

"Everything that I am," she let out an exhausted laugh, sniffing in between speech. "Inability to have stable relationships, sabotaging every good thing in my fucking life, self-harming, God, everything – fucking everything I've done."

"Blu –"

"So I am broken," she continued, inconsolable. "I now have doctor documentation to prove it."

"Darling you aren't —"

"Jace," she shook her head, eyeing me with caution. "This explains so much. It explains why my behaviour is so erratic and why I feel the way I do."

"Is it certain that you have it?"

"No." Her arms were covered in goosebumps as she shook. "I mean, I think there's a lot that goes into diagnosing someone, not just a fucking questionnaire." She laughed out loud.

Then, she cried.

I leaned back, watching the reality of her situation sink in. She was in utter hysterics, her eyes red and puffy.

I didn't know what to say.

Maybe if I went to a psychologist, they'd diagnosis me with something. Surely I was a broken mess too. But if they didn't, and I was just a deeply insecure person plagued by loneliness, then I was just fucked up.

That would be my label.

Simply, fucked up.

I cleared my throat. "Do you need to take medication?"

"I don't… I don't know." Her fingers wobbled against the form, her brown eyes darting around the page like a crossword. "Maybe? God, all my life I thought therapy was so stupid. I don't want to take pills, I don't — I don't like the idea of having a tiny capsule control my thoughts and…"

She trailed off, her words dying in her throat.

"If it'll help," was all I managed to say.

"If it'll help," she softly repeated back to me.

I watched her because that's all I could really do. I mean, I wasn't qualified to do anything but listen. If that's what she needed, then that's what I'd provide.

For how long, I wasn't sure. I wasn't sure about anything now.

But after an hour of her crying on and off, she fell asleep in my arms.

I held her. I held her and traced the lines of her scars, hidden beneath tattoos.

I held her, memorizing the curve of her lips and outline of her hips.

I held her because I could. Because in this moment, she needed me and I was able to right some wrongs.

So, I held her, because a gnawing feeling told me this might be one of the last times I would.

Age 26
Blu

Present

Flowers. Flower petals. White-Winter snowdrops. Watercolour. The sound of rain. Birds singing. Puddles and gloppy mud. Beautiful women. Beautiful men. Beautiful everything – Beautiful everyone. Stars. The night sky. Ballet. Music. Ballads. Sunshine. Lanterns. Wind. Green grass. Checkered tiles. Books. Time. People smiling. People laughing.

I could've listed a million things and it still wouldn't have done my new world justice.

For once I began to see it all.

For once, nothing was rushed – things were simple, precious.

For once, I wasn't a prisoner in my own brain.

For once, I found appreciation in the beauty around me.

And my God, there was a lot of it.

The day after I filled out the test questionnaire, I called Stacy and booked in three appointments.

For the past two weeks, I'd seen her six times. Six sessions that I poured my heart out to a stranger who didn't feel like a stranger anymore.

I filled out another five-hundred question booklet and regrouped with Stacy, prepared for the news. When she told me that borderline personality disorder held a nine criteria, and I possessed eight of the symptoms, I broke down.

"So…" I wiped away the stinging in my eyes. "What now? What's next? Will I be sick forever?"

"For one," she began, "You're not sick, Beatrice. We're going to work through this together, okay? You and me."

I nodded. I had a partner now. I wasn't alone. *It's okay. I'm going to be okay.*

"I'm going to start by prescribing you a small dose of mood stabilizers and if need be, anti-depressants."

Medication. Pills. My throat was dry. "Are um… Are they necessary?"

"They can be. We'll monitor your progress on the dosage for a few weeks. If at any point you feel like they are making you more anxious, in general doing more harm than good, come see me and we'll talk about other options, okay?"

My cracked lips felt like rough sandpaper as I rubbed them together, forcing pain.

Stacy leaned forward, giving me a reassuring smile. Her eyes were gentle, keen to help. "You're going to be okay, Beatrice," she said genuinely. "For what it's worth, I'm very proud of you."

I'm very proud of you.

The words a father should tell her daughter.

The words a mother should use to comfort her child.

Neither of those words were ever said to me. Until now.

I agreed to begin taking the medication with careful optimism.

"If it'll help." Jace's words repeated in my brain.

It's going to be okay. I'm going to be okay.

A Hue of Blu

Our progressing sessions consisted of Stacy asking me some questions that struck a nerve, and I had to leave the room for a few minutes. But always, she was determined to make sure I felt safe, unthreatened.

She moved her office to a bigger one, where there was an extension of her room that branched out into a small waiting area. Only with all my visits, she catered the space to me.

There were paints and crafts, a bunch of disposable cameras and film, but most importantly, a floor to ceiling window that opened to a landscape of greenery outside the clinic.

"It's important that you remember these things exist," she'd told me, "That there is a world outside your mind and it's really quite exquisite."

"I never realized I was sick," I whispered, staring at a nest of birds perched atop a tree branch. "I never clued in."

"Oh, Beatrice," she released in her soothing voice. At first I hated it. Now, it felt like a soft kiss from a mother to her daughter.

"You aren't sick, please stop saying that. You were never sick. BPD stems from deeply rooted trauma, and you've experienced so much of it."

"But maybe there was a way to avoid it? Maybe if I just —"

"You've been avoiding your feelings for too long. It's time you embrace them, embrace that they are a part of you and they're not trying to cause you harm. You are capable of healing," she urged, "And you are owed it."

Owed it.

I remember when I used to believe that the world owed me. That I could stake my claim on anything I wanted because it's what I deserved for all the shit I'd endured in my life.

Owed.

To think, the things I chased after were unattainable because they never belonged to me in the first place. And I tried to make it fit. I tried to make it work.

It was unachievable from the beginning. Some things were.

Jace was.

And it took me until his brother's wedding to realize that.

When I heard their vows and sat in the second row, tears in my eyes and watched him with wonder. I pictured us two, standing hand in hand under a beautiful gondola, professing our love for one another.

And then it hit me.

I couldn't see us doing that.

I couldn't even imagine the types of things he would say because he just... He just wouldn't have said anything.

Jace told me he promised to love me once, but he never told me that he truly did. Everything he said he felt for me were all indirect comments that never ensured security.

All Jace wanted from the beginning was to be loved, but he had no intention of loving.

At the reception, I stared longing at the couples dancing, twirling, singing... *Loving.*

He and I sat at table three and drank champagne, gazing at the world sparkling before us.

A Hue of Blu

Before us.

Not between us.

"Do you want to dance?" I tried. I remember at Winter's Lodge when he had asked the same of me. When he pulled me onto the club floor and held me close to prove a point.

To prove a point.

Because that's all it was. That's all it ever was.

He never did anything with me as the primary focus. I was never a priority, never first. I satisfied him, but I was never enough to fulfill him.

So when he refused to dance, I knew. I knew we were over. We'd been over for a long time now and I just didn't have the heart to accept it.

But we all had our breaking points. That was mine.

I saw the smiles people wore, the emotion that bled from every inch of their skin, and for the first time, I didn't envy them.

I was happy for them.

I was happy they found something I didn't. If it was possible for one, it was possible for all.

It was possible for me.

But as I stared at the beautiful man I'd come to know, I realized I never really did. He never really showed me. And it wouldn't be possible for *us*.

We were never made to last.

For so long I felt like I could only amount to the affection Jace showed me, that my worth was a ball of power he held in his hands.

I couldn't be who I wanted to be when I was with him, because for a while I was nothing if he wasn't mine.

The acceptance started after I realized I would never become who I was meant to be if he stayed in my life. I would never share the smiles these couples had, the smiles they gave one another out of genuine loyalty.

He consumed me when we were together, but he consumed me most when we weren't; when I had to worry about who he was talking to, who was better than me.

The right person would have never given me those doubts to begin with.

The right person would have danced with me in a sea of stars or burning lava. The point is –

They would have danced.

A week after Scott and Sabrina's wedding, I broke down on my kitchen floor and had a panic attack.

An overwhelming tsunami of emotions shot through every scar, every cut, every piece of my flesh that I buried beneath ink. But they screamed at me to remember. To remind me that I was a survivor and I could make it out alive, even if I was covered in wounds.

A week and two days later, I ended things with Jace.

[Finally].

He didn't take me seriously at first. He thought I'd come back.

"What did I do this time?"

But the second he met my eyes, void of complete and utter devotion, he placed his head in my lap.

"I'm sorry for everything, Blu."

Sweet words, sweet boy. I was familiar with them. They didn't hold the same weight as they once did.

Maybe because in just three short weeks, my dull, grey life was lit on fire. I started planting flowers in dead grass, watering the life that deserved to be there.

"Do you even know what you're apologizing for?"

"Yes," he sighed, taking hold of my hand. His touch pricked me like icicles. "I'm sorry that I wasn't ready to love you, even though my heart wanted to."

I kissed his lips then, softly, to savour the taste of poison and empty promises.

My final kiss that wasn't intended to start a new – It was to conclude an old.

My final goodbye.

He knew it too.

There had been plenty of endings, I realized, but could never admit. I couldn't. He was a part of me. I'd made sure of that.

I sought him out from the second I laid my eyes on his blue-green eyes, the storm that swam beneath his irises, the sharp jaw that cut my flesh when he fucked me with selfishness.

As time went on, Stacy and I worked through the deep, emotional manipulation I'd endured by all the characters in my life, including my mother.

I hadn't realized how much she relied on me to do everything she didn't *want* to do.

Not couldn't do.

Wanted to do.

I picked up the scattered scraps, overcompensating for lacking affection. Time after time after time, I'd volunteered to be a slave to those who provided nothing but pennies and dust. My mom, though bonded by blood, was not family.

Fawn was.

One good friend was better than a thousand acquaintances.

My father, in his own way, may have only loved me with the capacity he possessed, but that didn't mean he didn't love me at all.

I stopped blaming myself for his abandonment, because it wasn't on purpose. It wasn't my doing.

It wasn't my fault.

After countless sessions of rehashing my feelings, I accepted that Zac, Kyle, Tyler and Jace didn't know how to express the love I deserved, and a lot of what I experienced with them was a product of their own personal experiences. Maybe there was genuine care at a point, but it was clouded by unresolved issues that they needed to work through.

Not to say I didn't play a part. Surely I did. Clearly I did. But to take full responsibility for the hurt bestowed onto me would be harmful, detrimental. I'd been carrying that weight for so long.

It was time to let it go.

It was time to be free.

Months went by that felt like seconds, a full year around the sun approaching the horizon.

My social media was deleted. My job was enriching. New opportunities presented themselves in ways I could only imagine.

Jace and I hadn't spoken for seven months.

I thought of the time we spent apart, trying to fish for sadness, but I couldn't. Seeing the improvements in my life, how successful I'd become not just externally, but internally, it was almost difficult to dwell on pain.

"I don't understand why I liked him so much," I told Stacy a month back. "I was infatuated beyond belief, beyond control even."

She relaxed in her chair. "People who live with BPD often experience obsessive tendencies when connecting with those they're intrigued by. It was a normal response, Beatrice."

"Is that why I always fought with him over everything?" I leaned closer, "Why I was always so emotional?"

"I wasn't involved in your relationship; those arguments were between you both. But I can say that emotional regulation is something we've been working on because it's common that feelings are heightened."

"I don't feel as terrible as I used to," I admitted. "Focusing on the good instead of the bad has gotten easier."

She looked to me inquisitively. "Perhaps it's because you no longer feel the threat of abandonment any more."

"What do you mean?"

"From what I learned about you, Beatrice, you've always felt like you needed to please other people so they wouldn't leave. The foundation of your relationship with Jace seemed to be exactly that.

"You thought if you did everything for him, if you could *be* everything for him, he'd return. And for a while, it seemed he did."

"He didn't come back for me, he came back for him and his ego." The anger was slowly building, but I took in a deep breath and tried to keep it at bay.

Work in progress, I thought.

At least it was progress.

Stacy smiled. "You're doing very well with your emotional regulation, Beatrice. And if it is true that Jace only returned to you for his ego, then let it be true. We can only concern ourselves with ourselves, right?"

I pressed my lips together, nodding in response. "Right."

As the weeks went by, my job became more demanding, but I relished the work load. I attended day trips across cities for my job, taking photos of areas I'd never been to and pushed my limits as a photographer.

One trip in Spring, I decided to visit Thornberry to take exclusive photos of the greenery for our activities column. As I was hiking up the trail, I came across a man who'd propped up his camera in the exact location I hoped for myself.

"I'll wait until you're done," I said, clicking through old shots.

He had familiar eyes, green like sea moss with a tinge of Blu. His smile was kind, but deep wrinkles had set into his forehead. I had placed him in his late twenties.

"Photographer too? Or just for fun?" He'd asked.

"I work for Toronto Pix, under TTC Travels."

"Ah," he snapped a photo, then adjusted his lens. "How do you like it?"

I'd gotten better with small talk when talking to strangers over recent months. If I had the capability of dishing out all my personal problems to Stacy, I knew I was indestructible.

"It's a dream job," I confessed. I wore a smile at that.

"Lucky you," he adjusted his position, "I wish I could have stable income but I'm just a freelance photographer."

"Freelancing gives you creative freedom to take photos of whatever you like, though. No one can tell you what to do."

He pulled back from his lens and looked at me, the corner of his lips lifting as he extended a hand. "Baxter Boland."

Boland.

It had to have been a coincidence.

But the longer I looked in his eyes, the side profile cut like mountain peaks, I knew it wasn't.

"Do you know Jace Boland?"

He took a step back, assessing me now with caution. "He's my brother, how do you know him?"

How did I know Jace Boland, that really was the question. How did I want his brother to know me? Did I even care anymore? It'd been so long since we talked, our relationship seemed like a blink in existence.

"We were sort of friends," I settled on. "I'm Blu – *Beatrice*, Henderson."

In one swift movement, he secured his camera wrap around his neck and swore. "Blu," he said my name in disbelief. "You were the girl Jace couldn't shake."

I laughed in discomfort. "I think I'm insulted."

"No, no," he put out a hand, "That's not what I meant. He talked about you before, *fuck,* this is so insane that I'm meeting you like this."

"Likewise," I chuckled. *We* felt like a lifetime ago. "How is he doing?"

"Not sure, we don't talk much."

A part of my heart sank for him, even if the connection no longer burned with the passion it once possessed. His brothers meant everything to him, and those were probably the only relationships he insisted on keeping. *It must be hard*, I thought. I guess some things never change.

But I did. And his life was no longer my concern.

"He may be working on a business with his friend, but I heard that through the grapevine." He laughed so I mirrored his, but the protective part of me that sided with Jace lingered deep below.

So I said my goodbyes to Baxter Boland and found another area along another trail, forgetting the interaction as quickly as it came.

"It's weird," I told Stacy the following day. "I thought I'd feel more."

"Why?" She asked.

"I don't know, I guess because he was such a persistent presence in my life and seeing his brother reminded me of that."

"But you didn't feel much, you said."

"No," I shook my head, "I didn't. His life doesn't bother me anymore."

"And are you happy about that?"

I rubbed the tips of my dark blue hair, the only remaining part of me that held some semblance of my old self. The person who loved Jace Boland.

"I'm happy that he can't hurt me anymore."

"Well Beatrice, people can only hurt you if you let them."

I repeated her words like a mantra on my drive home, stopping at the pharmacy before darting for my bathroom.

"Am I really doing this?" I released, scooping out the black box dye I'd just purchased. The scissors were staring at me from a cupholder. I picked them up too.

"Fuck it."

The first chop felt like a knife in my gut, the second a wrench in my spine. But the more I snipped, the better I felt; like forcing out dead weight, weeding out the thorns.

When my hair was just below my shoulders, I mixed the dye solution and took in a deep breath. My blue hair was a part of me, the fractured girl who had no father, no mother – no one to love.

But I was no longer that girl anymore.

I had me.

I loved me.

As the dye coated my hair, tears escaped my eyes. They resembled rainwater.

I covered up the part of me that was Jace's rain.

I covered up the strands that wept over my insecurities, my flaws and defeats.

I covered up the sadness, the loss, the grief and the pain until I was no longer blue.

I was no longer Blu.

A few days later, I sat in Stacy's office, listening to her routine questions, when my phone rang.

A Hue of Blu

Marie-France Leger

The caller ID read: Jace Boland.

A million thoughts shuddered beneath my skin. Baxter probably told him that we spoke.

I lifted my phone to show Stacy who was calling.

"Are you going to answer?"

I stared at the screen, watching it ring. Time was slow, my breathing slower. What could he possibly want? What could I possibly give him that he hasn't already had?

He sucked the life out of me.

He drained me of all my energy.

He would do it again if I let him.

If I let him.

I silenced my phone and watched the call go to voicemail, whispering to myself, *"People can only hurt you if you let them."*

And today –

Today I didn't let him.

Tomorrow I wouldn't let him.

Onward, I'd never let him again.

"Well, that settles that," Stacy released, but I could tell she was proud. I was prouder.

"Tell me," she said, pulled out her notepad, "What's the worst thing that happened to you today?"

My hands were shaking, my heartbeat erratic, but I did it. I fucking did it.

I hung up on Jace Boland.

And I didn't call back.

My eyes fluttered closed, taking comfort in the blankness of my emotions. "I guess…" I swallowed, "A part of me died."

Because that's what it felt like. Turning a new leaf, healing. I drowned before I resurfaced. I struggle for breath before I inhaled fresh air.

But there was strength in my scars. I finally saw the beauty in that.

I chose happiness, just as I chose pain.

All choices nonetheless, all mine to make.

"A part of you died." She scribbled something on paper. "And the best?"

I shut my eyes once more, and melted in the thought of peace.

The smell of muffins. Red velvet cake. Bells ringing. Floppy hats. Cinnamon and spice. Fresh clothing. Lavender. Cobblestone walkways. Gardens.

A life I could live.

A life I *will* live.

When I thought about all the loss I'd endured, the residual ache lingered, but I was no longer suffering. All the precious parts of life conquered the dark, and I was the phoenix that rose from the ashes.

A ghost of a smile painted my lips as I peeled off one shackle at a time, the chains that I'd been bound to through years of agony, my own personal torment haunting me no longer.

Today, I chose me.

Tomorrow, I'd choose me.

Forever.

"The best part of today, Beatrice?" Stacy repeated, a curious look on her face.

A tear escaped the corner of my eye, but it was no longer rainwater.

It was the sun.

Goodbye, Blu Henderson.

"A part of me died."

The End

Thank you for reading "A Hue of Blu."
If for some reason you want to see Blu and Jace end up together, turn the page and read the alternate ending I wrote for this book.
----→

HOWEVER, I am very content with how I ended the book and to me, I'm proud of Blu [Beatrice] and her growth and I don't want her to ruin all her healing by running back to Jace.

That being said, the alternate ending is for everyone who still has hope for these two. I would never take that hope away from you.

I love you all.

Alternate Ending
Four Years Later

The painting was never removed.

"Controlling Chaos" reminded Jace of his demons, even though he no longer struggled with past grief anymore.

There was a time when he believed that life handed out aces to people who didn't deserve it, and standing in a polished grey suit, dimming the lights of Prix art gallery, he felt like he was one of those people.

When Mel took over the gallery two years ago, she employed Jace to work as assistant manager.

"It's the least I could do for a friend," she'd told him.

He greatly appreciated the opportunity, though it wasn't something he worked for. Maybe that's why he felt stuck in an endless cycle of nothingness, because life rewarded him despite his lack of efforts.

It'd always been that way, he thought. With everything, with everyone. The things he lost he could never get back.

But four years later and someone entered the gallery, stepping right in front of the painting he knew they both loved.

She didn't know he was there, she couldn't have. Her eyes were glued to the intersecting lines, the dot protected by a bleeding hue.

"Your hair's different," he said, recognizing that almost everything about her had changed.

She turned to him then, golden flecks in her brown eyes winking into his blue-green sea.

"You look different," she responded, though her voice was levelled and calm, a tone Jace was never familiar with.

"It's the suit," he joked, and she chuckled. No bitterness laced in her tone.

He stepped up beside her, gazing at the painting. "I run the gallery when Mel's away," he started. She turned to him. "I work here."

"You look like you own the place."

"I wish."

"Why wish?" she questioned, "When you can do?"

His eyes were gentle. "Maybe one day."

He wasn't talking about his job.

She knew that, even four years later.

A moment of silence passed between the two as they both returned their attention to the painting.

"Have you found your hue?" she whispered softly, her eyes following the cracks of the painting.

The memories of her flashed in his brain, but they were no longer a representation of the women standing beside him.

"I might have," he smiled, "What was your name again?"

She stepped closer, the corner of her lips curving upwards as she linked her pinky finger to his.

"Beatrice Henderson."

Acknowledgments

Thank you to the real life Jace Boland for coming into my life when you did. You inspired this. You're worthy of being someone's muse.
Thank you to the walking Pinterest board herself; my aunt, editor, and best friend. I wouldn't be a writer without you.
My best friends (you know who you are), I appreciate each and every single one of you. Thank you for always cheering me on and believing in me.
Thank you Mariah, my soul-sister, for softening my blue heart. You're one of a kind. Don't ever change.
To you, Mom, for always listening to me rant about the characters I despise and the characters I love. I told you not to read this book, but I'll give you a peek at the acknowledgments anyway.
Grandpa, my biggest fan and friend, I love you.
And lastly, to you, my beautiful readers.
I wouldn't be here if it weren't for you.
You've changed my life this year and I will always appreciate the love and support you give me day in, day out.
Remember that you are all the muse to someone's story…
Mine.
Always remember to find love within yourself, even if you feel unlovable. That is your greatest strength.
I love you forever.
I'll thank you forever.

Mar.

Mental Health Resources

Kids Help Phone
Text Services: Text "CONNECT" to 686868 (also serving adults)

Youthspace.ca (NEED2 Suicide Prevention, Education and Support)
Youth Text (6pm-12am PT): (778) 783-0177

Crisis Services Canada
Toll Free (24/7): 1 (833) 456-4566

Better Help www.betterhelp.com

National Alliance on Mental Illness (NAMI) HelpLine: 1-800-950-NAMI, or text "HELPLINE" to 62640.

Suicide Prevention, Awareness, and Support: www.suicide.org

Self-Harm Hotline: 1-800-DONT CUT (1-800-366-8288)

LGBTQ Hotline: 1-888-843-4564

National Council on Alcoholism & Drug Dependency: 1-800-622-2255

Rape Abuse and Incest National Network (RAINN) is the nation's largest organization fighting sexual violence: (800) 656-HOPE / (800) 810-7440 (TTY)

Psychology Today: https://www.psychologytoday.com/us/therapists

National Domestic Violence Hotline: 1-800-799-7233

Please do not be afraid to reach out.

Author Note:
Reviews mean everything to me! I love talking to my readers so please do not hesitate to shoot me a DM on any of the following platforms:

Instagram - @mariefranceleger
TikTok - @maariefraance

A Hue of Blu   Marie-France Leger

Printed in Great Britain
by Amazon